Mighty in Sorrow

A Tribute to David Tibet & Current 93

Edited by Jordan Krall

DYNATOX MINISTRIES INTL.

East Brunswick – Borneo – Fisherville

Published by
DYNATOX MINISTRIES (International)
http://dynatoxministries.com

ISBN-13:
978-0615990040
ISBN-10:
0615990045

CONTENTS

FOREWORD
NATURE REVEALED

The first David Tibet release I owned was not a Current 93 record. It was the 1986 release of *The Hastings Archives/The World as Power*. I was intrigued to hear the voice of the "Great Beast", Aleister Crowley, to some the very personification of EVIL; would this voice etched in plastic possess my very soul?

The record crackled and the blurry sound of a feeble, effete, well-spoken man emanated from the speakers. Surely this could NOT be the voice of the "Wickedest Man in the World"?

My friend Alex listened with me on this, the debut spin of the disc. It finished, he laughed and said, "What a load of shit, he sounds like Larry Grayson." I went to play the next record. The record player didn't work. It ceased to function for the rest of the evening; only the next day did it work again. Had we offended old Crow?

I didn't for one moment believe that To Mega Therion had influenced the workings of the record player. I have a cultural and anthropological interest in, but do not give any credence to, the occult or quasi- or traditional belief systems. I am a devout atheist in every possible way, but surprisingly this record was my initiation to all things David Tibet. An insert with a list of assorted releases was included with the disc, and they all looked very interesting to me.

7

So I collected Current 93 records along with the wonderful *Current 93 Presents* series, including such diverse recordings as Icelandic poetry, Tibetan chant and the sound of crystals. I wrote David letters asking questions. I wanted to know more about the more esoteric and obscure references in his lyrics and more about his eclectic passions. I was introduced to subjects, artists and writers that I would have never discovered for myself.

David's tastes and interests are well documented. Anything from the sublime to the ridiculous seems to have touched his psyche and imagination in some way. Everything from Noddy to the film *Legally Blonde*, Uriah Heep to Tiny Tim, from Count Stenbock to Madge Gill — over the years everything has been integrated and assimilated into his diverse oeuvre.

Many of us tuck away our guilty pleasures and arguably embarrassing predilections, ashamed to admit our bad or good tastes for fear of being laughed at or dismissed, but David is one those rarefied breeds—a honest person, he wears his heart on his (Paul Smith) sleeve. Everything is revealed in his very public announcements about his latest fixations and, of course, within his often candid and open lyrics.

His influences are bared nakedly to all, his fascinating glossary and encyclopedic knowledge of a vast array of interests, often obscure, arcane, archaic, innocuous and otherwise are there for all to see, ponder and investigate. This infinite multiplicity of ideas, concepts and obsessions often sit uncomfortably together or appear incongruous, but remarkably when added together it all makes sense, a perfect whole. A meticulously but randomly constructed, incredibly complex, intertwined, shiny, smooth, intricately planished, multi-layered completeness that has manifested into and within David Tibet... an indispensable influence, confidant and friend.

-Andrew Liles, 2013

SMOKE WINDING THROUGH PETRICHOR

Nikki Guerlain

Unchained eyes— kiss the sky
The Devil done burned
And the rabbit done died
In a pit of stone and fire
Sweat turns to ash— tears to dust

Dead Child, I'm alive like you are

Wishing the wind to call me home
To render me from this cage of skin and bone
To be in a fiery ecstasy— smoke winding through
Petrichor
In a Geosmin dream
The sunlight off the smoke of a bumble bee's wing

Summer eyes— rise to the sky
And out there somewhere— there's little kids
laughing
But I am crying
Because the Devil likes what a child spurns
And I've been left to harden

Dead Child— I'm alive like you are

Beating works and shaming regrets
Stealing the wind from a child's sails
Upon old rocks spirits go breaking
Summer's lost at such a cost

Another man born from a little boy lost

Another moth dies in light
As fire fills the sky
Another night falls
As another day dies

Dead Child— I'm alive like you are

MAY DAWN REDEEM WHAT NIGHT DESTROYS
Michael Griffin

I. Spring, fluttering above

Listen. What flutters overhead? Do these wing sounds portend the angels return? Or is it still the black-winged birds of darkness, talons ever dripping, malignant carriers of coming night? So long since last I heard the angels come. Who could remember their sound across Aeons?

Many times they've come, but will they always?

My legs chill, feet tingle, the first parts of me to sleep.

I walk the endless path, wide awake through uttermost endurance. Walk away, never rest. Never sure how long a cycle lasts. What seems forever isn't quite, and on my long, long path no milestones are given me to judge the nearness of another end.

Head down against beating wings, I press on. Always on. The wings buffet the air above me and all I can do is persist, unblinking.

II. Summer, the cycle insists

Into the void I try to see, yet all I discern is another eye staring back. The eternal recursion. Seeking, being sought. Wondering, wondered upon. Knowing only what I know, all else mystery. That which is familiar to me, mysterious to others. Step after step, on and on.

The Fundament vibrates beneath my feet, moved by what lies below. My every stride I feel the serpent riding hidden under the shell of the Globe, ever coiling and uncoiling in tremor-making expansion and contraction.

His broad spine supports the foundation of All Things.

His unwinding coil drives the clockwork that is Time.

His movements unfurl so slowly as to appear eternal. Nothing is without end. All forget this truth, even I, yet all must remember. The cycle will not be denied.

My path appears a perfect line, yet I know the curve is so long as to be imperceptible. What is crooked appears straight. The trees along the path seem infinite yet can be counted. No quantity is too large to number. Count the trees, my steps, all the dreams that give birth to the green worlds and the void.

Yet the circle is a circle, boundless. It returns to where it begins. The circle is inevitable.

The flow permeates everything. Ending so distant from beginning that all who glimpse the coming of the end forget it's a return. Even I forget. Endless walking, but not truly endless. What I approach is finite, a new beginning.

The circle is wide.

III. Autumn, the winds come

After enough time passes, I convince myself I am only a man. I am born, I die. I walk a path of my own determining, free to stop at any time. I might turn aside, seek others, find comforts as a man.

Briefly I believe. Always sorrow returns.

Winds surge, straining to rustle the leaves as winds are meant to do, but to no effect. These silver birches are barren of limb, their adornments no more than memory. Some forgotten ideal.

I am paced by invisible hordes, brief walkers who follow part of my journey. They fall into step, soon think they've seen enough to understand, then flit away. Some appear, cast fire at me, and quickly vanish. Through all, I persist.

Plumes of flame adorn the trees yet leave them unharmed, glassy silver carriers of rebirth's fire, the only increment I have. Always I lose count. The tree fires burn, they illuminate. Within the flickering light are many wonders, revealed only in the flame. Soft hints. Whispers of silver. On these I rely as my time nears.

Beyond the rows, green grass fields and beds of damp glistening moss extend as far as I can see. The green absorbs everything. It accepts all sound, deadens it to silence. Accepts heaven's golden rain, and from it grows.

As I near another ending -- I am near, am I near -- the Starres stop leaking and the Skye is calm and dry.

The end is coming. Is the end coming?

IV. Winter, darkness familiar

Mirrors flash in gaps beyond the trees. I strain to glimpse reflections, seeking in my own face reassurance. Before I can seize hold of what vision they might return, the mirrors vanish. All that remains as backdrop, beyond birch trees and expanse of green, is the pulsing black attraction of eternity's void.

Night comes, undeniable now, a moiré pattern of shadow moving over ground. My path darkens. Wings beat overhead, heavy and near. I trust these are the wings I hope for. I trust they will bear me away. Air moves, cooling me against the fires. A feeling somehow familiar.

Night is Destroyer, vanguard of a vanished Creator. The angels, like me, mechanisms of a dead King.

Everything changes, I repeat. All this must end. A cycle of rebirth. Day into night. The moon vanishes to reappear. Turning seasons of the year, unnamed divisions of Aeons tick away. These markers slowly echo, counting passage. The wheel turns, incremented but endless.

Is there no limit, no end to beginnings? I've nowhere to seek, no one to ask. My Creator subsided after long desistance, without instruction or explanation. All that's left for me, all but walking, is continuation and trust.

After countless rebirths, yet again I tremble.

Angels lower, flit and land, pale of skin, slight of body. So long anticipated, this seems impossible. Reality pales beside the dream.

Open wings, a gesture of welcoming. Blind eyeless faces, passage to renewal, to return. I step forward, somehow still unsure. I don't remember the last time, or any other before.

By the coming of music, I am convinced. The beacon is not beating wings, not silver fires. Not fears or doubts, nor any marker or sacred word. It's this, the vocal illustrations of bright angels. The song of hordes, of all universes gone before and yet to come. Brightness surrounded by black wings beating, the sublime in offset to cackling malignity, desire for paradise, hunger for scraps of pain. These inevitable consequences of Armageddon.

Pale benefactors sing against darkness; the black returns song, asserting against light. Together they are music.

I open my chest, offer the brighter angels my tender flame, the warm persistent essence of my core, the very glow which so long powered my circling.

I am an infinite universe. Nothing is infinite.

With these angels I encompass the King's will, his intentions as maker. We carry forth his grand design, those of us who still embody it, long past His demise.

The perfection I seek is to give in willingly, to seek this end. Darkness meeting light, eternal return. Trust the design. I can only trust. Allow their grace to lift me.

I close my eyes. Let myself fall.

A GARDEN OF CUCUMBERS
Ross E. Lockhart

"Abba, Abba," says the boy, shaking him. "Some men are here. Some men. From the village. Abba," the boy repeats. "Some men."

The prophet sits up, unsteady, slow, scratching his bony ribs. He yawns, his cracked and yellowed teeth, haphazardly repaired with gold and wire by a traveling doctor, ache in the chill of morning's air. He looks at the boy, swaying his head from side to side to correct for the room's spinning. *That dream again*, he thinks, *that grinning man, his leering black face. His strange, rhythmic words, the steady drumming of nonsense syllables.* Something twists in the prophet's belly, causing him to sway violently. He turns, vomiting onto the unfinished earthen floor beside his bedroll. "I wish it would stop," he mutters, clutching himself as dry heaves work their way through his emaciated body.

His stomach voided, the prophet sits up. The boy stands before him, an earthen mug in hand, offering it. The prophet takes it, presses it to his mouth, gulping the sweet wine with cracked lips and dry tongue. "Abba," says the boy. "Some men."

The prophet nods, holding the empty cup out to the boy, who refills it from a skin. The prophet drains the cup, a trickle of purple wine escaping the side of his mouth, rolling down into his dirty, gray

19

beard. The boy hangs the wineskin on a peg, then picks up a cloth bag and begins to sprinkle sand onto the prophet's emesis. "Boy," says the prophet, his voice a hollow rasp. "Come help me up." He drops the cup to the ground.

The boy leads the prophet to the chamber pot. The prophet squats over it, closing his eyes, pressing his naked, wrinkled back against the cold mud wall. He waits. Nothing happens. He picks dried flakes from his beard, his matted hair. He yawns. "Boy," he calls eventually. "Help me up." The boy takes the prophet's hands, pulling him to his feet.

"My robe," the prophet says, "my staff." The boy releases the prophet's hands, leaving him swaying as he gathers up the garments from the floor. He holds them at arm's length, shaking them free of vermin, and then offers them to the prophet.

"Abba," says the boy as the prophet pulls the robes over his head, dressing. "Some men." The prophet waves his hand dismissively, and then grasps the top of the boy's head, pulling him close. The prophet kisses the boy's forehead, and then staggers to the doorway where his staff leans against the wall. He clumsily shoves the coarse wooden door ajar, then stands, blinking in the doorway, blinded momentarily by the harsh morning sun.

The prophet's eyes adjust, revealing three men, silhouetted where they stand on the nearby bluff, perhaps two dozen paces away. The flanking two, burly types, fishermen or carpenters, impatiently tap rough-hewn clubs against their palms. The man in the middle is shorter, stocky, dressed in a merchant's purple. His beard is bushy, black. His hair held back with a slender metal circlet. Gold. The prophet crosses the distance, the boy following him. "Rebbe," the man says, extending his hands. "It's good of you to come out and talk to me."

The prophet leans on his staff, swaying slightly. His head lolls to one side, correcting the swaying horizon. He knows this black-bearded man, but cannot place him. *A businessman?* The prophet wonders, *A king?*

"Rebbe," says the man. "I've been having dreams."

"Dreams?" croaks the prophet, closing one eye. The words come, like they always do. "I see the country desolate, her cities burned with fire. The harlot is punished for her misdeeds. Foreigners devour her, stripping her, leaving her like a shack in a garden of cucumbers, a besieged city." He bends like a windblown reed, rolling to and fro, his hands clutching his staff. "Collapse is coming," says the prophet. "All will collapse, all will fall. Then the Messiah will come. If not tomorrow…" he trails off, staring at the sun. He sees the man from his dream, the black man, darker than any African, dancing before the corona. He claps his hands, his body gyrating. Women, unlike any the prophet has ever seen, bestial yet arousing, touch his chest, his arms. They move to sounds unheard.

21

"Rebbe, Rebbe," says the merchant, chuckling. "You aren't listening. These dreams I'm having, Rebbe, these dreams, they're different. There's this laughing, dancing man. This castle, these things," he motions as if counting coins. "Things like I've never seen, only dreamt of, material things. Wonderful things. This castle," his hands draw a box in the air. "Chariots, clothing, jewels. Women. Oh, the women." He traces the female form, an hourglass in the air before him, then pauses, as if looking at it, longing. "Not like my Aziza. You know, my Aziza." He traces the form again, a bulging circle through which sand would simply plummet. The man glares at the prophet, then grins, his glimmering gold teeth prominent. "This man," he continues, "this black stranger—"

"He is a devil," interrupts the prophet, growling.

"He is a prince," says the man. "The Black Pharaoh, the Lurker in the Night."

"A devil," repeats the prophet.

"He offers me these things, many, many things," says the man.

The prophet shakes his head, baffled that this man should share his dream. He brings one hand to his jaw, rubbing it. His teeth ache.

"And you teach austerity," continues the man. "Promising me that I will only find God in poverty. Bah, poverty," he spits. "God is the Crawling Mist, the Dark Dweller of my dreams, not your maker of empty promises."

"He is a devil," says the prophet.

"Rebbe," says the man, stroking his thick, oiled black beard. "The things you have said, your talk of collapse, of foreign invaders, all your talk of fear and fire. I hear about these things." He shakes his head. "My man Belkira keeps me well informed, he interprets my dreams, tells me of the rewards that await me. He also tells me what you say. Like what you said about my wife…" His hand falls to the sheathed knife at his hip. "Calling her a whore. We can't have that. Belkira says you must go, and so you must."

Belkira, the prophet thinks. *That magician. That false prophet. Then this is Manasseh, the king.* His anger rises, causing the earth's constant spin to feel even more violent, even more sickening. His guts twist. His grip tightens on his staff, and his considers swinging it at this man, this merchant-king, this devil.

"How do we know you are what you say you are?" continues Manasseh. "How do we know you're not buggering that boy? We don't." He shrugs.

The boy looks down, red-faced, embarrassed by the implication, then turns away to wander back to the hut. "So, you will leave, move along to the next village. We'll come back tonight, my friends and I. If you're still here, you'll wish you had left." The man nods to his burly companions, who grin maliciously at the prophet.

The prophet shakes his head, then turns. He wanders back into his mud shack, shutting the door behind him. He sits down on the bedroll. "I'm tired of feeling like this," he says. "Tired of feeling sick. Tired of being old. I just want it to end." The boy hands him the cup, refilled with wine. The prophet drinks, then reclines, closing his eyes. The boy takes the cup, and then sits down beside him, stroking the prophet's dirty, gray hair. Within minutes, the prophet is asleep.

The tree, the tree, the lightning-struck tree. The grinning man, his dark skin glistening in firelight, dancing around the hollow tree.

"Abba, Abba," says the boy, shaking him. "The men. The men from the village are back." The prophet sits up slowly, his head pounding. He holds out his hands, the boy presses the cup of wine into them. He realizes that the pounding isn't coming from within his head, but outdoors, from whence the flicker of firelight plays through the door's cracks and knotholes.

The boy helps the prophet to his feet. Grasping his staff, the prophet presses through the door, stepping out into night's chill. A dozen men surround the hut, torches held in hands. Most carry clubs, some swords, others, metal spikes or saws. One beats a massive drum. *Thrum. Thrum. Thrum.* Dark clouds blot out the stars above, lightning flickering on the horizon. The boy presses close to the prophet's back, peering out from behind him at the men. Manasseh stands at center, cleaning his nails with the tip of his knife, flames flashing, red and gold, in its etched blade. Red-bearded Belkira stands behind him, his jewel-covered chest-plate glimmering. Manasseh speaks: "If I remember correctly, Rebbe, we asked you to leave. We asked you nicely."

"Trample my vineyard no more," shouts the prophet, the words welling up within him. "Your hands are bloody. Wash yourselves, make yourselves clean, renounce your scarlet sins, for the Messiah comes soon."

"Your messiah is a serpent," calls Belkira, his voice shrill. "And you are a fraud."

The boy gasps.

The prophet's grip tightens on his staff, his head swaying as he looks from side to side. He hardly notices as the boy steps around him, that is, until the boy speaks. "The mouth of the Lord has spoken," says the boy, his voice clear, angelic. He stands between the prophet and the king, meeting the king's eye with burning intensity. "If you refuse to heed, you shall be devoured by the sword, and the Lord shall hide his eyes from you."

The prophet looks at the boy, a tear welling in his eye. He reaches bony fingers forward to touch the boy's shoulder, and then stumbles back as a brutish man grasps the boy by his hair, forces a rag into his mouth, and drags him away, kicking.

"Kill him!" shouts Manasseh, pointing at the prophet, his voice punctuated by Belkira's wicked laughter.

The prophet raises his staff, warding off the first of many blows, clubs wielded by rough hands, carpenters' hands. But soon it splinters, becoming useless. Clubs swing through the air, driving the prophet backward. He drops to the ground, throwing the halves of his shattered staff, scrambling away up the bluff on hands and knees as the shouting men pursue him.

The prophet runs, scuttling up hills, through brush and brambles, plants and rocks tearing his hands, his bare feet. The world sways as he clambers along. He glances over his shoulder, praying that he'll soon distance himself from the torches, the angry men, but they keep coming.

Ahead of him, the night explodes, a crackle like the voice of God accompanying a blinding flash as lightning strikes a tree. His vision blurred, the prophet presses his body into the charred hollow of the lightning-cracked tree. Splintered wood tears at his hollowed chest, his palms, his feet, his side, but he scrambles into the safety of the wood, pulling himself upward towards the hollow's skyward opening. "Why me," he whispers to the empty sky. "I didn't choose this. I wanted a simple life, a wife, a grove of olive trees, a garden of cucumbers. I didn't want this life."

Yes, you did, says the Boy's voice. *Dreamer, visionary, martyr.*

Looking up, the prophet watches the sky spinning in the chimney of the shattered tree. The clouds clear, the moon edging into view, a silver sliver at first, soon filling the opening, moving closer, until its pockmarked circle is directly overhead. The prophet closes his eyes, picking at his beard. He imagines the dancing, grinning man, gyrating, circling his hiding place, drawing Manasseh and his men, revealing him, exposing him.

His breath, echoing within the wood, mists in the air before him. He smells the charcoal, the ozone, the scarred, still-living wood. He listens: His heartbeat. The sounds of insects squirming. The approaching drum. Footfalls. The gruff, laughing voices of the men, surrounding him. Manasseh commanding. Belkira laughing. The nonsense syllables of the black man's chant. The sound of the saws, cutting into the tree...

WHISTLER'S GORE
Daniel Mills

The old churchyard
Two miles north of Plymouth, VT

*

ANNA BURDEN
Beloved Sister in Christ
Consort to the Revd Abijah Burden
Returned to the Lord
19th Jun 1798
Æ 24 years
Born in Ireland, County Sligo
She came late to the Faith
Being married to the Revd Burden
In her 22nd year of age
And received into the Fellowship of the Saints
Deporting herself with an abundance
Of kindness & womanly virtue
Before falling from the Post Bridge
Into the rapid waters beneath
Wherein she lies drowned
Untimely born and stolen away

Who is this that cometh from Idumea?
(Is 63:1)

*

PHINEAS OLMSTEAD
First son of the Col. Silas Olmstead
Felled by the Hand of God

28

Æ 16 years
Mon 30th Jun 1798
Heard to pass an unquiet night
Following upon the Revd's sermon
He journeyed to the far fields
West of the Gore
And did not take warning
When first the thunder
Rolled and clapped on high
And thus caught unawares
Did not return with the other ploughboys
And was not found until daybreak
By J Cuthbert, Smith

Am I born to die?
To lay this body down?
And must my trembling spirit fly
Into a world unknown?

*

In Memory Of

EDWARD CARTWRIGHT	PATIENCE
Taverner	CARTWRIGHT
Died	Amiable Consort
Jul 2nd 1798	Died
Æ 31 years	Jul 2nd 1798
	Æ 23 years

And though I waken to the
dream
And dwell no more upon the
Vale
I leave behind the burning skies
The One who yearns for death—
and fails

Pray do not mourn the end that
comes
But count it gladly as a grace
For in this death the Spider stirs
To mask with silk the Savior's
Face

*

ALL MUST SUBMIT TO THE KING OF TERRORS

JOHN CUTHBERT
Blacksmith, Deacon
An Honest Man & Strong
Upright in all matters
Devoted himself with saintly zeal
To the memory of his wife
And to the welfare of his countrymen
Perished in the flames
Jul 2nd 1798
Æ 27 years

Every knee will bow to me
And all the tongues confess
(Is 45:23)

*

ASHBEL ALLEN OLMSTEAD
Second son of the Col. Olmstead
Brother to the departed Phineas
An Innocent & Child of God
He apprenticed to John Cuthbert
And died in the fires of July the 2nd
That destroyed the tavern and the smithy
Returning to the ground
Æ 14 years
Reposing there in darkness
Where the silent waters flow
A land of deepest shade
Unpierced by human thought

The dreary regions of the dead
Where all things are forgot

*

ZERAH CARTWRIGHT
Brother to Edward & Jerusha
Departed this Dark Valley
Upon the 5th of July 1798
Æ 34 years
Having left the church
In the final days of his life
Upon hearing the words of the Revd Burden
And being granted a vision of realms beyond
He submitted himself to the Angel's yoke
And was washed clean in the waters
Wherein he fished by morning
And in which his empty boat was found

For there shall arise false Christs and false prophets
And they shall show great signs and wonders
(Matt 24:24)

*

BLACKBRIDGE

GIDEON JOSEPH	JERUSHA MARGARET
Capt, Massachusetts 1st Militia	Wife & Mother
B. Apr 12th 1753	B. Oct 27th 1770
D. _____	D. Jul 8th 1798

PATIENCE	FAITH
B. Jan 1st 1793	B. Sep 5th 1794
D. Jul 7th 1798	D. Jul 7th 1798
Æ 5 years	Æ 3 years

Born unto death
These babes await

31

The homecoming of their father
Capt. Gideon Blackbridge
A Hero of Bunker Hill
Who vanished into the wood
On the 5th of July
And could not save them
From their mother Jerusha
A midwife
Who christened them with pine pitch
And set the house alight
Before fleeing from the Gore
Found hanged at Adams' Point
8th Jul 1798

Now rest these babes in slumbers deep
The sleep that hath no dreaming
The sea o'er which their father waits
To join them in their weeping

*

SARAH OLMSTEAD LITTLE
Beloved Mother & Sister
Died the 10th of July 1798
Æ 52 years
Survived by her son
Ephraim Little, Stonecutter
Who writes now these words
And looks to the coming day
When ere the holy fire dims
And all things cease to be

That day is a day of wrath
A day of trouble and heaviness

32

A day of destruction and desolation
A day of obscurity and darkness
A day of clouds and blackness
(Zeph 1:15)

*

SILAS JAMES OLMSTEAD
Col., Massachusetts 5th
Born November the 12th in the year 1751
He acquitted himself with laudable valor
At the battles of Trenton and Princeton
Attaining for himself the rank of Colonel
Before the age of thirty
His was the first family to settle in Whistler's Gore
Where he oversaw the erection of a meetinghouse
And made provision for his fellow Christian
Throughout the winter of 88-89
A widower of long years
He raised two children from infancy
Only to lose them to lightning and to fire
Within a fortnight of one another
During these latter days
Died of grief
Jul 12th
May the darkness show him mercy
Where the Lord has shown none

Waked by the trumpet's sound
I from my grave shall rise
And see the Judge with Glory Crowned
And greet the Flaming Skies

^{Revd} ABIJAH BURDEN
A man of humility and moderation
Of benevolent aspect and amiable temperament
A teacher of the true faith, unsurpassed in learning
Unerring in his efforts on behalf of the lost
Husband to the late Anna Burden
Who drowned beneath the Post Bridge
And whose body was not recovered
In her death he glimpsed the coming of the
Kingdom
And was moved to preach the Final Gospel
In this his church on the 29th of June
Speaking to no man afterward
And taking neither food nor drink
He succumbed to these privations on
On the 14th of July
Æ 26 years
And thenceforth joined our brothers
In the dark that knows no suffering
Whereunto I soon shall follow
And fall into the grave prepared me
E. Little, Stonecutter

Behold, I come quickly
(Rev 22:12)

*

From the sermons of the Revd. Abijah Burden.
Dated June 29th 1798.

34

Upon that day of wrath they flayed the Son with savage blows and drove the spikes through his hands and feet. So, too, was he made to wear a crown of thorns, and in his despair, he cried out to the Father, beseeching the Godhead that dwells outside of time, of Whom Christ was begotten and Who shared His sufferings; aye, Who bears them still. For though Christ died and rose, the Father remains, trapped by His eternal nature in the moment of His Son's uttermost agony. Therein He knows only anguish and doubt and the terrible isolation of the dying. So falls to us this awful choice: the elect He preserves to join Him in the fire, while the damned He snuffs like candle flames failing. Where you will be, my brothers, when the Final Trumpet sounds? Where will you go, my sisters, when Death descends on spider's silk? Who is this who comes from Idumea?

THE SUFFERING CLOWN
Nicole Cushing

Black greasepaint – the vacuum of space. A half-dozen white asterisks painted, pox-like, atop the darkness – stars. When the suffering clown smiled, they stretched.

He sat on a chair in the middle of the supermarket parking lot, fidgeting with the tassels of a flannel blanket draped over his lap. It could only have offered token protection against the cold.

My four year old couldn't resist the temptation to investigate. We'd just spent a tense half-hour in the store, butting heads over his compulsive requests for any plastic trinket or box of junk food that crossed our path. When he discovered the clown in the parking lot, what else could he be expected to do but walk over and introduce himself (dragging me, all the way)? Children in Hanswurst and the surrounding environs are used to such oddities in parking lots. Here in Hanswurst, parking lots serve much the same purpose as a European town square. Anyone – politicians, performance artists, or even recruiters for armies or cults – can set up impromptu engagements there. The clown was obviously ready to put on a show for passers-by.

The flickering parking lot lamps provided an effect not unlike that of strobe lights, facilitating and impeding sight with equal measure. When the clown smiled his lips curled back, revealing twisted yellow teeth and bumpy gums. When the clown smiled, he stared at my son for too long, too wide-eyed. A full minute passed with his face frozen in that overly-congenial grin.

If I were the sort of man who watched horror films, I might blame the clown's creepiness on some diabolical nature intrinsic to his profession, but – after absorbing the entire scene – I realized his stilted, awkward manner owed more to illness than to any character defect. Indeed, he was as frail a specimen of buffoonery as I'd ever the misfortune to behold.

I doubt he could've tipped the scale at three digits. The loose fit of his silken yellow costume implied recent, significant weight loss. Clear plastic tubes delivered oxygen into his red rubber nose. A minivan was parked behind the clown's chair. Its hatchback was open, and I spied beverages and snack food inside (as though he was at a Hanswurst High football game, tailgating). To my chagrin, I also spotted a package of adult diapers alongside the food. The thin plastic grocery bag wasn't tall or opaque enough to obscure it.

The clown shouldn't have been out on a night like this – the sort of night I made my son wear a jacket and hat, whether he wanted to or not. Rain glistened on the cracked asphalt. An unseasonal thunderstorm had passed through less than a half hour before. The wind howled, sending clouds blowing through the night sky as though tugged by an unseen hand. Their departure unveiled the full moon first, followed by the multitude of stars in all their twinkle-twinkle splendor.

A pot-bellied man wearing a blue, grease-stained mechanic's shirt and threadbare trousers threw his calloused hand out for me to shake. The name patch sewn on his shirt announced him as "Butch". He looked up at the clearing sky. "Weather's breakin'. The show must go on! Just one dollar, mister."

My son craned his head up to mine. "Please Dad? Pleeeassssseee can I see the show?"

I turned to Butch. "You'll have to pardon us, but it's pretty cold and getting late. The boy's only a preschooler. His bed time's soon." It was as polite a refusal as I could muster. What I *wanted* to tell this man was that his clown was in no condition to work. What sort of entertaining little show could he be expected to perform while incontinent and demented? I didn't say that, though, because some clown promoters take it personally when you refuse their services. Ever since the economy tanked, it's been considered rude to refuse a brief, one-buck show.

"Please, sir, have a heart. This fella – König's his name – hasn't had the pleasure of performing for a single customer tonight, with it rainin' so hard."

"What's his act have to do with the weather?"

"The rain smears his makeup. We can't have that. Besides, for the audience to appreciate his powers, the night sky has to be clear. You see, this here ain't no ordinary clown – nosiree."

"That's what they all say."

Butch scowled. "This act is absolutely one-of-a-kind. No one else in all of clown history has attempted it, sir. This clown can kill stars... and I ain't talkin' about the Hollywood kind."

"Beg your pardon?"

"I don't know any way better to explain it, mister. If a kid comes up to this clown and smudges one of the white stars on his face into the black base coat, a corresponding star up there in the sky dims and dies. It's easy enough to show you, all it takes is a dollar."

"But I like stars," my son said. (I had to confess to feeling a swell of paternal pride when he said that; I could see that my boy had internalized the appreciation of nature his mother and I had worked so tirelessly to instill in him).

Butch sighed. "Look, it's not like there's any real shortage of 'em out there. We got more of 'em than we know what to do with."

I never could keep a poker face. My skepticism must've been obvious. I tried to let out a hearty laugh, but all that escaped was a raspy, nervous giggle.

Butch tried a new approach. He took a glance at my casual attire, apparently sizing me up as just another of Hanswurst's rednecks. "Hey," he said, "you hunt deer?"

"I can't say I have. I own a gun for self-defense, of course. I just don't feel the need to fire it at a dumb animal."

"W-well," he stammered, "I was just going to say, that killing stars is a little like killing deer – it's mercy killing. You see the problem with both of them is overpopulation..."

"The only thing I see overpopulating Hanswurst these days is parking lot performers. Now, if you'll excuse us, my son needs to go to sleep. We don't have time to watch this invalid attempt some cheap parlor trick."

König let out an incoherent, mournful wail. His awkward smile had been replaced with an even more awkward grimace.

Butch clinched his fists and cleared his throat. His face flushed. "Jeez, mister. What do you wanna do, make him *cry*? Don't you see the risk he takes on, coming out here like this? In his condition? I mean, do you even *care* what his condition is?"

Caught off guard by Butch's anger, I had no words to offer in my own defense. König's oxygen hissed. The lights teased us, staying on for several seconds before returning to their flickering ways. Finally, Butch continued ranting to fill the ugly void.

"He has *cancer*, mister. In his esophagus, his lungs, his brain, his liver, his pancreas, and his blood. Each day this little guy struggles to tread water in an ocean of pain. But he doesn't whine. The only time he gets pissed off is when he runs into an unappreciative audience. Don't you realize that this show is the only thing that keeps König from dying?"

My little boy looked up at me, eyes wide and glistening at Butch's disclosure. I felt like such an insensitive jerk. It all made sense. Hanswurst, Indiana was too remote a location to host a circus of any size. All the clowns in our region worked freelance for whichever promoter would be willing to take them on for a few weeks. Therefore, none of them had health insurance. If König wanted to afford even the least promising cancer treatments, he'd need cold hard cash (thus the extreme measures – courting pneumonia on a cold night just to snag even a handful of customers).

I took out my wallet and gushed apologies. "I'm so sorry. I, well, I just didn't know he was *that* sick." It was a lie that didn't convince König or Butch, but I didn't care all that much about them. At this stage of the game, I was just trying to preserve my reputation with my son. I was just trying to role model sympathy for the less fortunate. I didn't want him to go away from tonight thinking it was okay to humiliate a cancer patient (even if he set himself up for humiliation, with that bizarre outfit and those grandiose claims).

"Look," I continued. "I know that the show only costs a dollar, but seeing as it's been a rough night – and considering all that your clown has been through – what do you say I give you a five?" I presented the bill to the promoter.

Butch smiled and snatched the Abe Lincoln away. "Money's nice, but the most important thing for König is performing. The immune system is a funny thing, you know, mister? Nothing puts more pep in this guy than pickin' off a star or two before bedtime. For real, it does his body good."

I smiled. Nodded.

"The show will start in just a couple of minutes. Let me get it set up."

König let out a high-pitched gurgle and shook his gloved fists.

"Awww," my son said. "What's the matter, Koonig?"

Butch bent down to my little boy. "Oh, don't you worry, kiddo. Mr. König's okay. I know him well enough to be able to tell that this noise he's making now is a *good* thing. That's just his way of showing he's excited and happy that he'll be able to perform for you!"

Butch opened the backseat of the minivan and pulled out a tripod. Once it stood erect, he retrieved a series of metal tubes and went to work putting them all together. "It'll just take a few minutes to get this here telescope assembled before the show, so you can verify my clown's the real deal."

My boy and I looked at each other, then at König. I had to do a double take. His face paint hadn't changed, but something in the structure of the visage underneath *had*. His chin had become longer, his forehead higher. His ears had grown bigger. My son didn't say anything, but he took a step back.

König himself just stared at us and flashed his creepy little dying man's grin.

Butch clapped his filthy hands together. "Okay, now we're ready for some clownin'! Ordinarily, I'd go into my whole carnival barker routine building excitement about König's amazing powers, but we sort of covered that part earlier and we're not likely to get any more foot traffic around here until the cashiers on second-shift count out their till. So let me just tell you how this works. Earlier today, König sat quietly – all to himself – and *meditated*. This is what gave him intuition as to which patch of the night sky needed weeding. Then he took his magic clown paint and decorated his face in the manner you see before you."

"It's magic?" my little boy asked.

"Yup," said Butch. "Just like I said – if a young child places his or her hand on König's face paint and smears away one of the stars, a matching star disappears from the sky – never to nuisance us with its light ever again."

"Like killing lightening bugs," my youngster said, smiling and clapping.

I cringed. Did my boy really take that much joy in destruction? Maybe he hadn't internalized a love of nature, after all.

Butch smiled. "Yes, that's it. Exactly like killing lightening bugs. So, are you ready?"

"Boy, am I!"

I looked at König again, and was rendered uncomfortable by the inescapable perception that his skull had yet again undergone transformation when I wasn't looking. Now his face was heart-shaped, with high cheekbones. His chin was pointed – almost dainty.

My son approached the clown on tip-toe, trying in vain to reach his face. "Which star should I kill, Dad?"

"Woah," Butch said. "Wait...before you touch a star on König's face, I want you to see the matching star up in the sky." He gestured toward a step-ladder he'd brought in front of the tripod. My son jogged toward it, climbed up the steps and began to look through the telescope.

Butch smiled. "See all those stars?"

"Uh-huh!"

"Which one do you want to kill?"

"There's a real bright one. Let's make that one go 'way."

"Alrighty, then...with the help of König the Clown, I think we can do just that!" My boy jumped off the step ladder, and Butch moved it away from the tripod and put it in front of König's chair. "Now, climb up that ladder again and see Mr. König."

"How come I have to come over there? How come he can't come see me?" A bright child, my boy – asking such an observant question.

"Well," Butch said, frowning, "if you want to know the truth, son, König the Clown is *so sick* that

44

he can't even walk anymore." Then, with a single twitch of his meaty paw, he tore the flannel blanket off the clown, revealing the rust-pocked wheelchair in which he sat. The wheels looked low on air. Several of the spokes were fractured. It was a contraption from another generation, perhaps purchased for a few dollars at the local Goodwill. It should have been in a medical museum, not a rain-slicked parking lot.

My son looked like he was going to cry. Even *his* brain – so new to the world – could detect that something was amiss with the wheelchair. He couldn't place the antique medical device as something that was *old*, because his life experience stretched only a few years. But he could definitely intuit that it *didn't belong*.

Butch spoke up, shaking both of us out of our daze. "If you want Mr. König to feel better and be able to leave the wheelchair, you have to hop up there and help him kill stars. It's the best medicine in the whole wide world! König, do you want to point to the star on your face that matches up with the one the little boy wants to kill?"

The clown raised a trembling hand up to his right cheekbone, fingering the appropriate star.

"Okay then, son, all you have to do is smudge it out with your fingers."

My boy climbed the step-ladder and reached up to the clown's face. But the star wouldn't budge.

Butch sighed. "The bright ones are sometimes a little harder. I'll tell you what to do – why don't you

45

spit in your hand and use that to wipe the star away."

I felt the need to intervene. "Sir, pardon me but this *really is* unusual —"

My son spit in his hand.

"Stop that right now, mister! That's not how we behave!"

Ignoring me, the boy wiped his slobbery palm over König's cheekbone. A single white asterisk melted into the black background. When it was over, the marred makeup looked like nothing so much as one of the finger paintings adorning our refrigerator back at the house. Five stars remained, and by the smile on my son's face I could tell that they might also be endangered if I didn't immediately hoist him away from the step-ladder.

Butch looked through the telescope. "And....it's gone! Wanna come see?"

I set down the lad then hunched over and looked. Black emptiness occupied the space previously allocated to the bright star. I pulled my eye away from the lens. "It's just a trick," I said. "While our attention was focused on the clown, you must have moved the telescope to a different section of sky."

König wailed with newly-plump lips.

Butch sneered. "Tell you what, buddy — if by sunrise you *still* think we've bamboozled you, we'll give you back your money. Deal?"

Had I been a wise man, I would've asked him then and there just what he meant. As it was, I

46

turned my back to him, grabbed my boy with my left hand and steered our grocery cart back to our car with the right.

That night had simmered with unease. The following morning, this boiled over into terror. My boy was nowhere to be found. A sticky, smeared, gore-colored residue stained his bed sheets. It was as though he'd melted and a cosmic finger had reached down to make a swirly, preschoolish finger painting out of the remains. His mother balled her fists and shrieked.

My first call was to 911. For some reason they sent an ambulance. We felt just as puzzled as the paramedics were when they arrived at our house. It took another half-hour for the Hanswurst Police to arrive. They asked questions. Trying not to sound crazy, I let them know my concerns about König the clown.

The sergeant taking my report rolled his eyes. "You expect me to believe that a wheelchair-bound cancer patient did *that* to your son?"

"So you know him?"

He stroked his walrusy mustache with his chubby thumb and index finger. He took a too-long pause. When he finally *did* speak, his voice trembled. "You shouldn't ask the law a question like that, mister."

"What's that supposed to mean?

His face took on a sheen of sweat. "Who do you think is the most likely suspect in this case? Who had access to the boy during the night?"

"You really think my wife or I could do something like *that*? We have no motive. That's our son!"

He walked closer up to me. Almost belly to belly. "No," he whispered. "Off the record, sir, I *know* you didn't do it. But if you call 911 and the police come, then *someone*, someone *human* and *only human* – someone who's just one *discrete* human, I should add, has to be arrested, and tried. You should have just pretended this didn't happen, like the rest of us. As it is, I'll have to ask you to place your hands behind your back, sir." He took out his handcuffs. They were riddled with specks of rust, but appeared to still have enough sturdy steel left in them to restrain me.

"But you've no probable cause. On what grounds am I being arrested?"

"On the grounds of having reported a crime! A crime implies a criminal, and the only criminal the laws of nature allow us to identify in this case is either you or your wife. My choice of you, in particular, was admittedly arbitrary – c'est la vie. Now, if you'd rather skip the tediousness of incarceration and trial, I suggest you recant immediately. If you tell me that you made a gigantic blunder, perhaps mistaking your dog's vomit for the remains of a child, I'll forget that all of this ever happened and merely issue you a citation for making a false report. In most cases they'll plea bargain that down to a lesser charge. You'll pay a fine, perhaps perform some community service."

My wife sobbed and shook me by the shoulder. "J-just do like he says. Just make it stop! Just make it all *stop*! Recant, for God's sake, just like the good officer asks, sweetheart."

"But what about our son?"

The policeman answered. "If you recant, which I strongly suggest that you do, then you must never again speak of him. For all intents and purposes, he never existed. The same goes for that clown and his promoter. For the sake of your very sanity, you must convince yourself that they were just nightmares. This may sound harsh, but it's the way everyone else in Hanswurst has dealt with this kind of thing. It would be snobbery, on your part, to expect anything better."

I looked at the cop. I looked at my wife. "Then that's what I'll do. I-I'm sorry. I was mistaken, officer. Please forgive me." I trembled.

Maybe I was a snob. Maybe that's what led me to expect better answers than those offered by the authorities. Maybe that's what led me to defy the conditions of my arrangement with the police and investigate the grocery store parking lot by day, looking for any sign of the clown and his handler. Maybe that's why I took my pistol along.

Sunlight bleached the eeriness out of the place. Active commerce made it feel less haunted.

Nevertheless, my pulse raced. I couldn't imagine that they would have traveled far, given the advanced stage of the clown's cancer. I discovered that, in fact, they hadn't moved at all since the night before. I found their minivan parked in exactly the same place it had been.

By daylight, the vehicle looked old and decrepit. Its blue paint peeled. A handful of dents (some incidental, others disfiguring) suggested it might be ready for the junkyard. Rust afflicted its wheel wells.

Looking over a broader swath of parking lot, rust afflicted every car and truck within a six foot radius of König the Clown's minivan. All of the vehicles outside that perimeter were newer, or – at least – had been spared that particular state of decay.

The sun cast a glare on Butch's windshield. To catch a peek inside, I had to squat down to just the right angle. A gaudy, beaded curtain separated the front seats from the rear. Butch reclined in a tilted-back passenger seat. His fat stomach and legs were visible, his upper torso and head hidden by the beads.

I knocked on the windshield. Butch scrambled his hands through the beads, and then tilted his chair into a sitting position. He rubbed his eyes with his fists, getting the sleep out. Then he turned a crank and his window lowered. An odd smell wafted out – a nauseating mix of the artificial scent of clown makeup and all-too-natural body odor.

"Still think we cheated you last night?"

I hunched farther down so I could look him in the eye. "What'd you do with my son?"

"Son? You have a son? I'm afraid I can't help you out there, mister. When I met you last night, you were alone."

"You filthy liar! What the fuck *did you do*?"

He sighed. "Me? I didn't do anything. Now, König, on the other hand..." He ran stubby fingers through long, unwashed hair.

"What did *he* do?"

"Look, mister, I think you'd do a lot better for yourself in life if you just took things on faith instead of asking so many questions. I'm sure that if there were really anything that needed investigation, the cops would have been on it like white on rice!"

"They won't do anything. I don't know what your angle is with them. Maybe you're second-cousins to the police chief, or maybe you have photos of him in a compromising position. I don't know what game it is you're playing that lets you murder preschoolers, but I promise you I'll find out"

"You don't know what you're saying."

"Where's König? He's in there with you, isn't he?"

Butch grabbed a pack of Marlboros from his shirt pocket. Took out a zippo and lit up. "There are some things better left unknown."

I leaned forward, grabbed Butch's shirt collar with my left hand and put my pistol to his temple with the right. "Look at me, you little two-bit clown promoter. You're going to show me where König is right now, or else he'll be required to seek out new representation."

"You don't want to know, not really. You don't *need* to know."

I cocked the hammer.

Butch laid his head in his hands. "You're doing it. You're really making me show you König in the morning. Do you have any idea how many parents have shoved guns in my face? Do you know how many of them take those very same guns and stick 'em in their own mouths, once they see König the morning after a show?"

"Enough yapping," I said. "Show me the clown. Now."

He reached back and pulled up a small nob, unlocking the door. "You asked for it."

Yes, he was only a frail, sick clown – but I nonetheless found it necessary to brace myself for the need to shoot. At least, what I *expected* was a frail, sick clown. This is what I saw in the backseat: a bald, *buttery* man. Heavier than Butch, even. He wore the same yellow silk suit König had worn the night before. It billowed out at odd intervals, as though there were small animals racing around underneath; climbing around his torso. A series of muffled squeaks and high-pitched growls seemed to confirm this. The buttery man looked unperturbed by the ruckus. He sat with his legs folded underneath him, his eyes closed. Meditating.

"Where's König?"

The man fluttered his eyelids, as if waking. Then he spoke in a voice that was more than one voice. "Everywhere. In rising mountains and sinking islands, new worlds and dead ones. In the heart of the wood and in the skeleton of the universe. In any place that comes and ceases to be. Which is, if I may repeat myself, *everywhere*."

Not human. Not *only human*.

I began to feel my pulse in my jugular. "Who are you?"

"Everyone," said the hundred-voices-in-one.

Not one *discrete* human.

No merciful, dark night or face paint obscured the hideous sight of the buttery man's skull rearranging itself. Bones flexed and contracted, and his buttery skin flexed with them. They made popping and clicking sounds. The buttery man's head transformed from the thick, broad noggin I'd first seen to something more slender – but by no means emaciated. "Anyone or anything that is born and dies. Even you."

I studied the visage of the buttery man in the back seat until I discovered that his new face was my own. But the buttery man's body was still fat – far fatter than mine. "Not exactly to scale, is it? Hey, you like comedy? I do impressions. No charge, since you've come all this way."

I whimpered.

The buttery man was enjoying himself. "Abra Cadaver," he shrieked (intentionally, I think,

53

twisting the magic words into morbid ones). His face stayed as *my* face, but grew thinner. Bony. Likewise, the barks and howls under his clown suit quieted as the girth of his body dissolved. When he finished his metamorphosis, I was sitting across from myself, in a clown suit several sizes too big for me. My frame – the frame I was looking at – was frail. I could not have tipped the scale at three digits.

"Here's my impression of *you* dying from cancer ten years from now!"

"Stop it," I said, backing away from the minivan.

"Awww…," Buttery-König-Cancer-Patient-Me-Universe-Man said (in his voice that was more than one voice). "Don't leave. You haven't even asked me about your boy. Don't you want to see him?" He tucked his withered hands at his costume's collar and stretched it out from his body so he could see inside. "I know he's in here somewhere. He might be that melanoma that just showed up today on my tummy tum-tum."

As if to verify the clown's claim, I heard a squeaky, lisping voice coming from his (my) belly. "Help me, Dad. Please, Dad. Pleeeeassssee! It's dark in here!"

I took a step back, took a deep breath, and said the words that damned me. What other choice did I have? Who among us has resisted the urge to give up asking questions and just go with the flow? Who among us hasn't painted a surrendering smile over an inquisitive smirk? We've all volunteered for the part of the fool, going along with the conspiracy of happy delusion that keeps all of Hanswurst (and if König was to be believed, much beyond our little town) in its grip. It would be snobbery to expect anything better.

"I'm sorry to have troubled you, sir. There's no need to show me your anthropomorphic melanoma. It turns out I was mistaken. You and I have never met before. Perhaps that's someone else's boy. I have no son."

AIRWAVES BURST TO BLISSFUL

Josh Myers

For John Balance, Peter Christopherson, and David Tibet

I don't know.
I don't know.
I don't know.
I have to sleep.

This is my enemy.

There is bad noise around me. I have surrounded myself with countless machines, all echoing with sound, the sound of stars, the sound of planetary interference, the sound of thunder, the sound of murder. Organic sounds of fear and desperation. All played a thousand times at a thousand frequencies and swelling into one warm glow.

I have to sleep.

I close my eyes and there is barking. A horde of ravenous black and silver dogs surround the base of a crucifix. Behind them is a field of crosses, stretching up a sickly mountain and emanating black waves of dread. Waveforms and vibrations and explanations of why we feel discomfort.

I blink.

The man on the cross is not who he should be.

He looks with longing. He opens his mouth and the world swells with dryness. The fading light in his eyes burns into mine, sending a message, begging for mother's milk.

A beast sits on an arm of the cross. It barks and snarls and tells me, "Hello, I hate you."

I have to sleep.

Behind them, from the field of crosses, atop the sickly mountain, the ground cracks and breaks open. A new peak arises, one made of flesh and sin. The newborn phallic mountaintop sits in splendor and judges the man nailed to the cross. In obedience toward the emerging god, the field of crosses does the same.

Black waves of dread permeate his flesh and the dogs prick up their ears.

The beast that sits on the arm of the cross flaps its wings and bays.

Like sentinels from another time, the dogs erupt in a swarm of black and silver fur. They attack the field of crosses, ripping flesh and blood from wooden structures. Crosses collapse and writhe in agony, making hateful new shapes in their shameful rigor mortis. Crooked crosses in the blood and the dirt.

I have to sleep.

I was wrong.

The beast does not sit on an arm of the cross. The beast is a part of the cross. Its torso decomposes and petrifies, revealing a blend of wood and wickedness. Its wings lose their feathers and shrivel and drop off. A horn extends from its forehead. Its spine twists and aches and forms a great hump. Bones strain and crack as its arms extend to grip its cross-flesh and leer out at me, at us, at the world.

It smiles at the wreckage of the field of crosses. Dead and dying crosses, bent and bleeding in the shadow of the phallic mountaintop.

The dogs return to sit at the base of the sole remaining cross, the one with the beast and with the man. They sit at the base of the cross with the wrong man. Foamy blood drips from their jaws as they eagerly await their master's words.

The beast surveys the carnage.

Its shoulders sag and it lets out a sigh.

The man on the cross closes his eyes and smiles.

The beast flies into a rage. A twisted and gnarled arm extends and razor-blade nails slice a wound into the man's side.

The man smiles as blood trickles from the wound. Blood drips from his toes onto the heads of black and silver dogs. His blood mixes with that of the ravaged crosses.

The beast smiles and withdraws into the crucifix.

I am alone with the man and the dog and the man is dying and the dogs are without a master.

I have to sleep.

A buzzing fills the air.

This is not my buzzing. This is not my noise. This is not my machine, not my cries from distant planets, my begging for mercy, my screams from the center of the universe.

This is vicious and wicked and brings with it vicious and wicked things.

Clouds of insects pour from the bleeding wounds in the crooked crosses. A swarm makes its way through the wreckage. Locusts buzz and click and rattle. They carry with them a voice, and it echoes over the mountain.

The voice tells me things I know and it tells me things I must know and it tells me things I must never know and it tells me things I do not want to hear.

It is laughing at me.

I know it is laughing at me.

It is always laughing at me.

It has always laughed at me.

It will always be laughing at me.

I HAVE TO SLEEP.

There is another voice. Another voice cutting through the laughter. A sad, bored voice. A woman, reciting strange passages, addressing me directly.

More voices. All the same voice, but speaking at the same time, reciting different passages, the same passages, in different order and in a different way, yet all at the same time.

The voice speaks from the phallic mountaintop.

59

The voice speaks time and again, sad sermons at the wrong time.

The voice seeks to bring comfort for me and for the rest of mankind.

The voice recites lullabies for the end of the world.

I have to sleep.

They refer to all sparkling in darkness. All darkness, you know. But some light is not burned to death. We are able. This is a bullet for all times, and my thoughts. It hurts to think of him. Make me whole.

The world of me to enter my world spreading disease.

You have to sleep.

SHUT UP GOD. I CAN'T HEAR YOU ANYMORE.

These words mean nothing. Your words mean NOTHING.

Turn airwaves to blissful and banish darkness.

I must bring light.

Burn earth to heaven and rust heaven to dance.

You should beg for forgiveness.

You should fill out a formal request.

Errors have been and will always be.

It's not your fault.

This is who we are and what he is.

I have to sleep.

LULLABY
Edward Morris

For David Tibet & Nick Cave

Hush, dear one, hush. Those are not explosions, outside our cave. They are only branches breaking, with the weight of the black snow. The black snows have come again, but your Papa keeps us warm. There are still acres and acres of trees that didn't burn all the way. No matter how long this winter lasts, we will be safe.

Don't you cry, baby girl. Go to sleep. The promise of a new world will radiate outward from here, from under the Mountain of Sorrows whose name in the old tongue was once Alleghenia. The flame has not gone out. Guttered, yes, but not gone. We can still paint pictures on the wall in its cold light, and dig up the books the black robes buried long before. We can still find more.

Go to sleep, little baby. Go to sleep, little baby. Papa's long gone with his white suit on, soon back with meat that you don't have to look at before it's cooked. Don't need nobody, nobody, nobody but the babe.

Nobody but you, tonight, daughter, the way I found you at the airlock, looking into the sky with the tears streaming down your face as the Perseids began to fall. I told you what they were, baby, from the book your Papa and I found.

Your Papa and I watch the stars a lot. Your Papa says that one day, we might fall to them again. When we can range, and roam, and beat old dead missiles into ships. The way he says we can.

Out in the hinterlands, I think I see a slow star or two drop to Earth beyond the airlock, in the vast beast-whistling wastes. On the slope below our home, the stones which spell out H E L P may or may not be legible when those stars disgorge their pilots. Not for me to say. Merely to pray.

To pray we can. When you wake, baby, you can have all the stars. Rest your head upon the straw tick, and let the bees and butterflies of Dream circle round your eyes instead of tears.

THE MAN OF THE CROSSES
Ian Delacroix

The days were getting longer and longer. Dying over crooked roofs and spires, the sun drew traces of nonsense and decadence over the old structures and buildings. The city was a mass of wood, stone and brick. Its narrow passages, arches and alleys were full of nostalgias and broken hopes.

The Architect had left the city a decade ago, when the storm arrived, and now the chant of the wind through the stones was a mourning of selfishness and solitudes. His creations remained in the ancient district, hollow and deserted, like splendid ruins of a false past.

Even the Lord in Yellow, the prophet who mastered the Sect, had vanished. The followers and the Cultists have been disseminated through the region, spread in more comfortable cities, following other beliefs and worshipping new Gods, or believing in nothing but themselves. The teaching of the Lord in Yellow, forgotten.

The city was doomed to decay and rot. The same fortune had been written for his folks. The ones who were born in the city belonged to the city, its condemnation marked over their skin like a morbid stain.

Weird figures had been seen wandering down the streets, under a grey-coloured sky. Derelicts, vagrants, artists, apocalyptic poets. This was the way the town was dragging along the new millennium.

Veridiana couldn't find peace in her room.

Subterranean masks watched her from the walls with enigmatic eyes, but she scarcely gazed at them. Her eyes and thoughts were distant, beyond those cryptic walls and the matter of the house.

She had been seen at Maldoror, the Cabaret where the last of the unsuccessful artists – sculptors, gravers, musicians, painters, poets – gathered and performed their mystical, mighty and futile art.

She was one of *them*, she knew it. One of the derelicts. One of the failed ones.

«We cannot be forgotten 'cause we are utterly ignored», said once *Madame*, the oriental keeper.

She was right. Veridiana belonged to the city and she couldn't avoid its chant.

There was something more in those days, something that has nothing to do with the Sect, the Architect and his creations, nor the Lord in Yellow with his *Revelations* or the Art of failure. Maybe it was part of the same metaphysical structures or it could be due to different vibrations within the city.

Veridiana didn't know. She only cared about Danilo.

Someone was playing a wicked music at the Cabaret. An apocalyptical dancer was moving on the stage among sheets and shrouds, performing the decay. His body was covered in paint as in

Japanese Butoh dance. The flute followed his gestures with disharmonic sounds.

Among the dim light of the room there were few, absent minded spectators. The failed artists were all crowded around wooden tables.

Veridiana approached *Madame* at the counter. The old mistress had ended reading Tarots ages ago.

«He has vanished. It's been nearly three weeks now».

«Forget him».

Madame's eyes contained infinite colours.

«Now he is part of the city, dear».

«What do you mean?»

She looked into her eyes with a wrinkled smile.

«You know what I'm talking about, honey».

The mourning of the flute became unbearable. The room seemed darker than before to her eyes. The dancer moved through the shadows like a white larva.

«Forget him», repeated the old lady.

Veridiana looked at the stage, hypnotized.

«But if you really want to share the fortune of your brother, go to the *man of the crosses*», whispered *Madame* in her ears.

Veridiana turned, stunned.

«The man of the crosses», murmured.

The days were getting hotter and hotter. A never-ending open eye in a burning sky was the sun. The Cabaret would have been closed soon. No more apocalyptic performances, no more weird exhibitions of talented unknown musicians or morbid poems uttered in the dark.

The last show would have been the decadence itself.

Everyone knew that moment would have come but they were all pretending that nothing was going to happen. And besides they thought the drama wasn't linked with the *nature* of the city.

Veridiana wandered through the narrow alleys and dark passages of the old district, where the buildings were small and the roofs were made of stones. She has never been there for a long time.

Strange symbols were painted over the walls. She thought they were graffiti, but as soon as she roamed deeper in the core of the quarter, she realized that they were completely different signs.

Seals. Evocations. Chances.

They had a perverse logic, built up on a structure that reminded her of the disease inside the Puppeteers' marionettes, the hollow and unsaid contained in the Lord in Yellow's poems, and yet the pattern of the weird music she had heard at the Cabaret sometimes.

She shivered.

She glanced at the buildings that surrounded her, where she could recognize the hand of the Architect in the violent curves of certain lines, in the chant of disharmonies that screamed from certain colours. She wondered if the Architect and her brother had shared the same fate. Maybe it was *that* the meaning beyond the words of *Madame*. Maybe them, with the Cultists, the Lord in Yellow and his followers, the Puppeteers and the vanished ones with their sick art shared the same secret of the city. It was something that lay under the façade, the walls of brick and stone, the masks of wax at the gates of the cemetery or the whispers of strange poems spoken on the stage of the Cabaret.

The million masks of the town.

A hand of her slipped on her pocket, where one of the creations of Danilo laid. Her room was still filled with his bizarre carvings – mystical and biblical figures, scenes of coming storms, leviathans and angels and demons of clay – even the subterranean masks that crowded the walls and *watched* her without eyes have been created by him.

He was a sculptor and he had shared the decay of the city. He, like everyone else who was gifted, was more intertwined with the change than the others. The ones who weren't blessed with the touch of Art would have followed anyway.

Now she understood.

She reached the door of the deserted building *Madame* had told her.

She let her eyes get used to the gloominess, than went in.

The corridor smelled of rotten fish. The staircase was damaged. Pale rays of light came from the upper floor, where some birds – something big, heavy and dark – had set their nest.

Her eyes roamed to the other side of the stairs. She knew she had to go down.

The steps were filled with bags full of rubbish. Something moved through the littler, maybe cats, maybe something else.

The same signs she had seen on the walls outside were drawn inside along the corridors, but other symbols were there: crosses of different dimensions and shapes, engraved with a yellow paint over the plaster.

She went down the stairs, trying to avoid the rubbish to touch her skin, staring at the signs on the walls that were becoming more weird and obscene as far as she approached the end of the steps.

She reached the basement. The wooden door was out of her hinges. From the threshold she could hear the sound of the *sea* carried by a weak chant.

A step inside.

The room was gloomy and chaotic. A lot of strange devices and broken pieces of furniture crowded the space: cabinets, cupboards, bookshelves full of rotten books and rusted carpets with water stains. Litter was everywhere, pallid cats were moving through fish remains.

The walls were full of crosses. Pieces of wood created a spiritual and disgusting frame of chances. Branches intertwined in a hideous sculpture of feral asymmetry.

Veridiana couldn't say what was sick with that incredible multitude of crosses. Her unease was created by something underhand, something subtle and unconscious.

The *vibrations*.

That sculpture, that mass of crosses and chances relayed the same eerie vibrations of the structures built up by the Architect. It was the same pattern of dissonance and mysticism. Like the words of the lost prophet it was streaked in grey and scarlet. It was a subtle chant of the substance, remoulding the world, something that crumbled the flesh of the city little by little.

The *vibrations*.

Interferences were damaging the matter from its foundation.

Veridiana felt it inside her bones and she was overwhelmed by the depth of the revelation.

There was a city *under* the city, a second skin. Its frame was made up by various refractions. Humans couldn't see it. It was only a matter of light refraction theory. The hidden city was like a superimposed photograph. Or was the city on the surfaced the false picture?

The *vibrations*.

The man of the crosses was on the floor. He was a young skinned lad, not even in his thirties, his arms were thin and his fingers were gnarled like branches of flesh.

As an ordinary beggar, he was wrapped in tatters. He was lying in a floor of rubbish and litter.

There were shells, a lot of crosses made of shells among the rags that enveloped him.

«Are you the *man of the crosses?*»

Something moved among the garbage behind Veridiana. He didn't answer.

«My brother has vanished».

He moved with the rhythm of tides. The shells tinkled. His eyes were cavernous and ecstatic.

«I want him back».

«He belongs to the city».

His voice was the rotten chant of the sea.

«I want him back».

The shells tinkled again.

«Come closer».

She bit her lips.

He reached her with his gnarled fingers. The atmosphere changed. She felt as if the underneath city was pressing against the walls. The room trembled, but it was still. A new step to decay.

The eyes of the man of the crosses became many. She had the impression she was looking beyond their moisture and finally the darkness of the room and the power of the symbols showed her their multiplicity.

«You can find him through your sorrow», he sentenced.

Veridiana thought of what she had passed through in her whole life.

«The metaphysics of sorrow is the chant of the city, can't you hear it?» he added.

«The sacrifice is the threshold of knowledge».

The revelation was complete.

The days were getting more and more rotten. The sky has the colour of madness, a sick pale yellow of disease. The nights weren't better at all, the wind carried the smell of an unknown distant sea all over the city districts.

Veridiana stood in her room for seven days.

She had to think, to consider. The words of the *man of the crosses* echoed in her ears with the chant of the disharmonies. Now she knew the secret of the city.

In the past the Sect had tried to unveiled the pattern of sorrow – the Lord in Yellow's Seven Chapters of *Revelation* made sense now – but currently the Cultists were gone.

The Architect did the same thing through his art – the lines of his buildings showed the key of the enigma – and so did the Puppeteer with his sibylline marionettes and his odd performances that had been sent away soon.

She had preferred to ignore all those signs like anyone else.

She gazed out of the window the crooked streets and the hollow squares, letting her thoughts wander to the *other* city she had sensed underneath.

Images of her brother danced like ghosts on her mind.

She recalled a summer of decades before, when they were just teens. They were playing in the fields. From the hills they could see the entire profile of the city, with the river, the factories, the gardens and churches and the pinnacles and their hidden enigmas.

«How strange! I have never realized before that our city resembles an elongated cross», said him, suddenly.

«What?»

«Yes, look at it. It looks like a cross. The river is the main branch and the street of the merchants, with the seven squares, it's the other one. And there, near the Church of the Unknown Veil where the Sect gathers, you can find the intersection of the two main branches».

«Mhhh, you... you are right. How odd! Do you think it's done on purpose?»

«Of course. But I can't understand why».

Later that afternoon they found on the same hill a cross buried on the ground.

«Look. Do you think there is someone buried down there?» she asked him, reluctantly.

«I don't think so», Danilo appeared more interested than worried in their discovery. «The shape is unusual. I have never seen anything like this before, it doesn't resemble a Christian cross nor a Celtic one. And look what it's made of... what could it be? Is that stone?»

«It makes me think about...bones», she shivered.

Their eyes met, his glance was full of rapture and sorrow.

«It's late», she cried. «The sun is growing pale».

72

He followed the line of her gaze, where the buildings were creating shades of doubt.

«Have you ever dreamt about the sea?» he asked.

«What do you mean?»

«I always dream water. The city is full of it. The sea is everywhere. There is water instead of the streets and canals as a replacement for pavements. It's our city but at the same time it is *not*, could you understand? The buildings are deserted and hollow. I wander through the rooms following the swish of the waves against the walls. But every time I'm opening a door or I'm looking out from a balcony, the waters vanish».

Soon after that revelation Veridiana started to feel sick. She had the feeling that she was hearing a sort of liquid buzzing, some kind of deformed *vibration*. At the time she had thought it was something related to the cross they had found. But now, after all those years, she finally understood it was the city itself that had given her that vertigo. She had tasted its decaying nature for the first time that afternoon.

Her brother had come back several times to the hill, she had never returned.

Veridiana gazed at the masks on the walls. Her mind went back to her brother's first exhibition at the Cabaret – in those days it was not called Maldoror, it had a name she can't remember, something like *The Mourning Muse* or *The Suffering Muse* –, Danilo's creations were all along the main room while some twisted poets were reciting on the stage verses about tides and solitude and destiny. She reminded the determination in his brother's eyes and what *Madame* told her that night: «*Now* he belongs to the city».

Other exhibitions followed, new complex spirals into the abyss, Danilo's creations became more and more evocative and dark, his visions went deeper into the pulp of the human condition: the grief and the sacrifice.

Watching the masks, Veridiana asked herself how many secrets were hidden inside those faces of clay. She wondered if her brother's *nature* and hers were the same and if she could do what the man of the crosses had suggested. He had said that the chant of the city was the metaphysics of sorrow, and that the only way for her to share her brother's fate was to roam through the labyrinth of pain.

The days were getting weirder and weirder. The night was falling carrying the heavy scent of tides. A soft wind blew in the streets. In the old district pale cats wandered along the alleys, sending long moans of dissatisfaction through the dark.

The buildings appeared different somehow, less solid then before. The relics of the Architects' structures shined with a translucent mystical glow.

The Maldoror was open.

The stage was enlightened by a dim light. The last show, the ultimate performance, the final act would be held that night.

The Cabaret was more crowded than ever. It was like anyone in town felt something was going to happen. All the artists and wannabe left were gathered by this silent calling.

Madame was at the counter. Near her Veridiana felt nervous.

«You have made your choice, dear», said the old lady. There was something reassuring in her voice.

Veridiana tried to focus on her brother's works fixing the stage full of his sculptures.

Dreadful geometries intertwined in new configurations, shades formed lines and hollows on the strange figures. The most astonishing creation was a coral structure, spirals of decadence rose from a pedestal. A dark form was trapped among the spirals: a sort of fish with a manlike face, with a thorn of crosses on his head.

Her mind went to the day on the hill.

She could feel the vibrations, now. She could understand them and feel the fall of the city. In some way there was even some hidden beauty in the collapse.

She reached the stage and started her performance. Veridiana closed her eyes and began to dance under the rhythm of the morbid waving she could hear. It was a subtle and rotten chant. She followed the invisible patterns of decay, shaking her arms and her legs wrapped in the silk kimono. She moved like a creature from another world.

The audience was hypnotized. She couldn't see them – her eyes were shut – but she could *feel* them, the vibrations that they were all finally following were the ones she knew. The town was moving them.

Her gestures became more frenzied; she traced circles of thorns in the air to symbolize the stages of rotting the city has passed through.

She got undress soon, the kimono left on the floor, her pale skin offered to the underneath dimension. She trembled, and the entire Cabaret trembled with her. The walls, the structures, the atoms of the spectators, everything around her seemed to shrink and remould.

The blade in her hand.

She traced crosses and lost symbols over her skin, the blood dripping on the wood. Soon she found herself moving over a wet sticky floor. She didn't stop her dance, completing her sacrifice.

Rush of pain ran through her body. The crosses were burning over her skin, up to the bones. She peeled herself, passing though the different degrees of might and sorrow. And, finally, knowledge.

Then she opened her eyes.

She had found him.

Through a veil of light she could see him now.

Danilo was near the door of the Cabaret. His body in darkness. His skin was moist, his clothes and hair were covered in sand and seaweeds. She called his name. He came out of the dark. His body swayed while he was moving as a willow in the water.

A rosary of crosses was filling his neck and chest. Even his arms were full of symbols. Ancient patterns of beauty, of shared experience, of pain. He whispered and his low, liquid voice flowed upon her ears with a non-human language.

The last *vibrations*.

All lights vanished. The doors of the Cabaret closed forever.

ALL IN A ROW
Jon R. Meyers

I walked the battered streets from the bridge to the edge of the city. A black and white spiral rose parallel to my emotions as I looked around at the waste. This dirt was the filth that my ancestors left before me, for us. Society that once lingered was becoming more of a crucifix the older I became. Day in and day out subjects of poverty, human error, machines, human error, poverty, machines, human error, human error, human error.

As an infant I sat in a cloud of smoke.

I saw a bridge.

I saw a ghost inside of a halo.

I envisioned everything as we would once know on that bridge with that ghost on top of that halo in the dark. I continued to age. I continued to grow, older and wiser, stronger and more comfortable... But with or for what?

I wasn't sure.

I knew it would be hard to see passed the cracks in the mascara. It would be hard to pin the tail on the terror. It would be hard to move. It would be hard to breathe. It would be hard to sleep.

On socialism.

On death.

On Christ.

As an infant I sat in a cloud of smoke.

I saw a bridge.

I saw a ghost inside of a halo.

Broken street lamps. Shattered glass. Decaying bodies. Post-traumatic stress. Nuclear physics. Evolution. The cross. Holocaust. BLOOD. The river, so cold, so dark, and so red. A canvas, ever so black. A fix. A bridge. A ghost. A halo. A hole. In a city. Of piss. Of shit. Poverty. Human error. Machines. Human error. Poverty. Machines. Human error. Human error. Human error. Human error. Human error. Human error. Human error. Human error. Human error. Human error. Human error. Human error. Human error. Human error. Human error.

A crowd of gazing eyes sat below.
All in a row.
With knives and forks.
With spikes and chains.
With torches of fire,
held above heads,
With starved eyes, possessed.
Little white lies.
Little white lines.
REPEAT.
The people,
so hungry,
so pure.
Within a city,
of fog,
and mist,
gravity DOES NOT exist.

THROUGH OUR MASTER'S BLOOD WE SING

Kent Gowran

Trapped in stone we have withered inside, prisoners of a mercy, a solace we never sought.

Our master's blade bites into the earth, we are the secrets buried deep, life shaded shapeless, missing pages of the history of a flowering cadaver.

Sweat falls from our master's brow, crawling now clawing the earth, despair gripping a hopeless mind, the covenant of cursed seed shouting from the womb of sorrow.

Grace falls to us as the blade slips, rends the flesh, a rite of time, hard and cruel through our master's blood we sing, destiny realigns, our eyes look on and beyond.

I open my eyes alone the astral mind abandoned in this new wasteland, a painted mask of sadness, I am the progeny of desecration writ large the velvet tongued swine I name myself master now of this plane of despair.

Black rays shine loveless and cold, mine is an anatomy of frost never warmed by the sun.

THE PUPPET OF GRUDGES
Michael Allen Rose

I pull the string and the old doll emerges from its wooden coffin. It hesitates, physics defying me with friction's grip, for its sins are wet, and slick with memory. One by one, limbs spill onto the floor, legs, arms, head. I drop the controls. They clatter like bones.

I count my candles again. There are five. Remembering that man is five, and what came after, I decide I will add one candle to make six. My back hurts, and it takes time to cross the room. My joints ache, I bend like wheat in a storm and bow to the spectre of time.

Why can't I just walk away?

The wooden shelf in the corner appears a relic from another age, a last gasp of something beyond memory. Butterflies and clovers are carved into signs and sigils. I brush a curious fingertip over the relief and feel my skin fill up the subtle groove, tracing through the dust. My finger is covered in gray; without thinking I put the fingertip in my mouth and suck it clean.

I am cold, and I know before I am through I will become colder. The old trunk, her old trunk, stands nearby, a black mountain of longing standing as an island in the misery I've built. I pull it open. A child's blanket, stuffed with cotton. A quilt sewn through with the eschatology of limitation. It falls around my shallow shoulders. It will do for now.

The puppet's eyes stare at me lifelessly from yards away. It may as well be miles. I gather my form into something resembling a man and shuffle back toward the entrance to my attic, where I have set up shop. I am momentarily afraid to touch it, using the quilt on my back as a prop of procrastination, fidgeting and fussing with it. I take my time setting my objects about.

I wish to die inside of you, I said to her once. A mysterious smile, a kiss on the wind, a passing glance were my only replies.

The puppet is fragmented, a broken collection of pieces shaped of man and reeking of heaven. Without touching it, I examine the joints, the points of articulation. They are sealed with mud, grime from the chest. It has been a very long time. I pick up the knife I have laid so carefully next to the old chest and use the edge to pick out specks of dirt within the old hinges. I cannot help but smile, mimicking without forethought the whittled grin of the puppet.

I sit down, clenching my hand tight, the first fist I've made in years. Her picture stares at me from my other side, and I place the frame atop the chest. She looks like Mary Magdalene, an inner light gripping me as I look into a fabrication, a shoddy representation of what she is and was. My hands, shaking, knock the picture over. By instinct I set it right again. I cannot tell if she is a holy blessing or my greatest nemesis. Whether her very gaze has scorched my bones and allowed me to create new lies for memories, or whether I am completely lucid and moments away from salvation and ascension, all I can be certain of is my own fragile nature.

Part of me is dead. The nightmares that remain reintroduce that concept to me nightly.

For a moment, I see outside, as though the very walls have turned to glass. The sky is immense and terrifying. I wait for the sky to break open and drown me before I can continue. As I stare, I can see everything, the trees, the birds, the moon, a thousand years of natural existence before I was here, before this monument was built to love and became a manifestation of sin. I suddenly want to burn it all. I want to see the ashes blow, and the giants fall, everything becoming a twisted reflection of what I am feeling. I start to stand, trembling, and immediately fall back into a sitting position. Something snaps uncomfortably in my knee. I am old. I can do one last thing, and I set myself back upon the task before me. I will not allow myself to distract myself to the point of entropy.

The walls are still. The knife, the picture and the puppet all wait for me patiently. I have become the manipulator. I laugh a bitter, coughing chuckle from deep within the lungs.

I worshipped her. I made an idol of a breakable creature, and like all things capable of decay, she ended. I tell myself often, if I had been with her, if I had chosen differently in spending my time, if I had forced the universe into shape, making eddies and ripples, I could have fixed all this. What does a priest do when his god falls from heaven?

A buzzing in my ears. The sound of a snapping oak branch. The chest looks black in the low light of the attic. I do not remember painting it black. It looks like the survivor of a fire. Purified by ash. The color of death and rebirth. I shudder again and pull the quilt closer against my skin. I pick up the controls for the puppet and slowly, almost imperceptibly, it begins to move.

At first, the left foot twitches, like a baby bird, learning to walk. Hesitant, without grace, but slowly coming to stand up straight, followed by the left leg. The right leg is sticking straight, and creaks slightly as it bends into a human position. Soon, the legs stand, but the body is still bent over backward. The puppet looks like a bow, and I slowly pick up the torso, the arms doing spirals in the air, flailing for balance even though I have the wires in hand to keep it from falling. The neck looks broken, a dead flower hanging over in a drought. I force it up, and the eyes somehow look more alive, almost wet.

The puppet begins to dance, a creaking, shuffling dance, one foot in front of the other. The buzzing in my ears is louder now, and I can hear my heartbeat in between my ears. There is a bass drum beating inside my skull, echoing a steady rhythm, giving the puppet's movements a syncopated sense of purpose.

I cannot walk away.

All I can do now is stand, and despite myself, I smile gently down at the puppet. It is like a child, a smiling red mouth, a head too large for the body. The wires have aged surprisingly well, gleaming like razors in the fading light. The candles are burning down, leaving wax pools marking out the circle around my makeshift stage, and I begin to dance the puppet around the circle, marking out each of the points in turn, leaving tiny wooden footprints in the wax. My focus is on the puppet, my dance partner, but I cannot help watching the footprints harden and congeal from the corner of my vision.

The dance speeds up, and as it does, our motions become a blur, in sync together, my legs and arms moving as the puppet's move. For a moment I feel like we have become one, there is nothing separating us. I feel myself becoming more manic, reckless.

She's dead. A child's voice, from far away, shouting in my head. I ignore it.

I move faster, my feet feeling like they are about to burst with blood, my breath becoming ragged. The candlelight casts strange shadows on the wall, and I note that the puppet and I appear to be the same size, albeit distorted. Our limbs elongate and contract, covering and revealing all the carvings we used to do together. Our paintings. The art we made with our own hands. The dancing shadows wash over an old golden cross we made together from scraps of metal. It looks like a flurry of crows exploding from inside a church.

85

Now we are spinning frantically, the noise inside my head threatening to explode out of me and manifest in some destructive way. It builds and builds, and I think of her. The picture fades, I cannot focus, but she is looking at me and I am looking at her, our eyes meeting in a soul kiss. Nothing remains but her, the world disappears. I have built a strange dwelling here, where the walls are made of kisses and dreams. She is everything, omnipresent.

I am outside myself, looking in.

I become a black dog, chasing her as if she were a hare, fleeing under brambles and through shadows, faster and faster, until finally she turns to me. We are human again, and she is standing over an open grave. She holds up a hand. Four burning fingers are held up, the ring-finger missing. I feel something in my mouth. I open it and watch as her finger falls out, spinning and flipping through the air. It touches the ground and the world shatters, I'm looking at a picture puzzle made of glass, and behind it is blackness, and then I am back in the attic, the dance reaching a bestial, savage frequency.

Then, there is a moment of perfect silence and stillness.

"Forgive me."

I reach down and pick up the knife. A simple kitchen knife, nothing savage or fearsome, but enough to suffice. As we dance and spin, I note how much the puppet reminds me of myself. Similar facial features, a sloping nose, close-set eyes, and a receding hairline dappled with gray. With one swift motion, I bring the knife across the wire holding up the left arm. As I do, the little wooden arm falls limp against the side of the puppet, and I feel my shoulder dip and wither. I snap a second wire, this one attached to the left leg, and as I stumble, visions of apocalyptic fire burn behind my eyes, I am ending this and I feel like an avenging angel. There is a moment, crystal clear, where I wonder if I'm simply embracing my wild-eyed madness in an effort to bestow more importance upon myself than I deserve.

I can not begin to catalogue my sins, so I snuff them out.

The right leg is next, and I crash to the ground, my knees bearing the brunt of my fall. As I collide with the boards I grin through the pain and reach up to strike the blade across the final wire. It takes some sawing, the knife having grown dull from cutting through the stiff wires, but it finally gives and I feel myself drop down. Self-realization comes swiftly upon me and cuts deep, and I understand a form of enlightenment as I lay there in the deathly quiet.

As I lay, I hear a light scraping from behind my right ear, something dragging across the floor, millimeters at a time. I consider weeping, or laughing, or cracking into a million pieces. The sound of a broken carousel plays for only me, tiny pieces coming to life and pulling themselves into a mobile form. I feel it before I see it. A gentle pair of hands, small like a child's, grasp my right arm. I am being held softly, the hands trying to comfort me as a small wire is inserted just above my wrist. I am surprised to find it does not hurt, and though the thought of penetration disturbs me on some level, I quickly forget it and allow the hands to do their work. The right leg is next. I feel the wire bloom underneath my skin, becoming a part of me. A benediction comes to mind, a call for divine help, but my mouth no longer has the ability to emit any sort of invocation.

The small hands lift my left leg and fit the wire in, like a master-craftsman. My eyes are already growing dull, wood infused with mossy magic but unable to understand what I am seeing, I fail to feel the final wire as it connects with the flesh of my left arm. I have the impression of two feet in front of me, and then I am lifted up, cradled against the chest of my manipulator. I am placed into the box, like a child into a cradle. The quilt that had kept me warm during these last critical moments now swaddles me. The picture of her is placed with reverence over my eyes. She still looks like a saint to me, but I am unsure which one. Mary of Magdala still resonates as an image, but the seven demons might never have been cleansed, and so perhaps I am mistaken.

Man is five, god is seven. There is something of heaven in death.

Maybe I was her six.

As the lid closes and the darkness envelops me, I hear the chest being pushed back into the corner. I feel assured that my replacement will serve as my redemption. This is no sacrifice; this is simply what is right. That which seems grand and noble is but an affliction. I am at peace, and I kiss her eyelids on the photograph, sending a message behind the tapestry and into cruel seas of that which cannot be forgotten.

ANYWAY, PEOPLE DIE

Neal Alan Spurlock

"**I**'ve been seeing... well, I call them repeats," I said, watching the door to the waiting room out of the corner of my eye. I was currently consumed with the odd fear that my psychiatrist's secretary, a middle-aged woman with brown hair and a penchant for plaid dresses, might burst in on us at any moment. I was simultaneously determined that this anxiety go unnoticed by the man sitting across from me; I wasn't sure what the old secretary was up to, with her arch looks and hidden glances, but I was sure the doctor was in on it.

"And what is a 'repeat', Danny?" Dr. Stark asked. His precise, clipped words and monotone voice matched his name, as did his appearance. He looked as if he had been carved from some soft, white wood, then dehydrated and bleached through some arcane process, all color and moisture drained away long before I had ever met him. His skin, hair, and eyes were the same shade, and even his clothes, which tended always towards bone whites and ashen grays, seemed somehow dry and wooden. I had never really seen him smile or frown, but lately, over the last several sessions, he had looked haggard and unrested, the dark bags under his eyes standing out horribly against the rest of his face. I knew that I had similar bruises around my eyes, but mine were a permanent fixture, built up over years of broken, sleepless nights.

"You know how you're out sometimes, like walking downtown or whatever, and you see someone walking down the street that you recognize?" I sat up, still eying the door suspiciously. The beige love-seat had one of those slick, fake leather coverings, and I kept sliding down slowly over the course of the session. "But then you say something, or wave, and they just stare at you and walk on by? Because they aren't really the person you thought they were?"

"Yes, of course," Dr. Stark said. He sat with his long legs folded, the gray slacks and white shirt more bland than elegant. A small notepad sat on his thigh, which he occasionally picked up to write careful, cramped notes with the expensive gold pen he held in his left hand. "It's a common phenomenon. Our minds often fill in the gaps, as it were, when we see someone for only a moment or from the side. If they share some features with someone else we know, and we catch enough of those features, our brain tells us that it is that other person. They've even done studies showing that we will hallucinate, to a small degree, to maintain our first identification of the person, rather than abandon it when we see something wrong."

"Right," I said. Once, during one of our early sessions, I had tried to stop the good doctor's long-winded explanations, which sometimes came complete with citations and an offer to lend me the relevant journals. It had not gone well. The rest of that session consisted of an even longer, more convoluted explanation of why each point of the explanation I had just interrupted was important and relevant to my treatment. Since then, I just humored him. "Well, I have been having that happen a lot lately."

"You have been misidentifying people more often?" Dr. Stark scribbled something on his pad. Around me, the horrible beige room felt too small, claustrophobic. I had also complained about this before, only to find that the good doctor found it 'cozy'.

"Well, sort of," I said. "I keep seeing people who look like my best friend from high school. She's aged appropriately. I mean, she really looks like she looks now, as an adult. The first time it happened, I walked up and said hi. The girl probably thought I was a rapist. For a little while, I thought April--my friend--was playing some sort of trick on me, but the girl pulled out her driver's license and passport. It wasn't April."

"Have you just seen this girl?" Stark's head tilted as he gazed at me. I hated the way he looked at me, like I was a bug or some specimen being examined, rather than a human being. Still, there were only so many shrinks in Beggar's Grove, and this was the only one that took sliding-scale payments. Until the new paintings started selling, he was all I could afford. *If the new paintings start selling*, my mind, ever the stickler for detail, amended, and a new swell of anxiety over money replaced my fear of secretarial interruption. "Or are there others? Are they all people you were close to?"

"No, not at all," I said, shaking my head as I desperately tried to balance my checkbook in my mind. My palms felt wet, though the rest of me was cold. I tried to talk myself down in my head, applying some of the cognitive therapy techniques Stark had taught me. *It's okay,* I thought to myself comfortingly. *The worst that can happen is I get dinged for a late payment. It's not a catastrophe.* "I've seen four or five versions of a bagger from the grocery store, a few versions of a waitress from the Froth'n'Java, and I have seen my junior high principal no less than eight times. One of those times, he was a woman."

"The 'froth and java'?" Dr. Stark raised his left eyebrow.

"Coffee shop across from my apartment," I said. "Downtown? Green awning and outside furniture?"

"Right."

"So, I have been seeing more and more of them," I said. "And what's worse is that I catch them staring at me."

"You're watching them," Stark said. "Isn't it natural for them to notice and watch you back?"

"Well, yeah, I guess." Suddenly, I felt unsure. My fears that the repeats had some sinister motive or nature, and that they would come after me if I

93

revealed them, seemed a bit... out there. It was always like this with Stark. I started second-guessing myself, wondering what was real. "That's true."

"Are you still taking your meds?" Stark asked, and a sour taste filled my mouth. "We have you on imipramine now, right?"

"Yeah, yeah," I lied. I hated this question. The meds were supposed to be for my benefit, yet somehow I was supposed to feel guilty about not taking them. "Don't worry, I'm doped."

Stark frowned. "I really wish you would try to adopt a better attitude toward your medication. Your depression has been quite resistant to treatment."

"I know," I said. "I live inside this head, remember?" I tapped my forehead to illustrate. The meds worked, but only in a horribly bland and drawn-out way that bordered on the unacceptable. While my depression was eased in the depth of its misery, my processes felt interrupted, like I had stalled out and couldn't move on. Rumination, always a hallmark of my distress, was not relieved, leaving me caught in the same compulsive loops of thought, but without any emotional connection. The net result was that I didn't feel too bad to function, but I never got any better.

"Any irregular heartbeat or dizziness? Palpitations?" Stark's pen hovered, gleeful, ready to jot down a new symptom. "Nausea?"

"Hell, no," I said. "Should there be?"

"No, not normally," he assured me. "But there can be complications with any of the tricyclic antidepressants, which is why we tend to use them as a last resort. Just make sure to watch your dosage; overdoses are fatal more often than not."

"Okay," I said, and with that we were suddenly plunged into an awkward silence. The phone rang in the waiting room, and I heard the receptionist picked it up. She spoke in a hushed voice, and for a moment, I was sure she was talking about me. After a few tense seconds where I strained to hear her words, Stark broke the silence.

"In any case, I'm sure these 'repeats', as you call them, are simply a coincidence that your mind, ever-vigilant in its search for more reasons to avoid the world of other people, is investing with sinister meaning," Dr. Stark said.

"I'm sure you're right," I said, and at that moment, I was. "I mean, it's a pretty silly thing to get worried about, right?"

"Precisely." Stark's lips stretched over his teeth. If a smile could be dry, this one was. "Moving on to issues that are productive to worry about: how's the new painting coming?" he asked. "Any progress?"

"Yeah, I'm working on it a little each day," I said, lying again. That happened here a lot. "It's almost finished."

"And after you finish this portrait of your father dy--as he was at the end? Do you feel you will be able to move on?" Stark asked. "To change the tone of your work?"

"I don't know," I said. "I hope so. No one wants to buy any of the new series, but I just can't bring myself to paint anything else."

"Why do you feel like the style of your recent work is so different from your former output?" he asked. Different? More like decayed, twisted, putrefied, torn. Image after image of suffering, little snapshots of destroyed lives and worlds. "Do you feel it has something to do with your father's death?"

"Well, yeah," I replied, surprised it had to be said. "I'm an artist. Like any artist, I want to express myself. I want to see my insides on the outside. I want to take my visions and make them real."

"Just don't try to make them too real," Stark said, smiling in that way that never reached his eyes. "That way madness lies."

"Right," I said. "I'll see what I can do."

As I stood in my studio, the warm light of early evening guiding my brush, I dwelled obsessively on my session with Stark. *Jesus,* I thought. *Shakespeare quotes and helpful information on how to use your meds for suicide.* I sighed. *That must be why they pay him the big bucks.*

My studio, like the office where my sessions with Dr. Stark took place, was overwhelmingly beige. Unlike his office, however, it was not decorated in what I call 'suburban chic', a grotesque combination of bland, colorless surfaces interspersed with talentless pieces of so-called 'modern art'. My studio was beige simply because canvas is beige, and canvas drop-cloths covered every surface. At one end of the room sat a small desk, complete with a laptop that I never used except to send photos of new pieces to my agent. At the other end, a simple futon, thin blanket, and mini-fridge provided for my basic needs.

The center of the room housed the only important items: five easels, four of them turned to the wall, unfinished projects or finished work that needed to dry on each. One easel always faced the center of the room while I was working, so that my current project bathed in the incredible light from the half-ring of large windows overlooking downtown Beggar's Grove. If I needed to use the bathroom, I went to one of the various restaurants that littered the downtown streets outside my home. If I needed to shower, which was rarely a huge concern of mine, I would get a hotel room. Technically, I wasn't supposed to be living in here; it had been rented to me as an artist's studio, and the lease explicitly said the location was not zoned as a residence. Then again, there were lots of things I wasn't technically 'supposed' to be doing.

Or the opposite; according to my agent, I was 'supposed' to be working on something more commercial, something that he could sell, something like my old work. Something that, he kept telling me breathlessly, would save my career and, more importantly, his second mortgage. But I wasn't doing what I was 'supposed' to be doing. Instead, I was painting a portrait of my last memory of my father, sitting up in his hospital bed with the lights off, grimacing with pain that no drug could dull, and holding my hand loosely, as if he could barely muster the strength for such an intimate gesture. The cancer had whittled him down to little more than bones and eyes, but in the end it was pneumonia that finished the job of removing the last vestige of family I had from the world.

I considered myself an artist of the extreme. My goal is, or at least was, to express the human experience through its most intense moments. Once upon a time, my paintings had ranged in their subjects from women in childbirth to toddlers being dropped off for their first day of daycare. Sure, sometimes pain or death was part of that extremity, but usually through implication. It wasn't that I was choosing optimistic or pleasant subjects, subjects sure to gain interest from the mainstream; it was just that, in my 'artist's eye', I saw a vast range of human experiences and attempted to do them all justice. All of that changed last year when my father was diagnosed with pancreatic cancer.

I spent eight months with him, first at the home I had grown up in, its wood paneling and baby-puke green appliances comfortingly nostalgic, then in a hospital room that nearly drove me mad in its sterility. For eight months I did not draw, did not paint, did not take a single photograph or tuck away a single idea for later. For eight months, I lived, talked, and wept with the man who had given me life while waiting for him to die.

And finally, he did die, and I found myself at a loss, without a roof to put over my head or a dime to pay for it. Hospital bills and the funeral ate up what little savings I had left, even after selling his house. At first, I floundered from hotel room to bus station, traveling across the country randomly, until I ended up in this odd little town in California and this odd little studio. The town seemed to live in a constant state of expectation and held breath, as if the very soil were awaiting some miracle, as if the buildings and roads were working towards some unknown, final end. Something about the isolated strangeness of Beggar's Grove woke me up, opened wide my artist's eye, and I spent the next five months putting what I saw down on canvas.

And what I saw was horrible.

Death, in all its myriad forms. An old man discovering his wife cold and dead upon waking in their shared bed of fifty years, that single moment of realization and unfathomable grief captured forever in my mind and on canvas. An officer in the North Korean military, apathetic as a group of dissidents fell, their lives cut short by the rifles of a firing squad. A mother holding the hand of her child, her face resolute and sad and full of love, as the plane they are sitting in falls out of the sky.

Horror after horror was uncovered by my pencil and brush, and none of it sold.

My agent, Barry, was first understanding, then morose, and then, finally, desperate, imploring me to return to my subjects of the past, even going so far as to suggest a few of his own. A prize-fighter delivering the final blow. A soldier in the act of saving a fallen comrade. A set of obviously destitute parents at their child's college graduation. But the suggestions fell on deaf ears; I had one, and only one, subject worthy of my attention now. So he pushed me to see a therapist, even offering to pay for it, though I had no interest in his charity.

Once I became tired of arguing, I started seeing Stark, but neither the medications he handed out so freely nor the weekly sessions really seemed to pull me from this obsession with unnatural, unjust death. I drank more, slept less, and felt more and more alone in an alien world, spending days at a time in my studio, only relenting when hygiene or hunger demanded that I went out. I lost weight, and my face, once considered handsome by many, became haggard, eyes hollow and cheeks sharp, my brown hair and beard tangled and dirty.

Finally, it came to me, the painting to end this series and, hopefully, free my artist's eye for other visions. My father's final moment with me, spent talking in the dark as he coughed and groaned. I could express that final horror, that final moment of understanding that my father was going to die, and then be free of it. Or, at least, so I hoped.

Adding a final curve of shading to my father's left eye, hollow and dark, I decided to call it a day and turned the painting toward the wall so that its eyes did not follow me. This habit, developed in my teens, had eventually turned into a phobia; the staring eyes of photographs and paintings could send me into a frenzy of panic. The spartan arrangement of my studio and its utter lack of decoration stemmed from this phobia; almost all good art is of people, and almost all people have eyes. Each painting dried completely for three weeks on an easel, was photographed digitally, and the file was emailed to my agent. It was then added to the growing pile in the corner of the room, to face away from me forever or until it had a buyer, whichever happened first.

I grabbed my pack of cigarettes, shaking one out and lighting it as I poured myself a single, celebratory drink of cheap scotch. *Another day lived through,* I congratulated myself. *Another day where I didn't gargle a handgun.* I considered each such day a personal victory, though whether it was my victory or that of the world which tormented me, I had no clue.

I carried my drink and cigarette to the window, where I stood, smoking and sipping. Below me, the intersection of downtown Beggar's Grove was jumping, with parked cars lined up and down both streets and pedestrians wandering the sidewalks. I could hear snatches of conversation, and I strained my ears to hear more, moved by some voyeuristic urge to be included in the ebb and flow of public life, even as I avoided it. My eyes wandered until they fell on the Froth'n'Java. People went in and out of the coffee shop, sometimes sitting at the outside tables with their purchases, and sometimes wandering on down the sidewalk, content to window-shop as they drank their overpriced lattes and too-rich mochas. My glance followed a pair of giggling high school girls until the door swallowed them, then drifted back until I saw, sitting in a dark suit and eating a biscotti, myself.

I stiffened and glanced at my drink incredulously. I looked back, and there he was. He wasn't exactly me. His clothes, for one thing, were ridiculous on my thin frame. His hair was cut short and formal, a businessman's cut, while my own hair fell to my shoulders in unkempt patches. He had good posture, sitting tall and self-assured as he ate his snack and drank from one of the cafe's glass mugs. *I never do that*, I thought, my shocked mind focusing on the trivial out of some desperate sense of self-preservation. *I always get a to-go cup. Always.*

But he was still, obviously and plainly, me. His complexion, the twist of his nose, the eyes, the half-smile as he overheard some amusing anecdote from a neighboring table... all of these tiny details were mine, me, myself.

Then the man who was me finished his food and stood. He brushed off his hands, just as I would have, put his dishes in the small bus tub near the door, and walked nonchalantly to a pricey little blue sports car parked on the street adjacent to the coffee-shop. A growing dread, far beyond simple fear, filled me as I saw that he walked and moved exactly as I did. The tell-tale stride that signified a lowered center-of-gravity, the slightly bent hips ready to push off an attack... techniques my father had taught me during the bully-tormented days of junior high school and long ago ingrained as habit.

As the man who was me opened the door to his car, he looked up and met my gaze. He smiled, and as he nodded at me, I felt dread turn to terror.

Two days passed, and with the painting finally finished and turned to the wall to dry, I stretched out on my futon and tried to read. It was getting harder and harder to control the anxiety that rose every time I looked out the window, but some morbid curiosity drove me, again and again, to the wooden sill. For ten or fifteen minutes I would stand, watching, as people milled through downtown and the cars passed through the intersection. Then I would turn, the acid rising in my throat from my constantly churning stomach, and flee into the corner to pour a drink, crawl into my blankets, and attempt to forget what I had just seen. An hour would pass, maybe less, and I would be at it again, staring through the window and trembling.

At last count, roughly half the people I saw were me.

They walked, ate, drove, and drank, sometimes several of me together, laughing and talking in a single voice. Yesterday, I saw two of me, one wearing a low-cut dress and carrying a purse, the other in a white t-shirt and blue jeans. They strolled hand in hand, smiling, happy, and obviously in love. I had to look away when they embraced and their lips met in a tender kiss. An identical trio, all me, sat outside the coffee shop wearing clothes more suited to adolescence than my actual 'thirty-five going-on sixty' wardrobe. I wondered if they saw each other differently, if the clothes made sense and looked good to them. Perhaps none of them noticed anything wrong at all, as they pulled garter belts over the legs of a hairy man limping his way toward middle-age.

None of them ever seemed to notice their uncanny resemblance to each other, but once in a while, one of them would lift his gaze to my window, meet my eyes, and nod. My own cryptic little half-smile, the bane of my mother's existence before she died, would twist his lips, and I would be afraid.

BEEPBEEPBEEPBEEPBEEPBEEP--

"Ahhh!" I leapt up, my heart pounding in my chest, blood humming in my ears, and scanned the room. The horrible sound came again, and my addled brain, sleepless for days as the ratio of my appearances outside shifted, finally realized it was my phone, a simple land-line I kept for emergencies and for Dr. Stark's office to call when they needed to change an appointment. I steadfastly refused to get a mobile phone, though my agent kept trying to buy me one. 'Who would I call?' I would ask him, and he would sigh. 'Where do I go?'

I ignored the continued ringing and poured myself a couple of fingers of scotch. As the days passed, my fear had increased. Fear of leaving the house, fear of running into myself and the horrors that could--would, I resolutely believed--happen after that meeting, and another indescribable dread that welled up from deep in my gut, refusing to identify itself. As my fear increased, so did the drinking. Good thing I had a well-stocked stash next to the mini-fridge.

Eventually, the answering machine, an ancient device that my agent had been scandalized to learn actually used magnetic tape, clicked on. I heard my own voice, bored and slightly annoyed. "You know who this is, and you know what to do. Do it." A loud beep, followed by a familiar voice.

"--identity, you see," Dr. Stark said. "It's all about identity. Who you are, who you think you are, the little story you tell yourself, about yourself."

I sipped my drink absently, not surprised that it had begun in the middle of a sentence. Many people, apparently confused by the space-age technology of a glorified tape-recorder, started talking before the beep. *I need to seriously consider getting a new therapist*, I thought. *This guy has a screw loose.* I chuckled dryly at the thought. After all, who was I to talk?

"Jung talked about identity as being social, and thought and mind as being translocal," Stark went on. "He hypothesized archetypes, great conceptual structures that exist in our collective unconscious. These archetypes are the cause of phenomena like mass hysteria, the existence of nations, and the rise of religions. Even more, he thought that these archetypes acted independently of us, but through us nonetheless. In a seldom-cited and controversial paper called 'Wotan', he explained the rise of Hitler as the awakening of one of these archetypes. He said that Germany was a nation possessed by an angry god."

Now I really knew I needed to find a new therapist. Ranting about Hitler on my answering machine was officially crossing a line. I settled back onto my futon and sat, leaning against the wall. On one hand, his call was annoying, but on the other, it was entertaining, a distraction from the ever-present dread that had been building in me over the last several days.

"Heidegger also wrote about identity and art. His ideas about poetry, in particular, are about the revealing of being, of authenticity." Stark's voice seemed to be dreamy. Maybe he had been drinking or sampling some of his own pills. "Art, in his mind, was about the revelation of identity through the creation of things--objects in the world--that, through their authenticity, reveal the true self, the

Dasein, Being." His voice sounded odd...softer, somehow; less hoarse. Younger, almost. *Maybe the old bastard is finally getting some sleep,* I thought, remembering the bruised eyes of our last session.

I sipped my drink and thought about what he was saying. In a sense, I had always thought that my art was an attempt to externalize myself, to reproduce myself, or the various selves I found myself being in different situations. I'd strived to reproduce them as something outside of me, something that could be separate. Every drawing, every stroke of paint and twist of charcoal, was an attempt to create an eternal self-portrait, something that would illustrate and illuminate. Something that would reveal my self to myself.

"This all connects to eschatology," Stark said. His voice was definitely different, and changing by the word, the resonance becoming something shallow and high-pitched, as if the tall doctor's frame was getting smaller. "The belief that the end of the world is just around the corner is perfectly justified; as many thinkers have pointed out, the only world we know is through our own eyes, ears, and mind. Each and every one of us is, at most, a handful of years from the end of the world, because each and every one of us is dying."

I brought myself to my feet shakily, the dread in my belly mixing with the liquor and sleep deprivation to make my legs stupid. There was no doubt. Stark's voice was changing, becoming another voice entirely, a voice I had just heard sarcastically saying 'do it' over the hiss of magnetic tape.

"So the revealing brought about through art acts upon the world," I heard myself say through the speaker. "And that world is ending."

I walked slowly over to my desk. Little indicator-lights on the closed laptop, the phone, and the answering machine lit the way through the canvas maze of my studio. I felt the sweat on my back, my t-shirt sticking to my skin, but the rest of my body felt cold. I reached out and grabbed the phone, bringing it up to my head in a single, swift motion.

"Who is this?" I yelled. "What do you want?"

A dial-tone sang into my right ear.

My forays to the window had stopped. No more point in looking.

Everyone was me.

Three more days with no sleep and little food. The first day I spent tearing apart my easels, all except the one holding the drying portrait of my father, cannibalizing the wood to barricade the door of my apartment. The repeats were going to come for me, and I wanted to be ready, though each time I looked down at the street, the army of me simply seemed to be living life. I would watch myself, clad in a dress with long, curly hair, window-shopping at the used-clothing store on the far corner. Two of me would sit, drinking coffee and chatting, then get up and go about their day.

Cars, trucks, and vans rolled up and down the streets, each driven by various versions of me. Despite the fact that none of my variations seemed concerned about me in the least, from time to time, one would look up, meet my gaze, and smile. They knew of my presence, and while I didn't know their intent, it seemed right to assume the worst.

The second day I spent on the internet, despite the fact that I hate the damned thing, trying to figure out what was happening. Searching through sites about the paranormal and occult yielded little real information. While doppelgangers and other entities that imitated the form of a human populated the folklore of various cultures, an entire city of them seemed unprecedented. I also did searches on Jung and Heidegger, the men Dr. Stark had mentioned in his bizarre phone call. While I found Jung's ideas easy to follow, Heidegger was another thing entirely. The man seemed to have cruelly devised a new language, using completely innocuous and normal words in obtuse and subtle ways, and then obstinately refused to stop writing that way. I eventually gave up on finding anything that would explain the situation, but I did notice something that sent me rushing to every news and social website I could to confirm my suspicion: Carl Jung and Martin Heidegger looked just like me. As did everyone else, on every site I looked at. Whether it was a drawing, painting, photograph, or video, every single human figure was me. Sometimes I was a woman, sometimes a man, sometimes old, sometimes young, but always me, as I was right now, underneath the hair and clothes.

At this, I stopped really feeling afraid. I was too tired. The discovery was too large in scope to comprehend. All I felt was tired, resigned, and oddly amused. *Why me?* I wondered idly. But then again, maybe it wasn't just me. Maybe, all across the world, others were staring out of their own windows, seeing themselves and only themselves, acting out the dramas of life around them. Maybe it was everyone, and the selves we saw were merely reproductions, simulacra sent to torment us by living out every possible life that could have been ours, but for the roll of the dice in some monstrous demiurge's hand. I put on some music, grabbed my bottle, and went back to the futon, eager to sleep. It took less of the burning fluid to bring on blessed oblivion than I thought it would, but it still took a lot.

I awoke, startled and shivering. My ears strained, but I heard no sound, and around me was darkness, the only light an ambient glow from lamps on the street below. I heard nothing and fell back onto my pillow. *It was nothing,* I tried to reassure myself. *Just a dream.*

I tried to go back to sleep, but eventually my insistent bladder won the day, and I rose unsteadily to my feet. *It can't have been more than a couple hours,* I thought as I walked to the small sink where I usually washed my brushes. *I'm still drunk.* The foul odor of three days of physical waste rose up from the sink like a punch in the face, and I had to squeeze my eyes against the fumes as I emptied my bladder, the steam rising in the cool air. I made an effort at running water down the drain, but it didn't help.

Relieved, I walked back out into the studio and turned on my lamp. The canvas all around had been disturbed by my stumbling, and beneath it I could see the hardwood floors I had been trying to protect from dripping paint. I stood for a moment in the center of my studio, slightly rocking back and forth on my feet. My eyes closed, and I briefly wondered if I was going to throw up, whether fear and liquor and the stench of days-old sewage had overwhelmed me. But my stomach soon reported the all-clear, and I opened my eyes. Before me, turned to the wall, was my last easel. I felt a wild desire to look at my newest creation, and slowly, carefully, I walked to the easel, lifted it, and turned it around.

There, in a hospital bed lit only by the quarter-moon through a window, I sat. My eyes were hollow, and my face was creased with old pain, pain that had been eating me up for months and for which the drugs did nothing. I could remember feeling this way, somehow, my father's last moments becoming my own, and shuddered.

I hurried to the stack of paintings, the new series, leaning against the wall in the corner. Almost slamming myself into the wall, I could feel my stomach twist as the room spun for a moment, but I forced myself to open my eyes and look. As I took each painting and turned it around, I felt no surprise, only a growing grief like nothing I had ever felt and the panic of the last several days draining out of me, leaving me limp, hollow.

On one, I was a starving South American child being beaten back as uniformed men, who were all me, took my mother, who was also me, away forever.

On another, I was a shaven-headed prisoner, strapped down onto a medical table, receiving a lethal injection from a sad-eyed me wearing medical scrubs.

On yet another, I was a soldier in uniform caught in the moment of shooting another me, dressed in torn velvet and rags, through the eye. I could feel the pain in slow motion. First, the shock of the gunshot, then the bullet penetrating my eye, splitting the aqueous and vitreous humours with a sizzling pop and sliding into me, inch by burning inch. I also felt the despair of the soldier, forced by circumstance and the chain-of-command to commit an act I could not live with.

Another, and another, the paintings fell onto the floor as I turned each one and revealed a new horror in which I was both perpetrator and victim. The despair in my chest grew until it erupted from my mouth in a loud sob, and I finally turned away. I pulled myself to my feet, weeping.

The sun was rising, the light in the studio becoming a soft orange as new shadows stretched out on the walls behind me. I could hear the sounds of cars. The world was waking up.

I stumbled to the window, tears and drunkenness blurring my eyes. Below me, Beggar's Grove was coming to life. The door of the Froth'n'Java opened, and the chairs were brought out, their green darker than normal in the morning light, and the young barista was me. Cars, free of traffic in the early-morning, sped through the intersection in front of my studio, and the driver of every one of them was me.

I felt suddenly quiet. No more tears. No more sadness. No more fear.

I reached into my pocket and pulled out a large, amber prescription bottle. *Imipramine,* I read. *Take only as directed. In case of overdose, call emergency services immediately and induce vomiting.* I opened the bottle. It was full. I had stopped taking my meds weeks ago; I hated how they made me feel. They prevented the extremes of experience, and how could I call myself an artist of extremity if my own experience of life was blunted? No highs, no lows, just an infinite, gray middle. I opened my mouth and upended the bottle. The first mouthful of sour gel caps went down easily, but the second stuck in my throat. I walked over to the futon, picked up the bottle of scotch, and took a deep pull to wash down the pills. The burning liquid made me choke briefly, and for a moment I was afraid that I was going to vomit the precious pills out onto the hardwood floor and canvas. I managed to force it down, and made my careful way back to the window.

I stood there, watching the day begin and washing down the sour pills with cheap whiskey. Soon they were gone, and I simply took pulls off of the bottle until that was gone, too. Then I just waited, the sun quickly rising, revealing the waking life of downtown.

Soon it was full light. Pedestrians had begun to walk along the mall, various versions of me wearing various uniforms and living various lives. As I felt the first heart palpitations and a wave of dizziness fall over me, I saw one of me clutch his left arm, writhe for a few moments in pain, and then fall to the ground. A second later, a bright-green truck veered off the road. Its driver, a dreadlocked me, slumped over the wheel as the truck slammed into another me who was walking three small dogs, their long leashes stretching far enough to leave them unharmed. I saw myself, dressed in a cute red blouse and slacks, hair pulled back in a bun, attack a business-suited me, choking me with my bare hands. Both fought until they fell to the sidewalk, dead.

A gasp passed my lips, as pain shot through my chest and left arm. My heart was pounding, fast and irregular, and I wanted to lie down, but I could not look away as a dozen of me died a dozen deaths. They were screaming as cars slammed into each other and pedestrians fell to the ground, and I

114

heard my own voice all around me, raised in horror and pain.

Black patches filled my vision, and I began to laugh as I watched the world die.

MALICE AND MAJESTY
D.P. *Watt*

It was a grey day in that grey town. Everything bled a bleakness and despair that begged redemption. Those modern mummers had appeared that day, all dressed in their grey ruin, their faces as faded as their suits. I had offered them cake and alms a plenty, but little good it did me on that forsaken afternoon, heavy with the ritual of two thousand years and the hopes of every soul that had existed. I would not sign their documents; I would not buy their wares. They traded only in the empty greyness of that grey day. Their grey performances left me cold and lonely.

I warmed a brown soup from a grey can, in a blackened saucepan, and sat watching the grey drizzle as it drowned my yearning heart. Then something shifted within me, like the first stretch of a proud beast as it wakes from slumber. The grey shapes passed by my window like cardboard cut-outs in a colourless toy theatre. My body ached for the rich air of the hills, my eyes the lush green of the trees and grass; my legs forced me to seek sustenance and I was thrust out into the deathly dullness in search of spirit and life.

At first I simply joined the greyness, another body wrapped against the rain, adding only movement to this washed-out scene. My feet splashed along the black tarmac, heralding, in their

116

beat, some purpose. And then I caught the great rhythm that bounded through them, and beneath them; in the pulse of passing cars, in the distant cries of children at play, in the low rumble of a plane overhead. They rose into a great cacophony, a chorus of voices, human and mechanical. And there, behind them all, still my feet, tap, tap, tapping, like some little drummer boy; tap, tap, tapping; eager for the blast of cannon and the soaring fear in heart and limb; the shot and the blood; the smoke and the screams.

Within the space of a few streets the November sky brightened and I was heartened by the signs about me of a world in transformation. The paving slabs were cracked with the slow and relentless work of root and weed, reclaiming the oppressed ground with the touch of eternity. The houses about me were cracked and splintered—the marks of collapsing stone and rock miles beneath us, flowing and falling in vast cycles of time, sending out its tiny signals of shock and ruin in ancient pulses. The chimes of the church, buried amidst the fog of fumes and the murmur of traffic, sounded out its call behind me, but I was destined for other worship.

The rooftops about me, and down into the valley ahead, glistened with the rain of the late afternoon. The sun's fresh blast upon them awakened that army of shields, beneath which each family nurtured the hope of their embryonic community, and trampled the bones of earlier

117

civilizations. The gleams of windscreens were an array of spears and the treetops in the forest ahead were the bold pennants of an encampment; all an army as ancient as battle itself, the enemy—us— always at hand.

As the world became possibility once more there appeared my guide—a cat.

She was an enchanting long haired tabby with a pleading face framed by a furry scarf of warmth. She had stepped from history; more at home on the yellowing cardboard of a Victorian Christmas card than here in the suburbs, amidst the baying of dogs in the distance and the hum of cars from the ring road, and the beep of reversing rubbish lorries at work about the busy neighbourhood. Her world was all light and freedom, darkness and the bliss of the hunt. She was at once so playful and adorable yet terrible with sovereign cruelty; yes, that was her entirely, a fluffy ball of malice, mockery, might and mischief. Her arrogant swagger had me captivated as she padded the path with the timeless lope of an eternal hunter; hers was aggression in miniature, the murderer's passion locked into the heart of a little automaton that could harm only the small things of the world. Her heart pumped with a craving for blood that her paws—no doubt hiding claws most keen and sharp—were ill matched to enact. Oh, little tyrant, would that you were as tall as a mountain, that you could slake your thirst upon our useless frames. Though we would be little sport for your feline vengeance, we might, with the corpses piled high around your recumbent form, be sacrifice enough—in our thousands—to assuage your deadly spirit, for a day; a day awash with blood and terror.

She led me from the collapsing concrete world, where walls had been her castles, fences her palisades, and territory lay ready to be claimed in the flurry of fur and claw. Back into the timeless gardens she would fall, finding in her soul a hunger that evolution could not erase. Onwards we drifted until the pathways collapsed into ways barely trodden, where even the beaten ground ghosted into the faintest of lines through field and pasture. Her ways were old, plotted by scents and senses I had lost long ago. She was queen of the wilderness and I followed in awe, an idiot jester at her invisible court.

Still onwards she took me, into the woods, whose dark canopy whispered with forever's legends. Sometimes she seemed to grow tall in the distance, reclaiming her kingdom, at other moments she shrank into the ground, hugging her land with eyes and ears alert to the bristling life about us—a life I was blind to; a life that I craved.

The trees broke into a clearing, a perfect circle of bright grass with a low mound in the middle—she took up her throne. Deep within there were either the bones of kings or the gates to a fairy world—she kept her secrets though, and the keys, all I was given were her sad eyes of famine.

Strewn about the idyllic clearing were the struggling forms of nature's various disguises; the toad, its long limbs broken into monstrous crucifixion; the rat, its plump abdomen plundered and its eviscerated entrails cast across the grass to augur futures already plotted and well advanced in their dreadful designs; the hare, his lithe body a great question to existence, his throat pierced by deep, sharp teeth, that had drunk deeply of his vigour; the owl, wings blasted in the melee and great eyes unplugged and dangling against his heaving feathered breast. And there too all the tiny creatures that had flickered with life; the battered moth, whose delicate dusty wings had so enthralled as it sought the moon; the earthworm, simply sliced in two; a great black beetle, whose hard armour had been prised asunder to reveal the mechanism of its glassy wings. All was alive with the mutter of flies, the air bursting with the rich oils of blood and the giggle of pain. The twitching forms danced me into their midst; their soft cries orchestrated the beating of my desperate heart. Was my flesh not pure enough for this half-feast, might I not be so unstrung too, convulsing the last of my energy, all for her cruel delight?

For there, upon the mossy mound, amidst the beautiful carnage, was the Great Malice, Her Mighty Majesty, licking her paws and preening her bloodied fur. She smiled with teeth and laughed with a flick of her thick tail and then sauntered into a laurel bush, as though to change costume for the next scene of her glorious pageant. Where she had lain there erupted dark soils and fungal forms, roots of trees and bulbs of flowers awaiting the mystery of spring. The earth ruptured and brought forth the pale flesh of my beloved, caked in the moist shrouds of the ground. She was bruised with the chase, her soft skin aflame with scratches and scars. She was coiled upon herself like any newborn, her umbilical cord a throbbing root of an ash tree. Her eyes were tightly closed, hiding the furnace of possible worlds therein and the collapse and conflagration of galaxies that is the life of every sleeping mind. Her hair crawled like armies of red ants across the green swathe until it became the bright yellow of the thousand suns that flickered behind her eyelids, then the black oil of the pits beneath our feet where a million creatures had fused into fuels for the future toil of generations, and finally the delicate chestnut brown of the bounty of this planet, always poised between fruitfulness and sterility.

I stared. I lusted. I cried. My thoughts broke into primordial desires and I was flooded with a stream of chemistry. I was weighed down by sin, and alive with the promise of forgiveness—everything was sacred, nothing was sane. You who live with hope in your hearts know the sorrow—you for whom damnation is as certain as resurrection is for all other beings.

I bounded to her side, scratching at that earthy womb, bringing her fully back to being. Her mouth yawned and the night leapt out, stars bursting from the moisture of her sweet breath. I cradled her; she, who tortured me with a billion forms of being, who lay before me the entire rich feast of existence, only to leave me hungry for everything. I felt the fire rage within her, as it also began to flicker in me. I felt her cold skin, that millennia in the desert heat would never warm; that crisp rime also crackled across the surface of me—an ecstatic ripple, promising the epochs to come. We were flame encased in frost.

I lay my head upon her thighs, the beat of her burning blood in my ears. I smelt the damp vitality of the earth upon her and her legs embraced me. I heard the soft movements of the plants about us and the slow creep of moss and lichens above us, as they sealed our union within the delicate layers of the ground that slipped around us like fine robes.

In the savage night's unfolding, we were enfolded. Would that fur and flesh, shell and skin, might dissolve and the tawdry bricolage of this faded creation begin itself anew from deep within its own promise. Such is the hope to be found in dust and dirt, in all the creeping tendrils of existence, root and vein, river and bacterium. Living and dying—hilarious opposition; in the depths of this sleep there is no division, all weakness is might and all majesty only poverty; soil is gold and the rain, precious as diamonds. We are the seeds of all futures—let your tears rouse us.

MOURN NOT THE SLEEPLESS CHILDREN

Bob Freeman

Fog crept like a living thing across the graveyard, mindful and with purpose. It masked the cemetery's landscape with malicious intent, stealthily concealing whatever evil lurked within the ineffable mist. Watching from the balcony of Grandstaff Hall, Brianna Moore surrendered to the fear that grew inside her.

A pall hung over the inhabitants of Grandstaff. For a score of nights the fog had come, thick and oppressive, and with it the mournful repine of some godforsaken spirit. It was a maddening clamor, like a demonic din rising up from the very aperture of Abbadon itself.

The young governess' attention was drawn to the ruins of the old Kirk at the periphery of the cemetery grounds. Lantern light struggled to cut through the assaulting mist and the sounds of human voices floated up to her from the sacellum. She was unsure of what troubled her more, the anticipation of the wail's return, or the presence of the man in the company of the Grandstaff Lord below.

"We'll not be waiting much longer, Old Crow," she heard Lord Grandstaff say. His was a commanding voice, used to issuing orders and seeing them carried out in due haste. The serpentine tongue that responded commanded equal attention, but for altogether different reasons.

"I need not hear the banshee, Sir Stuart, for already I sense a presence among us wholly unnatural. It feeds off the fear that emanates from Grandstaff Hall. It is a type of psychic vampire, if you will."

"Aleister, I knew you were the man to call in. Your knowledge of the esoteric knows no peer. I trust within your magical arsenal you have the means to dispose of this beastie."

"I would need to gather some things from Boleskine. I could return within a fortnight and see to the exorcism of your earthbound spirit. Of course, there would be the matter of compensation... travel, the expense of the material components, my time and, I should add that my considerable expertise comes not cheaply."

"Yes, yes, old friend," she heard her employer say. "Coin is of no consequence. I would be free of this damnable apparition once and for all."

Brianna returned to her room, distraught. A fortnight? she thought. She feared she'd not last another night, let alone two weeks. She crossed the cool marble floor and stoked the fire against the autumn chill. When the wailing began she was quick to bed, burying herself beneath thick woolen blankets and praying that morning would come faster than was its natural course.

"**G**one," the lady of the house moaned, "all gone."

"Pardon me, ma'am?" Brianna asked. She was exhausted, having scarcely slept for nigh three weeks. Standing in the Manor kitchen, she had been surprised to find Lady Grandstaff toiling over a pot of tea.

"The staff," she muttered, "all gone save for you and Ewan." Ewan Pitcairn was Lord Grandstaff's retainer.

"Gone," Brianna repeated in a low murmur. The thought had occurred to her... to flee into the night. But when all was said and done, she had nowhere to go.

Lady Grandstaff turned to face the governess and Brianna was struck by how much older the woman appeared. Her eyes were dark and puffy, her dark hair now touched here and there with gray. Three weeks of ghostly manifestations had taken their toll.

"What shall we do, ma'am?" Brianna asked, lowering her gaze to the tile floor.

"We shall persevere, dear child, for we are Grandstaffs and that is what Grandstaffs do," the proud woman proclaimed. "If you would see to the children, Brianna, I will see that my husband gets his morning tea."

"At once ma'am," she responded, shuffling off toward the great stair and the children's wing.

The long hall toward the children's rooms was dark wood and ill-lit. At the far end of the passageway was a high window that would normally spill daylight down the hall, but a heavy drape was pulled tight. Brianna's footfalls fell silent, masked by the oriental runner that stretched the full length of the space. Nearing the twins' room she heard their animated speech. Taking pause, she listened.

"Walter, must the voices return to bother us this night?" a thin voice asked. It belonged to Wallace, the fair-haired twin. Where Walter was energetic and robust, Wallace in turn was frail and weak. Wallace was the sharper of the two, blessed with an innate knowledge of the world around them. Walter, though no dullard, deferred to his twin in matters of intellectual dissection.

"Must you be such a frightened ninny, Wally?" Walter chided his brother.

"But they've not kept their promise," Wallace said.

Brianna could take no more. She burst into the room.

"What promise?" she demanded. "What do you hear at night?"

"Miss Moore," the boys said in unison, startled by her sudden arrival. She flew across the room and snatched Wallace up, holding the boy about the shoulders and drawing him in close.

"Speak up you little heathens," she raged, flashing an evil look toward Walter. "What do you know? What devilry have you been up to?"

Wallace was beside himself, tears streaming down his cheeks, while his twin backed away to the far wall.

"No?" Brianna fumed, tossing Wallace aside. She turned and stalked toward Walter. "What about you Walter? Have you something you'd like to share with me?"

"I'm not scared of you," the boy said, puffing his chest out.

"Tell me Walter," she fumed, "or so help me…"

"So help you?" the boy said with a wry smile. "There's no help for you. Not after what you did when you were dollymopping the dockers."

"When I…" the governess stammered, "…I… how could you…?"

"Know?" Walter said, finishing her bewildered statement. "I know because they speak to us on the wind. At night. When the banshee comes. Oh, we know all about you, Miss Moore. We know all about how you spread it for a tanner, or less when you were hungry. And we know what happened the night of the blood moon, of how you…"

The sound of shattering glass somewhere deep inside the manor silenced the young Grandstaff. The reprieve did little to alleviate the governess of her ire and embarrassment. A distant scream followed and Brianna raced out of the room and down the hall, distancing herself from the twisted and evil smiles shared between her twin charges.

The governess was led by the sounds of muffled whimpers into the dining room. The room was darker, curtains pulled tight against the beckoning day. Shards of fine porcelain lay scattered across the mahogany floor, and in the midst of the destruction, the Lady of the House knelt, rag in hand, sopping up steaming tea from the floor and rug.

"Lady Grandstaff?" The woman looked up and Brianna gasped as she saw the hand-shaped red mark across her face. "Oh, ma'am, I'm so sorry… here, let me get that for you."

What was going on around here, Brianna wondered? Were they all going crazy? Had madness settled in and taken root in all their minds? How long before something truly horrible took place? How long before… No, she thought, not that. Why even consider that?

"I… he…" Lady Grandstaff stammered.

"It's all right, ma'am. I understand," the governess sobbed.

"Do not cry for me, Miss Moore," the Lady said.

"I do not cry for you, ma'am," Brianna said, fearing to look up. "I cry for us all."

The rest of the day was filled with tension. On edge, the whole household seemed ready to explode. Nightfall came, and with it, the horrific wails of the demon spirit. Four days later, Lady

Grandstaff would be gone. Two days after that, Ewan too was nowhere to be found. Soon the house was filled with naught but the brooding visage of the Lord of Grandstaff Hall, a morose and despondent governess... and the sound of laughing children.

Brianna Moore watched as the fog returned once more, rolling across the aphotic grounds. How many nights had they been besieged, she wondered? Thirty-eight? Forty? It wouldn't be long now. Soon the wail would begin and she would once more sink into madness.

She hadn't seen the twins in three or four days. Had they been spirited away? Or had they simply run off, no longer able to withstand the strain of the conditions they were living under? Or worse? She feared the boys now, perhaps more than the wailing demon without. How could they have known about...? No, she couldn't even bring herself to think upon those horrible days. Nor could she face the twins. She had been shamed by mere children... children with a knowledge that burned her to her very soul. She had been unable to go to them. She lacked the courage to look them in the eye. Had this decision doomed them? Was her own set to toll as well?

A resounding knock upon the great door roused her from her melancholy. She descended the stair and made her way through the maze of rooms, pausing when she heard voices coming from the parlor. The visitor had already been let in. She crept forward, opened the servant door but a crack, and peered inside the stygian-lit room.

Lord Grandstaff sat hunched in a high backed chair, more throne than seat. Before him stood a pompous aristocrat, bedecked in full Scottish regalia, leaning regally on an elaborate cane.

"I wondered if you would return, Master Therion. Have you come to exorcise the demon that plagues this house at last?" the beaten patriarch bemoaned.

"First, Lord Grandstaff, is the matter of payment. The spells which I intend to unleash in your service come not cheaply."

"I assured you that the cost would be no object, my old friend" the Lord responded.

"Old friend," the guest muttered. "Old friend... is that what we are then, Sir Stuart? Old friends? Tell me, how long have we known one another?"

"Well, I'd say," the Lord mumbled. "What? Nearly thirteen years, I suspect? Since our Malvern days."

"Yes, quite right," the man responded, indignant. "Malvern... wretched place, what with all that buggery."

"Here now, Crowley," the Lord started, leaning forward in his withered throne. "What is this? Do you begrudge the trifling flirtations of schoolboys?"

"Trifling?" Crowley scoffed. "Then what, pray tell, Lord Grandstaff, of our later years then? Trinity... do you recall our camaraderie while installed upon those hallowed grounds of learning?"

"Damn you, Old Crow," Grandstaff huffed. "Damn you and your warped and twisted mind."

"Boys will be boys, eh, my Lord?"

"You asked for everything that befell you, you damnable wizard," Grandstaff barked. "In this, my hour of need, you fall upon me like a sick and wounded pup? Did I not defend you, you awkward, socially inept wretch? When the fists flew, who came to your aid then?"

"You're a revisionist, old friend," the guest raged. "It was by Will alone that I overcame my enemies and by Will alone did I master not only my fear, but by which I have begun to unlock the most esoteric of mysteries."

"Why did I send for you? I should have known," the lord grumbled, rising weakly to stand before the pompous magician. "You were a pathetic schoolboy, deluded and maladroit. I see that maturity has eluded you and you are little different. I had hoped for better, but it seems I am to fend against this fiend on my own terms."

"Your arrogance has remained unchanged as well, *Lord* Grandstaff," Crowley scoffed. "Do you think it an accident that you are beset by this malefic entity? You belittle me, the only man in Britain that might give you aid, just as you saw fit to see me debased when we were but aspirants. This shall be your undoing."

Brianna was drawn from the two men's dialogue by the sounds of the twins' laughter down the main hall. She looked back to the parlor and saw that Lord Grandstaff had brandished a weapon, an ancestral claymore from his private collection. She was torn between rushing in to her lord's aid and to investigating the children's whereabouts. The added sounds of a woman's soft murmurings led her away from the parlor, entranced by the sounds down the hall, sounds drowned out as the mournful wails descended once more upon Grandstaff Hall.

The governess passed through the butlery and paused to listen in the kitchen. The youthful mirth, tempered with a palpable darkness rose from the winery door just off from the dining hall. She crept forward uneasily, trepidation clinging to her heart. The banshee wail that laid siege to Grandstaff weakened her resolve, but when the mournful repose of a pained woman once more danced amid the sounds of youthful revelry, she steeled herself and slowly opened the door, descending the dark stair toward the lord's private stock.

Dark shadows performed a minuet with the candlelight that caressed the narrow climb. She traversed the stairs with care and set her feet firmly upon the doglegged landing. The boys' rapture had ceased, leaving naught but the whimpering of the shadowed figure before her. Drawn out on the service table she laid, arms outstretched in mock crucifixion. Her flesh glistened wetly in the half-light.

"Blessed Virgin," Brianna gasped.

Before her lay Lady Grandstaff, naked to the waist. Her chest, a gaping wound that hid not the organs within. Lungs rose and fell weakly, the heart pulsating with a dangerous rhythm. The governess felt her stomach's meager contents rebel and she spewed hot bile upon the cellar floor. She was frozen in place, feet unable to carry her away from this scene of utter horror.

"We feared the ribs would have been difficult to remove, you know," young Wallace said, stepping from the shadows with his brother in tow. "Strangely enough, it was the skin itself that proved more bothersome." His hands and face were covered in blood, his teeth and lips stained crimson from his inhuman activities.

"How... why..." Brianna stammered, what little sanity that she had been able to cling to slowly slipping away. "You're monsters."

"No, silly cow," Walter scolded. "We are reborn. We have answered the call of our true mother. Her lullaby has raised us from the dead sleep that this house has fettered us with. Her song has called us home and we are reshaping this dwelling to meet her desire."

"You're mad," the governess spat. "The both of you. Driven mad by the very demon that haunts this place."

"A whore for sixpence with blood on her hands," Wallace spoke, "dares to call us mad."

"Shut up!" she screamed. "You don't know me!"

"Don't we, little dollymop?" Walter giggled, licking his fingers clean. "Were they someone else's hands clamped 'round the throat of the newborn babe that clawed from your putrid womb?"

"Shut up, damn you!" Brianna wailed. "You don't understand! How could you?"

"We understand plenty," Wallace said coldly. "We're all damned in this house."

Brianna froze as she heard a metallic click behind her.

"I couldn't agree more, foul spirit," a serpentine voice slithered weakly from the stair. An explosion cut through the tension as a shadowed figure fired a revolver into the room. The slug caught young Wallace squarely between the eyes, showering his twin with blood and gray matter. The governess turned to face Mr. Crowley, his eyes cold and piercing, their gaze the very essence of championing death. The Englishman let loose with another round that sent the boy Walter scurrying for the cover of darkness.

"Hell is waiting for you, Old Crow," the boy called out. "Your wickedness is a one way ticket into the arms of your true lover."

"In the name of all that's Holy and all that is Profane," Crowley called out, "you'll be sent back to the bowels from which you've sprung!"

"What are you doing?" Brianna mouthed, unsure if she even spoke the words aloud in the midst of the spectral cacophony and the reverberations of the weapon that the magician wielded.

"Saving your life, I think," Crowley answered. He reached out and pulled her to him. The governess was surprised by the strength of his grip. She clung to her benefactor even as thoughts of her being trapped between two devils filled her head. "We should ascend with all due haste, my frazzled beauty," he said, urging her up the narrow stair. "I've but two shots left and I'm afraid these wee bairns have decided to raise the stakes in this gambit."

The governess' eyes were drawn toward the child Walter and she was stunned to see the boy rising up and scurrying over his mother's eviscerated corpse. He no longer looked human, what with the addition of scaled tentacles that had sprouted from his ribcage and the mottled fin that now bisected his skull, fanning out along his spine and forming a grotesque tail that whipped about like a thing independent of its host. Behind him, his brother writhed in pain, but she could already see the wound delivered by the mage's pistol knitting itself whole once more.

"Oh bloody hell, do something!" she exclaimed as she clamored up the stairs.

"I am open to suggestions," Crowley responded as he let loose with one of his two remaining bullets.

"Your reputation…" she shouted, gasping for breath as she raced forward, crashing through the winery door and into the kitchen, "… precedes you sir." She sprinted through the dark room and down the hall with reckless abandon. "Can't you cast a spell or something?"

"Don't believe everything you read in the papers, Miss Moore," he chided. She was sure he would have been amused were they not running for their lives.

The governess crossed the grand entry and slammed hard into the door. She tried to open it, but it held fast. "Damn it!" she exclaimed, pulling with all her might.

"It's been nailed shut!" Crowley barked. Brianna cowered behind her Byronic savior as he turned to face the creatures that were slithering toward them.

"By who?" the governess asked.

"By me, Miss Moore."

Brianna and Crowley looked toward the parlor door and saw the man standing there. Lord Grandstaff stood tall, oblivious to the seeping wound in his stomach put there by Crowley's revolver.

"Why?" she pleaded, eyeing he and the inhuman creatures that had once been her charges.

They had ceased their advance and now sat coiled, as if ready to pounce, at their father's feet.

"This has all been my doing, I'm afraid. My children needed to eat. You see, my wife and I had struggled to bring forth an heir to ensure the legacy of Grandstaff. Something had to be done. We had been to every physician, consulted every expert at our disposal. Still, nothing. My beautiful wife was barren. You can imagine our heartbreak. So, with nowhere else to turn, I called upon the Ancient Ones. I made a pact with them and they delivered not one but two children from my wife's barren womb. Their hunger was small at first. Slowly they went through their wet nurse, then a small parade of governesses. But their hunger was growing. Something more needed to be done."

"Why bring me into this, Stuart?" Crowley asked, keeping the gun leveled on the Lord of Grandstaff Hall.

"Because human flesh was no longer enough. They needed something more. They needed to feed on someone more satisfying…someone with power. So I devised a ruse and I invited you here, appealing to your inflated ego and your appetite for the supernatural."

"The banshee, she is the Ancient One you bargained with," Crowley spat. "You offered her something she couldn't resist… a foothold in this plane of existence, a base from which she and her offspring could grow in power. You damnable fool, you've placed all of Britain in jeopardy, if not the entire world."

"You are without a doubt an adept of the first order," the lord choked, grimacing through the pain of his stomach wound. "I knew you would not be able to resist a challenge such as the one I had presented, not the funds I waved under your nose. For all your knowledge and proficiency Aleister, you have always had a weakness for sycophancy."

"He's right you know," Crowley quipped with a wink toward the governess.

"And me, Sir Stuart?" Brianna asked. "What part in your game did I play?"

"The children feed on fear, as well as flesh, but they also are nurtured by darkness, and we both know your sins, dear Brianna."

"Very well, Grandstaff," Crowley said, "you've played your game and lost. We're not cattle for your brood. Blood has been spilled enough this night. The girl and I shall take our leave and you shall darken our paths no more, or by all the gods of Heaven and Hell, I shall see you cursed in a manner that shall boil your very soul."

"False bravado, Mr. Crowley. I still have the upper hand, and hungry mouths that need fed. Walter, Wallace," Lord Grandstaff said to his inhuman children, "your feast is prepared. You may eat."

The beasts lurched forward, propelled off of powerful tentacles, moving swiftly across the marble floor. Twin jaws dropped low and protruded unnaturally, the children's teeth now razor sharp and housed within demonic maws.

"I think not," Crowley said calmly. "Magick is an act of Will in concordance with action." He stepped in front of the governess and steeled himself, staring down the grotesque younglings. He thought of his years of training at the feet of lesser men, men who had knowledge but not the Will to use it. He would show them what true Will could produce. He reached down into the depths of his being and ignited the spark of magickal energy that was alive within him. Crowley spread his hands wide, bending the ring finger of each and slowly bringing his thumbs forward to touch the fingertips, completing a magickal circuit.

Brianna stepped back, feeling the surge of preternatural energy emanating from within her benefactor. It frightened her in a way that even the beasts that charged toward them couldn't. Her mind told her that those ungodly creatures were an aberration, but the energies flowing outward from this man, this magician, it resonated in her soul and warned that such power could lurk behind a human face.

The beasts were nigh upon them, their black tongues licking at the air, their tentacles slithering forth, their eyes ablaze with hatred and insatiable hunger... hunger for human flesh. Brianna Moore cowered behind Crowley, he being, she thought, the lesser evil, and as he spoke words that she could not comprehend, and as she felt the heat of magickal flame as it sprang forth from the magician's hands and into the faces of the demonic twins, she prayed not to God, but to an infernal spirit. It was in that moment that she knew she was lost.

"I believe that is more to what you had in mind," Crowley said to the governess with a wink He offered his hand to her. He was shaking almost as badly as she was, but for an altogether different reason, her from mind numbing fear, he from preternatural exertion. The stench of brimstone filled the acrid air and flames had taken root and began to slowly spread throughout the great Hall. The bodies of the twins were blackened and smoldering with their father on his knees beside their lifeless forms.

"What have you done?" Lord Grandstaff bellowed. "My boys! My beautiful boys!"

"Stuart," Crowley said.

Sir Stuart Grandstaff, Lord of Grandstaff Hall, looked up at his former schoolmate with a mixture of anguish and bitter hatred. He clutched at his stomach and the bullet wound there with a grim determination. Crowley hovered above him, revolver once more in hand. He steadied it, centering it on the Lord's forehead.

"She'll never let you leave here alive," Grandstaff moaned. "She was their mother. She will have her revenge."

"Do you think I fear her, you fool?" Crowley asked.

"What are you waiting for," the Lord growled. "Do it."

The revolver exploded, the bullet ripping through the Lord's head, tumbling through his brain, spraying bone and gray matter out the back of his skull.

"Black blood upon the altar!" Crowley said, "and the rustle of angel wings above! Black blood of the sweet fruit, the bruised, the violated bloom—*that* setteth the Wheel a-spinning in the spire. Death is the veil of Life, and Life of Death; for both are Gods."

Brianna came to stand beside Crowley and the magician slipped his arm around her waist and smiled.

"It is finished," he said.

"Aleister," the governess said, "the banshee's wail. It's silenced."

"Grandstaff didn't realize that when he brought her forth, it was his life force that she fed off of. When I silenced him, I laid that hellspawn to rest as well, at least until the next blackheart comes along intent on making a pact with the devil."

EPILOGUE

Brianna watched as Grandstaff Hall burned. Crowley had scoured the Hall for prizes that he could not give up to the pyre. Art, silver, jewels, cash, and rare books as well. All these he carted away with him. His offer to take the governess in as both pupil and concubine was rejected, though she had allowed the magician to seduce her into an act of Tantric coupling. She had been a prostitute in another life, after all, and before the heat of the conflagration and the fire that burned in her heart after nearly having her life taken from her, she relished in the wantonness of it. A new lease on life had been offered.

She reflected, gazing into the fiery shell of what had been and wondered as to this new road that was now laid out before her. She had a bit of cash but no course. Perhaps America beckoned? Yes, that was it. America. Land of opportunity they said. She could have a fresh start in a new country, with not but fading memories of a wicked past and a devilish misadventure with the so-called Wickedest Man in the World. Not so wicked, she thought, as she turned away from the hellish ruin. Not so wicked at all.

ADAM CATMAN

Andrew Wayne Adams

No less resplendent for the candied end he's eaten, the Prince of Eden speaks: "Love be to my wife, she of the scarlet galoshes." The tree is full of such fruit, apples and more, all in suits of hardened sugar. The one he ate had a razor in it. His light bulb is filling with blood, the filament ablaze like a worm of white fire above the rising red.

Feline attendants lick his feet. I am one of them. My whiskers bristle like swords. I roll my tongue between two toes, collecting the sweat that is as wine to us, the crud that is as bread, all sweeter than ever now that he's falling. Another cat tries to worm in where I am, and I claw him, arched and hissing.

Unaware, I have just introduced territoriality into the world.

He looks to his wife. She is swinging from a tree branch, red boots kicking at fruit. Her light bulb brims with blood. The filament burns within the churning crimson, turning it into a sun, the light bulb like a furious exclamation point above her head.

She drops from the branch. He goes to her. The cats follow him, darting after his feet. I bite and scratch at the others, trying to be the first, the only.

His hand still clutches the candied fruit. An apple, one big bite in its side. She raises it to both their lips. As they lean in, their light bulbs touch.

The bulbs of blood explode.

The blood falls upon their heads. It streaks their faces. Their eyes turn to wood. The apple falls. It bruises the moss. The cats stop licking and wander off.

Not me. I stay. I lick.

Something sour in the sweat now. It withers my tongue. Trickles of blood arrive from above, bathing the toes dark red. I lick the blood.

Then comes a huge fleshy dog with wings, hooves, antlers, pincers, peacock feathers, etc. I hide behind a hedgerow of mushrooms and watch as the dog leads husband and wife away. They go out through a rusty gate. The slender streaks of blood running head to foot are like pinstriped suits on their former nudity. Their oaken eyes stare everywhere at once. They mutter gibberish to each other.

If every man and every woman is a star, then these two have gone supernova.

I come out from behind the mushrooms. I find, in a glove of bruised moss, the apple with the bite in its side. I see the razor in its flesh, a razor with a million parts, discontinuous shards glittering like nodes in a net.

I eat the apple, seeds and all.

And say hello to an angel.

Time passes. Dilates, shrinks. I am time.

Now, now, and now.

I am a cat. I know this now. I know the names of things. I am what the man was, the knower and giver of names. I go unnoticed. I am small. I stalk through the garden, watching the unconscious meat fold and erupt.

Raw piglets burst mewling from a flower, and I lick their eyes open. I build fences around the corn and wheat. I walk on my hind legs, wearing pants and a vest.

I am looking for God. He has been absent here since the humans left. He has gone to be with them in the bogs of clay. I wonder if He knows about me, if He sees my barns and fences and the stones I heap over dead things.

The other cats have taken to dressing like me. They mimic my bipedalism, my agriculture. Their heads hold only a buzzing fly each. My head holds roads and warring seahorses.

Why has God not sent His dog to fetch me? These others, they are empty, their houses and chapels mere anthills. It is innocent, the way they mimic me. Like children. Can it be that God has mistaken me for one of them? For just another gnarl of bone and fur bubbling dumbly in His erstwhile garden? It could be. Anything could be. And so the dog could come for me at any moment (such as now, now, or now) with its wings, hooves, antlers, pincers, peacock feathers, etc.

Sometimes I go to the rusty gate and look out upon the trenches of black iron. I see men and

145

women trembling like maggots within the sinuses of a cadaverous earth. God is out there with them. He must be. He is not here, so He must be there. Unless there is some other place, and there always is. But that other place is a playroom in the Halls of Autism. And if He is there, then He is nowhere.

I know, as surely as I know the names of things, that God is in the playroom.

I stop looking.

I take to wearing a laurel wreath and calling myself Caesar. The others take to marching in step behind me, scarlet armbands marking them all alike. They trample the pastel tissue of old meadows. Their chants are a kind of silence. They demand my rule. I yield, am imperial. I send youths to die in the embrace of eastern ferns. I laud a certain bone structure, decry another, and oppose the two, dropping truncheons and shields into the mix. I invent cryptic regalia, all stelliform and skeletal, and strew them wherever there are eyes. Whimsy, whimsy. I lick the blood (thick and swimming with minnows) that pours from the ears of those who hear me, and everyone hears me.

Time.

The garden is not small. It is the size of the world. I push my men (they are men) onward, trying to find the outer walls. One wall I know already, the one with the rusty gate. Soon I find the second wall. Longer to find the third. Now I order all life into thirst for the fourth and final.

I fall toward the final wall. Fall into the west.

What is this wave rolling into the last quarter? I no longer recognize it. Dirigibles knit a new sky over the old. I am in one of them, looking out through a convex lens. There is a mountain ahead. It is the final wall.

The airships descend, black hulls pouring down like countless apple seeds to take apart the soil. I remain aloft, the head that watches.

On the mountain, the tree. It is the one from long ago, its branches loaded with candied fruit. Different fruit, now, less of the fat red apples, more of citrus and ice, but with the same sharp science lurking inside the skins.

My men (lions), who are my body, file out of their landed ships, onto the mountaintop. They eat fruit.

Above my head, a light bulb fills with blood.

From my place in the sky, I see the entire garden at once. It is a vast flowering body — an awareness — a thing of wings, hooves, antlers, pincers, peacock feathers, etc.

I see now.

Bulb blown, I fly beyond the wall—the first, the only—and crash-land in the bogs of clay. The bogs of clay get up and walk with blood on their face.

'there comes a midnight hour…'

Jayaprakash Satyamurthy

Doors. Rows of doors, off-white. Some left blank, featureless but for the handle, the keyhole, the number plate just above the frame. Some with proud plaques displaying names followed by strings of acronyms, others with icons of some deity or the other, or hung with decorations, some with welcome mats spread outside, or potted plants beside, or statuettes. Still they convey a sense of uniform intent, even in their differences. Doors to keep things in.

All those doors, all those corridors, all meeting at right angles, joining more rows of doors. They are like teeth set in the mandible of machine, a machine to live in and be eaten by and spat out anew, remade in the image of the pharaoh. For we are all pharaohs now in our hearts, all our hearts are hardened and we live in vast mausoleums, packed with all the dead things we need to live our dead lives.

Look, I can tell you're new here. Your mask, it isn't the usual kind. No, neither's mine, but I've learned to hide the differences – see, this little bit of muslin hides so much, this hat brim lowered just so covers much else. Here, you can have my hat, I have more, all different.

You live on the sixth level? I live right next to you. We're neighbours.

Look at all these doors! That one there, that's the elevator door. That's the door you want right now. It opens up and you see another door. I dream of opening a door that just opens into more doors one day, just doors receding from today to the Second Coming, and I step out into the final unveiling. In the meantime, there are these two doors, one opens the regular way and the other slides – this way. Yes, just slide it closed after you. No, I'm not coming up. You're welcome, you can really keep the hat. You know my room. Drop in sometime.

But wait! Just be careful! Don't go wandering the corridors when the moon wears an orange mask. The doors sometimes open then. Better to bide your time and wait for the other midnight, when the masks come off. But I'm holding you back. Bye-bye, now!

Hours, sliding by, intolerable friction of time on the side of my mind. Faces: what do they think they are? Faces? No such thing. Time will show. Minutes, scouring the surface of my thoughts, the parade that never relents.

I'm glad you dropped by. No, it's not a bad time at all. There is no bad time, time is a burden, a cage, a closet, time is sandpaper scraping at the skin of consciousness, but there is no time that is bad. Time just is. Or was. Or will be. It scrambles by so much, it's hard to know what tense it exists in, itself.

The committee welcomed you? That is interesting, it must have been interesting. They are interesting, they constitute a committee of welcome to welcome people into spaces that they have no rights over and then they impose strictures and caveats and call this process one of welcoming. Very interesting. Then they slink back behind their doors. Those doors are the maws of their domiciles, the windows are the eyes of the household. The walls are masks behind which entire lives are concealed. But beware the midnight hour; except of course that one final midnight.

Let me tell you about these towers. They rear up into the skies; have you thought of this space you float in, perched up in this slowly swaying, slowly crumbling pile of rubble? Once it was just sky; empty space through which sunlight floated, picking out dust motes, warming passing birds. Or it was occupied by treetops, residential towers for a different kind of society, all felled now, all gone. Let me tell you about these towers: they have no foundations. They are swaying between earth and sky, and they are of neither. Here, you are not of heaven or earth. You are of the ether. Things with no roots can grab you, can sink hooks into you and make holes in the side of your mind and crawl in.

You've been thinking about your mask? I know, I know, they must have hinted at you to get one of the standard models. This year's styles. Must keep up. But we've found a way, you and I, haven't we? We make masks of our own faces, we hide behind the truth, a ruse so blatant they do not see it. And so our true faces become lies, lies that will be removed when the time comes. Time rushes by, like a river in spate, flooding the banks of my mind, wearing away at the bedrock of my intellect. But I have already spoken of time. Now we shall converse of masks and deceit, of disguise upon disguise.

Always these corridors, always these doors. The corridors are a lie; they lead nowhere. Every path is a cul-de-sac – except one, but the time for it has not come, yet. The doors are a feint; they are not here to keep you out. Every door is an invitation, like a sweet, soft voice hissing in paradise. They want to keep you here, they want to draw you in. When you enter, you may yet be yourself, some kind of self that was raised in its own water and soil in some hayseed carnival tent hick town blown into some crumpled rumpled rucked mucked corner of the map no one ever smoothes out and looks at. When you come back, if you aren't careful you'll be another. A pharaoh. A kind of god-thing made into flesh, mortal for a limited time, rapt in skin and bone, dead in life in a mausoleum with your dead money and your dead friends and your dead religion and your dead life.

But we've spoken about these things. We've spoken about masks within masks, the deceit that hides the deception. We've spoken and spoken and spoken and the hours have wound long and tight about us, choking us like serpents of vengeance, the minutes have crept across our skin, raking bloody trails, like small barbed creatures of authority, time has flown through and past us, eating away at our cognition, wearing away our minds with each passing instant.

There will be a time. Do you not know that there comes a midnight hour when everyone has to throw their masks off?

Life is being mocked. This cannot last forever.

'**S**he was weird, but I took to her immediately. No, let me rephrase that. She was weird, so I took to her immediately. I don't even know why I'd migrated to the big city so late in my life, too late to build a fortune or even much of a life. I suppose I'd spent so long on the peripheries, hiding my mask from the light, that I just wanted to reach out, like a blinded, wounded prehistoric beast lying dormant in a deep, hidden place for long epochs before it finally stretches out a single, quivering tentacle, wondering if there are still creatures like itself out there.

For the most part, there weren't. But I took my savings and I took my little collection of odds and ends – seashells, riverbed rocks, pine cones, sandstones with bits of fossils in them, a few photos and sentimental souvenirs I had of my late wife (my first, last and only love) and a few things from my long-dead career as a doctor: an old stethoscope, my certificates, the signboard that had hung outside my consulting room – and I visited a dozen brokers until I finally found a place I could afford, a small two-room affair up in a residential tower. She met me the first evening I got there, showed me to the lift, gave me a hat.

She was decidedly fey. (I like using the word; it dates me, establishes me as someone of a certain generation. Who says 'fey' anymore? Only the very aged, and those who are themselves fey. No one else has need for such a word, for such precise pinpointing. It is enough for them to say 'different' or better yet 'wrong'.) Not gamine or svelte or any of those other words which focus solely on the body: fey. Strange, unworldly, giving an impression of possessing the gift of second sight. It was probably her eyes, brilliant and unsettling even through what she passed off as a mask. Not brilliant like an actress' eyes, framed in eyeliner and given that special glow by subtle lighting and post-photographic effects; I don't want you weaving pictures of some overly fond old codger drooling after some Audrey Hepburn lookalike. She was messy, lank-haired, lanky, given to rambling rants and now and then to staring into space, head tilted at what must have been an uncomfortable angle. And her eyes were brilliant because they suggested a brilliant, skewed mind with a brilliant, skewed regard. I took to her immediately because of those eyes, that gift of a hat and the rant about doors and corridors. I sensed that she saw things, the true, alive things, not the made-up, dead things.'

'Life in that tower was a nightmare.

The residents were all of one mind, yet they rarely got together. When they did, they picked out one or two targets for all the venom that gathered in their fangs, absent targets, those whose masks were outmoded or obscure, and spewed bile and vinegar on these targets in a joyous, rapt, terrible exultation.

I had learned not to draw attention to myself, to walk soundlessly and blend in with a variety of textures and shades. So I roamed the corridors, catching glimpses of the dead lives hidden behind doors, windows and walls. Sometimes doors were ajar, sometimes windows swung open, sometimes I caught a fleeting glimpse through a wall – I had the gift of second sight too.

I saw senior police officers ungird their bulbous bellies, sink back in sybaritic comfort and chortle as they sucked smuggled liquor from ornate bottles and watched footage of illicit deeds captured by surveillance cameras. I saw clerks lock themselves away from their families, jamming huge, spiked dildos up their anuses as they watched films of dogs or horses being guided to penetrate waiting men, kneeling on elbows, behinds spread wide. I saw schoolchildren gathering in squares of straggling garden to capture small creatures – insects, rats, kittens, puppies – and burn them with pilfered lighters, slice their flesh with cleavers stolen from kitchens, smash the remains and bury them in sandpits, I saw young couples slink up to rooftops to put out cigarettes on each other's fevered flesh or engage in acts of mutual coprophilia.

I saw other old people, men and women, sneaking around like me to catch these fleeting, fractured glimpses, withered hands moving implacably over ever-hungering genitalia.

Soon, I stopped sneaking about. I stayed home, I kept a close watch on my own heart, I pored over my small collection of tokens and mementos and I wondered about the midnight hour when all of these denizens would remove their masks. And I wondered about my own mask, and what may lie beneath it after all these years.'

Come with me. It is a bad time, a bad time to be out, a bad time to be in, a very bad time to be up here. The moon is wearing her orange mask.

They will be out tonight. Out in the corridors, stalking, their masks buffed, their nails sharpened, their senses keen with the thrill of the chase. Doors will open before them, they will enter rooms, unearth secrets – not the secrets you have been seeing, but secrets such as those you and I hide. Our memories, our dreams. Our beating hearts. Our alive things. They want to rip the beating hearts out of our chests, to watch black hearts' blood jetting out of the cavities they have made of our trunks, staining the walls, the roof, the tables and chairs, the small, fragile precious things gathered in our rooms.

Gather your small precious things. Come with me.

There isn't much time to lose. Come, this way, where the corridors become uncertain, meeting at angles nearly obtuse or acute, this way where the shadows are liberated from the gaze of ceaselessly staring strip-lighting, where darkness regains some of his swagger and authority, this way where the rows of doors suddenly ends, where a corridor joins another at an impossible angle, come, let us leap – you can hold my hand. Close your eyes, it makes the first time easier.

Now we are nowhere. Nowhere is a safe place, they cannot find it, it has no things within and they cannot go easily to places where there are no things, places that are only ideas. You are safe here with me, in this idea of nowhere. We shall wait out the night of culling and then leap back in. I know what you are thinking, but no, we cannot stay here indefinitely. There is nothing here to sustain us, we would have to keep sneaking back out to find and bring back the things we need, and in time the things we brought would accumulate. Then, this place would no longer be nowhere.

Now sleep. That's the best thing to do. Take your little souvenirs out, run your fingers over them, unlock your memories and drift to sleep.

It is the night of the culling, the night of the masks.

They come down the corridors, masked heads held high, searching for the stain, the mark, the sign of difference. All doors open before them and they enter chambers filled with secrets and horrors – but these are not the secrets they are looking for, these are not the horrors that they fear. See their masks gleaming, the colours brilliant, see them marching like an army of automatons with jeweled heads.

Look! There is one unknown! Some wretch who lingers on the edges of their tower, living on refuse and waste, too stubborn to conform, too scared to escape. See how they fall upon him, these staunch burghers, these good folk of the eternal middle class, these attorneys and bankers and civil servants and engineers and teachers and contractors, hear their cries of wild glee, funneled and filtered through the mouth-grilles of their masks, hear the pell-mell of their feet as they run towards the delivered victim.

They fall upon him like crows upon a dying, poisoned rat on the city streets, screaming, fighting each other, vying for the choicest pieces. His screams are awesome, terrible, but they are drowned in the exultant cries of the mob.

When they leave, nothing is left of the culled victim, save for some scraps of clothing, perhaps a bone shard or too. But look – one more has joined their parade, one more marches alongside them, his head encased in a mask that gleams like a jewel as it hides and shapes the things within.

It is the night of the culling, the night of the masks.

'I don't know how long we stayed in that place – it felt like an eternity, but a welcome eternity. Nothing was distinct, yet everything was lit with a pale glow, although glow is the wrong word, too unequivocal. There was a certain medium of visibility, but it was not clear what it showed. An impression of space with no dimension. Yet, it was a comfortable place, for me, a comforting place. There was nothing truly amenable there, it is true, but nothing adverse – and that can be a great comfort, a great release after a life lived in opposition.

I sat on a surface that wasn't and looked at my little souvenirs for a long time, eyes poring over all the dear familiar details, mind unlocking a host of memories. A life against the grain, and so a hard life, but not without its own inner felicities and plenitudes. And few can say as much, of this I am sure.

I was thinking to myself that this no-place, this nowhere my protector had brought me to would be an ideal afterlife in many ways, save for the absence of the dear departed.

Then I slept, and I dreamed of them and it was perfect.

I awoke to find her pacing tensely. 'Oh, you're awake. I was just about to try waking you up.' 'For what?' 'The time has come. We must return.' 'Must we?' 'Yes – you cannot live on dreams, can you?' 'I have lived for nothing but dreams, I think.' 'For, not on,' she said, unusually terse. I stood up and she took my hand, pulled me along in some direction in that dimensionless not-space. We came to a pause, then a leap.

As we emerged back into the familiar corridors, moved from that anomalous intersection in its flickering illumination into the familiar perfection of right angles and precise turns, lit by that familiar light, artificial and unequivocal, it came to me that she had been so unaccountably brisk with me because she, too, was loathe to leave nowhere.'

'I took to wandering the corridors and the outside perimeters with her, at times when no one was abroad – during the long watches of the blank afternoons, children at school, workers at work, home-makers at home, or during the quiet hours of the night, the quiet hours that shade into sunrise, the hours when, once again, no one is abroad but instead rapt before their television screens or simply deep within dead dreams.

In these hours, the empty spaces seemed different, as if unmasked and off their guard. An immemorial sadness seeped through everything and I truly felt as if the soul of man had died long ago and we were all just revenants and animated carcasses, hauled about like automatons under the remote control of false idols we ourselves had created.

In the open spaces we would find the small creatures the children had tormented and bury them, putting them out of their misery if needed. Once, we found a small black kitten that had been smashed repeatedly against a brick wall. Miraculously, it still breathed. I felt it, gingerly, using some of the training I had received, a lifetime ago it seemed. Its bones seemed intact, but it was in shock. I took this little one home and weaned it back to health for weeks. My friend brought me food and drink, for my little ward and for me. Slowly, he started to move, to walk and play, batting at my fingers with his paws or stalking imaginary foes across my carpet. His eyes stopped dripping and he started to fill out. He was a jet-black cat with lustrous green eyes and a bushy tail. As his hair settled from the spiky, jagged mass it had been when I first found him, it transformed into a lush, glossy velvet that I loved rubbing my hands over. He had almost no voice at all, but he had a deep, rumbling purr that gave me more comfort than anything else that still remained with me: memories, mementos, even my unusual friend, even my certainty of eventual death.

I spent less time with my friend on her nightly rambles after I brought Edmund – for that was his name – home. Instead, she would knock on my door sometime after dawn, a light syncopated rap that I soon came to recognize. I would let her in and she would sprawl, disordered and still trembling with nervous energy, across a couch and tell me of the night's gleanings. Sometimes she found things discarded in the corridors or in the compound – old televisions, worn-out mattresses, a box of toys, defunct mobile phones, hideous knick-knacks thrown out to make room for newer, more hideous knick-knacks. She too these things to places far away from our building, places where other marginal people found ways to re-use them. She told me of a wider network, a broader reality that existed around the margins of the world of the masked.

If I was younger, if I still had my wife with me, I would have given anything to become a part of this shadowy group. As it was, as soon as I could quit the public hospital without arousing suspicion, my wife and I had moved. We claimed that I was joining a private clinic halfway across the country, but instead we had moved to the outskirts of a small town just a few kilometers down the highway, a quiet, unimportant place where we could lead a quiet, unimportant life, becoming as invisible and self-reliant as we could in our little house, set well back from the main part of town.

It wasn't the death of my wife that had prompted my move to the big city. I still don't really know what it was. I suppose I was just curious. And now I had had my curiosity fulfilled and I was starting to think that I should perhaps leave for the peripheries once again.

'She's been gone for three weeks now.

I am to blame. Little Edmund and I are to blame.

It was that night again. The night of the culling, and we were going to the place of hiding. This time, along with my little souvenirs, I brought my little friend along. But the kitten balked at the final leap. I hadn't really expected that. I imagined that he would take naturally to the unknown, to the places between places. We overestimate the sinister and ethereal aspects of our feline companions; in truth, they are so much like us: warm-blooded, comfort-loving, lazy and loving, only with more elegance and grace than most of us can emulate.

So: Edmund leapt out of my pocket (he was bigger, but still fit in the large outside pockets of my old overcoat) and went careening down a corridor where lights flickered and lines intersected at skewed angles. I cried out in terror and shock and fell to the ground as I attempted to whirl around in pursuit. My cry echoed for what seemed like infinity and as it died out I heard footsteps, voices gaining in volume, growing nearer.

'Stay here,' she whispered to me, the shortest speech I had heard from her yet. I watched dazed, panting, useless old fool spread out on the tiles, as she dashed after the wee sleekit thing, her own footsteps an impossibly slight counterpoint to the culling mob's. In the distance I heard a yowl of feline outrage, then that one frail set of footsteps racing back, the sound of panting and of Edmund's grumbling. I realized that the sound of the mob was gaining in volume from a different direction altogether. I stumbled to my feet and turned my head this way and that, positioning sounds in space and realizing that mob and girl would converge at the point where, I old codger, waited any moment now. I stood at the brink, waiting for her, for him, for them. Waiting to pull them both into my arms, close my eyes, and leap. Into nothing. Into safety.

By now, you have formed some idea of what happened. Let it suffice. I will not relive that awful moment. Suffice it to say that she delivered my charge to me, then, the mob having found us sooner than I had expected, heroically served as a decoy and sacrifice while Edmund and I found our way to safety.

Sound does not carry through to the place that is not a place and for this I am deeply grateful.

When I finally left that place and made my way back to my own rooms, I found that she had left a note for me. She must have left it on my table when I was not looking, that night when she had come to fetch Edmund and me away.

'There is a pattern, and we all have a place in it. Even the threads that seem to go against the weave, even the threads seem to have come loose, the points of potential unraveling. There is a pattern and it is not to be denied or hidden forever. I have found my place in this pattern, I have loved life, even this hidden, uncertain life in these mazes of corridors, these rows of doors, these galleries of masked faces, I have lived life and loved every moment of it and I have welcomed the end as well, not for the torments that will pass in a flash, but for the chance it has bought. Remember, we all have a place in this pattern, even the loose threads, even the points at which the pattern seems set to unravel.'

There comes a midnight hour, and I am here to see that it does.

I may be wrong; but I think when you spend enough time in that other place, that place which is not a place, you start to see beyond the transient distractions that obscure things. I think that's what happened to her; I think she saw things as they really are. I have been back to that place five times since they took her away. I think I have started to see my place in the pattern.

I sit here and sip from a cup of chamomile tea, brewed in the long, silent watches of the night. Edmund sits beside me, purring softly in his sleep. My room is warm and comfortable, the mementos of a life lived outside the margins all around me. Relics of my one great mortal love. I look at our wedding photograph, now crumpled and faded. I touch the place where her face is printed. I close my eyes and think of the strange girl who once showed me the way to pass through these corridors safely.

I know there will come a time of unmasking. A time when they shall be culled. And I will be there at the very beginning, starting everything when I stand in a corridor where the lights flicker and the lines join uneasily, I will stand there, waiting, as the mob gathers around me. When they have me surrounded, powerless to flee, I will stand tall and proud and peel away the face that was my mask all my life.

And the truth will burn away all their lies.

THE WITHERING ECHO
James Champagne

"9 The thing that hath been,
It is that which shall be;
And that which is done
Is that which shall be done:
And there is no new thing
Under the sun.
"11 There is no remembrance of former things;
Neither shall there be any remembrance
Of things that are to come
With those that shall come after."
-Ecclesiastes, KJV

"I am like a puppet sitting here. It's not just I;
all of us are puppets. Nature is pulling the strings,
but we believe that we are acting."
-U.G. Krishnamurti, *No Way Out*

I.
Spherics of the Quivering Obelisk

I found the box containing my father's old records about a week after he died, when I was going through his personal belongings, checking to see if he owned anything worth keeping. They were in a shadowy corner of the basement of his house, next to another box (inside of which were five black painted candles arranged to resemble the shape of an upside down pentagram, along with a black leather-bound book, the front cover of which featured a reproduction of one of the pentacles of Solomon). On the front of the box of records my father had placed a yellow sticky note with two words written on the front in his childlike scrawl: "For Raoul." Obviously, the albums were intended for me. So I took the box home, wondering if there was anything of great value within it, maybe something I could sell on eBay or at that used record store downtown, the one that catered to hipster audiophiles and trendy DJs and whose name I could never remember. My hopes were quickly dashed upon a cursory investigation of the collection, though. It was mostly just a lot of old Christmas albums, some exotica from the late 1950's, a few records from long forgotten psychedelic bands (such as Mother Hive Brain Syndicate and Tanith Blues), along with one or two big name acts, but these latter records were in such dire shape that they wouldn't have gotten me anything at all: the mold blanketing the cover of my father's copy of the *Meet the Beatles* LP made it look as if the Fab Four's faces were being devoured by some sort of parasitic Martian fungus.

There was at least one album that caught my eye, however. It was named *The Withering Echo*, but I didn't know if that was the name of the band or of the album. The front cover of the sleeve showcased a top down, bird's eye view of a labyrinth, done in black and white, with the words *The Withering Echo* superimposed in the center of the maze in small red letters, while the back of the sleeve had nothing on it at all: just a black void of nothingness. I opened the sleeve, which seemed to still be in good condition, and an insert fell out, a small piece of white paper with only one sentence on the front of it: "The Withering Echo performed live at St. Dajjal's Cathedral." I reached into the inner sleeve and pulled out the record itself for a closer inspection. It was a black vinyl disc, and there was no further information about the album contained on it: no year was given, no record label was listed, nor were any band members mentioned or song titles indicated. It was most curious.

I took the album over to my record player and put it on, wondering what it would sound like. To my surprise, the sound quality was very good. The album had obviously been recorded inside a church of sorts (as the insert seemed to indicate), as there was a pronounced echo to the sound. The album began with a pregnant silence, a silence that was eventually punctured by a long, drawn-out note being played on a lone violin. At first, it was almost impossible to hear this note, but as the song progressed it began to go higher and higher in pitch, and the echo of the room made it sound as if multiple violins were joining in. The higher the pitch got, the more discordant the note became, making me think of a microscopic world of insects boiling in Old Testament agony. Soon other instruments began joining in. My ears detected flutes, pipes, and other members of the woodwind family, and these were played in a chaotic, somewhat shrill manner. There was also a bit of moody piano, and some percussion, mainly what sounded like the pounding of tribal drums, a Lwa cardiogram. The "band" didn't appear to even be trying to play a coherent song: it sounded as if each musician was playing something different, not even bothering to match each other's playing, to find a common groove.

Then, about four minutes into this opening song, a voice entered the fray. Like the violin note that had begun the album, at first this voice was very quiet, but gradually its volume began to increase, as if it were rising forth from a universe of plague pits. It was a male voice, with a pronounced British accent, yet it was impossible to tell if the singer was young or old: it was a timeless voice, seemingly immortal, both childlike and world-weary. The man didn't so much sing his vocals, it sounded more along the lines as if he were reciting poetry, poetry of the highest and most refined decadence. "Toothy tears of rain descend from the eyes of God/ two trails of black crystals on Infinity's face. We live in Golgotha-Time, sweat tears of blood in Golgotha-Hours, decompose gradually in Golgotha-Seconds." Those were the opening "lyrics." But the singer could have been reading numbers out of a phonebook and it would have been just as entrancing. His voice had me spellbound, as hypnotized as King Herod had been by Salome's dance. In the singer's voice I heard captured all the great collapses of history: the cyclical decline and fall of the Holy Roman Empire, Adam and Eve's fall from God's grace, and the primal Fall, that of Lucifer, the angel who had rebelled against Heaven itself.

And this singer's voice, along with the musical backdrop which accompanied it, filled my head with the most incredible visions: in my mind's eye, I saw a room whose ceiling was made out of dirt, whose walls were made of gray stone, a room lit only by candles. On one wall there was an alcove, and resting atop a pedestal in this alcove was a lonely human skull, a skull whose mouth was open in a silent scream. Crouched before this alcove were two vaguely humanoid shapes, grappling with each other in what appeared to be some sort of obscene shadowplay lovemaking. In the center of the room was a large black obelisk, and this obelisk was quivering like one of Harlow's mistreated monkeys, and from its base it was weeping a pool of blood.

This was just one of many visions conjured in my mind by the evocative music created by the unknown band. Other visions included that of a world gone mad in the hands of a lunatic god, torn apart by the brutal struggle between two fifth-dimensional djinns. I saw buildings grow monstrous toothy faces and come to sickening life, people drowning to death in cars filled with urine, giant black cockroaches oozing out from trembling sidewalks, children screaming as their skin turned into ice cream that promptly melted in the harsh glare of the multiplying suns. In short, I saw a world stripped of all reason, all order, reduced to a primal demonic chaos. I don't know why the unknown singer's voice made me think of such things, but for some reason, his singing evoked in my mind these strange rotgut images.

The singer intoned the following words like a sigh: "Nothing ever dies: anything that ever happens leaves a fingerprint on time, a withering echo that reverberates for all eternity." And with that, the first song ended. After a brief period of silence, there was a bit of skeletal applause, the clapping sounding like a landslide in an ossuary. It was obvious that this band, whoever they were, had not been playing to a large audience. Soon enough they launched into a second song, which in many ways sounded much like the first one.

The most striking aspect of the album was the ever-constant echo in the background. The echo produced by both the sound of the musicians' instruments and the singer's voice seemed to linger in the nave of the church, lasting for much longer than a regular echo should have, so that by the time the band had begun their final song, one could still slightly hear traces of all the songs which had come before it reverberating in the background, in a way I find difficult to describe. Perhaps it would be best if I simply said that by the end of the album's first side (and, as I found out after my initial listening experience, *only* side, as the other side of the album was blank), it sounded as if the band were playing all of their songs at once, as if the musicians on stage were being accompanied by the ghosts of their previous songs. I marveled at this curious effect, and wondered what clever architect had designed a church such as this, one capable of producing this intoxicating and, it must be said, slightly disturbing echo effect.

There were, however, incidental noises on the album itself which I found to be slightly jarring. Every now and then, in the space between the applause of the audience and the band starting their next song, I could detect a curious rustling sound that seemed to be coming forth from the audience itself, which made it seem as if the band were playing not only to a bone hoard, but also to some enormous, monstrous bird. I can't quite say why this was the image that these sounds conveyed to my poetic imagination. But there were other incidental noises that I also found unnerving, and they appeared on the album towards the very end. As the band finished their second to last song, I could hear, over the din of sickly echoes, what sounded like a door being open and shut in a hasty manner, followed by the sound of tiny footsteps running across the room. Then the footsteps seemed to descend a staircase and recede into nothing, though their echoes lingered in the room like every other sound, tiny echoes that reminded me of spider bites blistering on the body of angels. The song ended and the audience applauded. Then, in the space between that applause and the start of the final song, I heard the door open again, in what sounded like a hesitant, uncertain manner. More silence, followed by another set of footsteps, these striding across the room as opposed to running across it. By the time these new footsteps descended the staircase, the band began playing their final song, accompanied by the echoes of the earlier songs in the manner I just described a moment ago.

The most unsettling of these incidental sounds occurred at the very end of the album. As the band wound down their final song, the singer spoke one last lyric into the microphone, repeating the lyric that had ended the first song: "Nothing ever dies: anything that ever happens leaves a fingerprint on time, a withering echo that reverberates for all eternity." Then he fell silent, and gradually the musicians stopped playing. Soon the only sounds left were the echoes of their performance, echoes that slowly withered away to nothing. Silence again. Then, from somewhere that sounded like it was far below the stage, a harrowing scream came forth, a bloodcurdling noise that made my body shiver like the flame of a candle being blown out. The scream was quickly cut off by a noxious gurgling noise, and soon the only sounds left on the album were the mutated echoes of these two sounds, a male scream and a gurgling noise, the death rattle of two deformed lovers plummeting down a wormhole of annihilation, and the album ended with a locked groove, so that these two sounds were repeated over and over again in an infinite loop, a sick-tone echo that only ended when I took the needle off the record.

I listened to that album about five or six times, that first day. It captivated me like no album that I had ever listened to in my life, though why I cannot say, as it wasn't the sort of music I normally listen to. I wasn't even sure what genre of music it could be classified as. In regards to this *Withering Echo* album, I felt like an entomologist who had stumbled across a new, unidentified species of exotic butterfly. It both enthralled and terrified me, filling my soul with a kind of horror that could only be described as sacred. It quickly became clear to me that I needed to do some research into this album, to see if I could unearth any information about it.

Like most people of my generation, I began my quest on the Internet. A quick search on Google turned up nothing at all, so I tried other websites like Allmusic, Discogs, Wikipedia, even sites that specialized in listing prices for antique records. All these searches were fruitless. Next I contacted some friends of mine, record collectors who prided themselves on the fact that their collections held some of the most obscure and outré sounds ever committed to vinyl. But none of them were able to provide me with any information in regards to *The Withering Echo* album either. Frustrated, I began to wonder if I possessed the only copy of this album on Earth.

Not being able to find out any information about the band or the album, I decided to at least see if I could unearth anything about the venue in which the album was supposedly recorded at, St. Dajjal's Cathedral. The name of that church seemed vaguely familiar to me, and I dimly recalled seeing it appear in a certain book which I had read a couple of years ago. I walked over to one of my crowded bookcases and ran my finger along one of the shelves until I found what I was looking for, in between copies of Francis Parker Yockey's *Imperium* and Oswald Spengler's *The Decline of the West*: *Antichrist Throughout the Ages*, written by Professor Eugene Kilpatrick, published by Durtal Press in 2002. I took the book off the shelf and looked at the cover. In between the author's name and the book's title was the following artwork: an engraving from Jean Duvet's 16th-century Apocalypse series, plate #14, "The Worship of the Seven-Headed Beast," done in red and black colors. The engraving depicted a mob of people worshiping the Beast of Revelation. The Beast had a lion's body and seven heads, each of which was attached to the end of long, scaly, snake-like necks, and these heads resembled those of horned and bearded goats, dragons, bears, and cruel lions. I had purchased this book a few years ago, after having read one of the professor's other books, *The Omega Cults*, a tome whose immaculate scholarship had left a lasting impression on me. Sadly, Prof. Kilpatrick, who had been a teacher at Fludd University in Massachusetts, had lost his mind shortly before the publication of that latter book, so it appeared that these two books would be his only published work. But I digress.

The reason I sought out *Antichrist Throughout the Ages* now was because I recalled a mention of St. Dajjal in that book. I opened it up to the index and searched under "D." Sure enough, there was his name, and I quickly flipped to page 179. There, I read about the Masih ad-Dajjal, "The Imposter Messiah" and "lying Christ" of Islamic eschatology. Dajjal itself is a common Arabic word that means "to deceive," and when applied to the aforementioned figure it signified him as a false prophet, the Muslim equivalent of the Christian Antichrist. At the bottom of the page was a footnote that mentioned a saint in the Middle Ages who had named himself after Dajjal, and how more information about the life of this heretic could be found in Prof. Roland Cavendish's *Divine Madness* (published by Fludd University, Massachusetts in 2005). I didn't own a copy of that book, though, so I decided to make a little trip to the local library.

At the library, I found a copy of *Divine Madness* near some old Francis Bacon manuscripts and sat myself down at one of the polished oak tables, a notepad opened up next to me so I could jot down any relevant information that I came across. *Divine*

Madness had a whole chapter devoted to heretics of the Middle Ages, and a few of these yellowing pages dealt with the shadowy history of Saint Dajjal, of which little is known to us. Biographical information about him was scarce, other than that he lived in the eleventh century, was born and raised in Al-Andalus, and that his birth name had been Abu al-Shigrath al-Maliki. Originally raised as a Muslim, he eventually converted to Christianity sometime after his 23rd birthday, and he changed his name to St. Dajjal (spelled "Dajal" in some historical accounts). Like the religious figure he named himself after, he had been blind in one eye. Although some miracles were attributed to his name, these good deeds were outweighed by a whole list of supposed heretical acts, including his claim that he was the risen Christ, the Second Coming itself. Because of these heresies, the Vatican refused to recognize St. Dajjal as a saint, and he had never been officially canonized, though he had had something of a cult following back in the day, and even after his death a small cult of his followers lingered on. A footnote on page 52 mentioned a book entitled *Heretic Churches* by Prof. Tiffany Thule, and how this book contained an entry on St. Dajjal's Cathedral, erected by one of the dead saint's admirers during the 18th century. My face lit up like a jack-o'-lantern when I came across that information, and I went over to the card catalog to check to see if the library I was at had a copy of *Heretic Churches*. I was in luck: they did. I found the book, sat back down at my table, and continued my research.

In England, in 1711, an Act of Parliament created the Commission for Building 50 New Churches. However, only 12 of these planned 50 churches were actually built... according to orthodox history, at least. Some maverick architectural historians maintained that St. Dajjal's Cathedral was one of those intended 50 churches, though there was little in the way of solid evidence to support this conjecture. What is known about the church is the following: St. Dajjal's Cathedral was built between 1732 and 1747, and it was designed by an architect named Edward Dulac. The cathedral cost 40,000 pounds to build in all. In terms of architectural style, it would be classified as Georgian English Baroque, and it bore a strong resemblance to Christ Church, Spitalfields, which wasn't all that surprising, seeing as Dulac had been a student of that most infamous Dionysian architect, Nicholas Hawksmoor. The book showed a picture of the church: it had a rectangular body, 80 feet in width and 132 feet in length, and I was impressed by what the book said was the church's most captivating feature, a dramatic Georgian steeple that rose high above the cathedral's massive Doric portico entrance (supposedly the gargoyles built for the church were also works of the highest artistry). However, having very little personal interest in ecclesiastical architecture, I skimmed most of the book's passages dealing with the structural attributes of the church.

Far more intriguing in my mind was the history of the land that the church itself had been built on. In Roman times, it had housed a temple used by Druids for blood ritual ceremonies devoted to Plutonic gods, while during the Medieval age, it had been the location of a number of plague pits (in 1891, 8,500 skeletons had been excavated from beneath the cathedral). There were also stories that the spot had once served as the execution site for women accused of witchcraft during the 15th century. As for the church itself, while it was supposedly built with the intention of being a Catholic church, it had been rumored to have secretly been a place of worship used by a society of avant-garde Scottish Freemasons.

Later on, back at home, while listening once again to the *Withering Echo* album, I decided it would be in my best interest to pay a visit to St. Dajjal's Cathedral. A quick search on the Internet informed me that the church's address was on Arka Street in the Lamia Hill neighborhood of the town of Owlminster (pop. 1,118), which was itself located in the Severn Valley, near the town of Brichester, about a day's train ride away from my home. Perhaps the church was still open to the public, assuming it was still standing, and maybe I could find a priest there who could tell me something about the recording of the *Withering*

Echo album. That afternoon, I purchased a train ticket to Owlminster, and the following day found myself on a train headed in the direction of that town, the *Withering Echo* album secured in my suitcase.

II.
The Locust Summers

On the train I checked my watch, saw that the time was a little after ten. In about four hours or so, I'd be arriving in Owlminster. Until then, I had time to kill. I tried reading the novel that I had brought along with me, a dog-eared copy of Helena Morrison's *Astral Dustbin Dirge*, but my mind was so preoccupied that I found myself unable to read more than a few pages before my attention drifted. I didn't even know why I had purchased that book in the first place: perhaps it had something to do with the fact that the author's face reminded me a little of Diana, my ex-girlfriend, who had broken up with me a few years ago. I put the book down on the seat next to me and looked around my compartment. It was small and cramped, but at least it gave me some small measure of privacy. Aside from a bed and a closet, it also had a tiny bathroom and a window.

Outside, I heard the train whistle go "Choo Choo," and I suddenly found myself experiencing a flashback. I thought back to my childhood, so long ago, back when I had lived at Black Pudding

Manor, which had been the name of the estate owned by my family. It had been such a lovely home, and I bitterly regretted that my parents had to eventually sell it and move out, after falling on hard times. Ah, but what memories… sipping tea with Mummy in the lounge next to a roaring fire on the cold winter afternoons, playing croquet on the front lawn with my father during the spring, and, most especially, lighting bonfires with my sister Fanny during the sweltering summers, in a futile attempt to ward off the swarms of locusts who frequently converged on our family's estate during the hotter months.

A childhood recollection: myself, at the age of 8, skipping about the vast front lawns of the Black Pudding Manor, a rolled up and burning torch in my hand, lighting bonfires all around myself while Fanny, age 6, claps and laughs in delight at my antics. In the skies above us, black clouds of locusts swell like apocalyptic omens, preparing to swoop down and devour everything in their path.

Just thinking about poor Fanny brought about a pang of sadness in my mind. Her death had opened a wound in my heart that could never be healed. Closing my eyes, I could see her face again: that cherubic face, with those blue eyes that were such profound testimonials to innocence, that grin that could warm the most frostbitten of hearts, and a head topped by a mop of golden curls. Fanny, my dead little sister, the constant companion of my early years, perhaps my only true childhood friend, now long lost, drowned in the ocean of death. Oh,

181

how I missed her. What joys we both had, in those locust summers. What fires we had lit, in those locust years. Fanny, why did you have to die?

It was the "Choo Choo" of the train in the present that sent me hurtling back into the past, reminding me of the grim events surrounding the death of my sister (who had been my only sibling). I could never forget that day, as it had been seared into my memory like the brand of a Spanish Inquisitor, its memory forever wandering through the labyrinths of my brain. It had occurred around 20 years ago, when I had been 9 years old and Fanny had been 7. It had been a warm day late in July, the sky overcast with dark clouds, clouds which heralded storms to come that evening, clouds which had reminded me of the locust swarms in their black thousands. Both Fanny and I had been on summer vacation, and during those months of relaxation we had enjoyed spending a great deal of time playing outdoors. Our parents had no problems with this, as they believed it was important for growing children to get lots of fresh air and exercise. Still, our mother had always warned us to stay away from the vast marsh located at the edge of our estate. This marsh was a sprawling, treeless wetland, a great expanse of shallow water. My sister and I had been fascinated by this forbidden marsh: we had often stood on its sandy banks and looked out at all of the plants sprouting forth from the water, mainly reeds, cattails, and other forms of herbaceous flora. On overcast days like the one on which Fanny died, gazing out at the marsh could fill one with a sensation of comfortable melancholy, a cozy desolation. And at night during the summer, the marsh gas would sometimes burn and create ghostly dancing lights, mischievous will-o'-the-wisps and impish sprites, whose chaotic antics were a delight to observe.

Our parents had not been home that warm afternoon; rather they were in town, shopping for some wicker lawn furniture. Left to our own devices, Fanny and I decided to go play in the marsh. So we changed into our bathing clothes and headed outside, into the oppressive heat. The day was so warm that statues of animals located on the grounds of the estate had begun to actually melt. But Fanny and I were used to the heat. As soon as we reached the marsh, Fanny stepped right into it; the water only went up to her hips. That day she had been wearing a blood-red bathing suit and top, and on her head she was wearing a big straw hat, that I think belonged to our mother, or perhaps to one of our servants, such as our maid, Ginny. In the meanwhile I, being not as adventurous as my sister, remained on the banks of the marsh, where I could keep an eye on her, but all Fanny had been doing was wading through the water, laughing and splashing at it with her tiny hands.

A few minutes after our arrival, I had heard, in the distance, the lonely "Choo Choo" of a passing train. I had looked up and seen a black iron train riding by, along the tracks located near the edge of Black Pudding Manor, not far from the borders of the marsh. I had stared in awe at this train, unable to tear my eyes away from it, as if I were hypnotized. I loved trains, despite the fact that at that point in my life, I had never even been on one. Soon enough, the train had passed out of sight, and I had returned my attention to the marsh, returned my attention to Fanny... only now I could no longer see her.

I had begun to panic. Had Fanny drowned, whilst I had been transfixed by the sight of the train? In a frantic state of mind, I had waded into the marsh. It didn't take me long to find her: there she had been, floating face down in the fetid water like a drowned homunculus, her straw hat bobbing by her side like a boat lost at sea. Her pale body had been covered with strange objects, but in my panic I failed to notice them: I had grabbed my sister and pulled her back to land, to the banks of the marsh. There, I had turned her over and made a most shocking discovery: not only was she dead, not only had life fled from her fragile young body like rats streaming away from a flooding town, but her body had been covered with giant white leeches, leeches that had to be at least 7-8 inches in length. Some of these leeches were of a pale composition that matched the paleness of Fanny's corpse, while others were a crimson red, my sister's blood clearly visible beneath their pulsing, translucent skin.

I had quickly pieced together what had happened: while I had been watching the train, Fanny had evidentially stumbled upon an underwater nest of Wamphyri-Leeches, who, thus disturbed, had quickly latched themselves onto her and sucked her body dry, draining all of her blood in seconds. The fact that it had most likely been a quick and painless death did little to assuage my grief. I had run back to the manor to call for the servants, but by this point nothing could be done to save her: she was beyond medical attention. On that splenetic, sweltering, and overcast July day, amidst the chaos of my sobbing parents and the screaming servants and the animals melting, two major events had taken place in my life: my sister had died, and I had also developed what was to become a lifelong interest in nature's blood-suckers (I am an assistant professor of hematophagy at Disshiver University, currently working on my thesis, which will be entitled "Brethren of Desmodus: a study of sanguivores, vampire bats, leeches, bed bugs, chiggers, ticks, mites, vampire finches, candirus, mosquitoes, and other blood-feeders").

In any event, my grief did not end there. Poor Fanny had never even received a proper burial, as her body had vanished from the town morgue the following morning. Even more curiously, the coroner in charge of handling her autopsy had also not shown up for work that day. When the police had investigated the coroner's home, they had discovered his corpse, which had seemingly been drained of most of its blood. The police eventually concluded that the coroner had spirited Fanny's body away from the morgue, did God knows what to it, disposed of it, then killed himself in a highly unorthodox manner. It was a very sordid affair, but what it boiled down to was this: they had lowered an empty coffin into the ground on the day of Fanny's funeral, a coffin as empty as the hole that had been left in my heart by her death.

Back in the present, I shook my head, forced myself to stop torturing myself with the past. Although I would never allow myself to forget Fanny's death, I also realized that it had occurred many years ago, and what was done was done. Better to focus on the present, look forward to the future, and refuse to let myself be haunted by the phantoms of my past. Still, my eyes were brimming with tears, so I grabbed a Kleenex from a nearby tissue box and wiped my eyes dry. I always hate pulling a tissue from a tissue box, though, because when I do so, the tissue underneath the one I just pulled out comes forward like a ghostly arm, waving goodbye to a lover it will never see again.

I decided to pass a bit of time by gazing out my cabin's window and watching the world go by, but it wasn't as if the scenery were all that captivating. All I saw was a dull expanse of farmland, sloping hills, brooding forests, and not much else. Every now and then I'd spot an interesting sight, like when the train passed by the ruins of an old and abandoned vinegar works, the sight of which, when viewed in the bleak light of the gray morning, filled me with an immense sensation of melancholy and desolation. But for the most part, the only things to see outside were endless parades of electrical pylons, run-down gas stations, tiny and decrepit towns, comatose windmills, lice-ridden trailer parks, lonely orphanages and sterile insane asylums. Eventually we'd be passing through the Iron Mountains, which separated the Severn Valley from the rest of England, and that promised to be much more scenic.

A few hours later noontime rolled around, and the train began winding its way through the Iron Mountains. I decided that now would be a good time to get a bite to eat, figuring that I'd get a better view of the mountains from the dining carriage. So I left my cabin and headed in that direction. As I stepped into the dining carriage, I became aware of a change in the air pressure of the train; when I swallowed, I felt my ears pop. Well, after all, we were up in the mountains, so that wasn't very surprising. The dining carriage itself was fairly large, decorated in such a way so as to create an atmosphere that suggested both luxury and coziness. Against the west wall of the carriage was a buffet table. I went over to it, grabbed a plate, and selected my lunch: a sandwich, a small bowl of lukewarm vegetable soup, and a snack-sized bag of crisps. Then I found an empty seat and table near one of the dining carriage's large windows.

While I ate my lunch, I peered out the window, and I could see that the train was riding over a large wooden trestle that was built over Pascal's Gorge. At the gorge's bottom, about 100 feet below us, my sharp eyes spotted the wrecks of a number of ruined tourist cars, all unlucky victims to the Iron Mountains' treacherous curves. All around the train rose the soaring black peaks of the Iron Mountains, which the train tracks twisted and slithered around like a giant metal snake, or tunneled through like some burrowing worm. These mountains were curved at the peak in such a way that they resembled the canine fangs of some enormous animal, and when the rays of the sun struck the snow atop the peaks, white became red, blood-red, a vampiric alpenglow. To my poetic sensibilities, it looked as if the train were passing through the bristling, bloody maw of some titanic leviathan, the mountains serving as bloody fangs.

Upon finishing my lunch, I decided to return to my cabin. Once I was back there, I decided to try doing some more reading, this time non-fiction, Bill Schutt's *Dark Banquet: Blood and the Curious Lives of Blood-Feeding Creatures* (Harmony, 2008). After that I listened to some music on my iPod, The Mamas and the Papas' "California Dreamin'," which is one of my all-time favorite songs (even though I've never been to California or, for that matter, America). Eventually, whilst listening to the music, I fell asleep, but the nap was cut short by a robotic voice on the train intercom, informing the passengers that the train had arrived at Owlminster.

III.
Great Black Time

The train pulled into the station in the heart of Owlminster, came to a complete stop. I rose to my feet, stretched, felt a few bones in my legs pop. I gathered up my luggage, then left my cabin. A moment later I was exiting the train, along with a few other surly passengers. As I stepped onto the platform I checked my watch, saw that it was past 2 in the afternoon. I looked around the concrete platform, which was almost totally deserted, with the exception of one little girl loitering near one of the exit ramps. I looked around at the surrounding buildings, which seemed to tower above my head like tall black coffins standing upright. Still, it seemed like a nice enough city, despite some of the rumors that I had heard about it, and these rumors were the kind of things that one often heard about pretty much any other town: how warrens existed beneath the streets that were home to a race of trans-spatial moles with humanoid faces, or how a deserted Masonic hall in one of the town's seedier districts was actually a portal used to call forth elder demons from alien spheres. Nothing I hadn't heard of before.

Before I had set out on this little trip, I had

189

consulted with a friend who had been to this city before as to where the best lodgings for travelers could be found. He had suggested the Argos Inn, which was situated in the Lamia Hill district, only a few blocks away from where St. Dajjal's Cathedral was purported to be located. The only problem was, in my haste to leave I had forgotten to take along a map of the city with me, and I had no idea where Lamia Hill even was. I decided to ask around, see if I could get any directions from the local populace.

Satisfied with my plan, I made a beeline for the little girl standing near the exit ramp, the walls of which were covered with posters advertising something called "The Little Pooka Cabaret." As I got closer to her, I could see that she was bundled up in winter outer wear, even though it wasn't all that cold out outside on that October afternoon. A red cap was located on her head, while a mauve-colored scarf was wrapped around the lower half of her face, obstructing it from view. As a result, the only part of her face that I could see were her eyes, which were a chilly blue color. I approached her in what I hoped was a non-threatening manner, one of my hands raised in greeting. Soon I was only a few feet in front of her. Up close, even though most of her face was covered up, I could tell that she was around the age of 6 or 7. What she was doing hanging around the city's train station, I had no idea: maybe she was waiting for someone.

"Excuse me," I said to her, a smile on my face

as I stared into her eyes, eyes that struck me as strangely familiar in a manner I found disconcerting. "I'm looking for a place called the Argos Inn. Could you perhaps tell me how to get there?"

The girl's eyes widened, and her body began trembling like a little leaf. It was as if I had just told her that I were the Devil himself, coming to claim her soul. I took another step towards her, about to tell her not to worry, that I meant her no harm, when she suddenly turned away from me and ran off, away from the train platform, and a second later I saw her disappear down a nearby alleyway.

I sighed, hefted up my luggage, and stepped off the train platform. I began wandering around the city, and very quickly became lost. The streets of Owlminster were like no streets I had ever encountered in my life: they were constantly curving and twisting out into erratic spirals, and I found myself walking past the same streets over and over again, past innumerable boarded-up apartment buildings. Finally, I encountered a constable, who was able to give me the directions I needed. A few minutes later I was well on my way to the Argos Inn.

I arrived at the Inn at around 3 in the afternoon. It was a very narrow building, about six stories in terms of height, made of dull gray bricks, its outer walls covered with patches of mold here and there, which reminded me of the mold which had covered the surfaces of some of my father's old records. I stepped into the building's main lobby. It was a dimly-lit room of a medium size, with an old and rusted fountain in the center. On the left wall was a door leading to an even more dimly-lit bar, while the check-in desk was located on the right, near a door which led one to a tiny gift store, a store in which everything inside seemed to be covered in several layers of dust. The elevators and stairs were located at the north wall, facing the Inn's main entrance, which was on the south wall. An old jukebox in one corner of the room was playing Current 93's song "The Death of the Corn." I headed to the check-in desk, which was being staffed by a very thin, very emaciated young man, whose skin was almost shockingly pallid. As I approached, he stared at me with bulging, unblinking eyes.

"Can I help you, sir?" he asked in a hoarse voice. I told him I wished to reserve a room for the evening. He said that rooms were available. I paid the requisite amount of money, and a moment later he was handing me a key, to a room on the fourth floor. Before I headed to the stairs, I asked him, "Excuse me, but do you know anything about a St. Dajjal's Cathedral?"

"St. Dajjal's?" the clerk asked, scratching the top of his head as he did so. "Can't say I've ever heard of it, sir."

"Are you sure?" I asked. "It's supposedly on Arka Street in this very district. It's a very old church."

"Can't say I've ever heard of it, sir," the clerk repeated, shrugging his bony shoulders.

"Never mind," I muttered under my breath. With the room key in one hand and my suitcase in the other, I walked over to the ancient elevator, which I took up to the fourth floor. I walked down a shabby hallway with creaking wooden floors until I found my door. I unlocked it and stepped into the room, closing the door behind me as I did so.

It was a small room with two windows, a bed, a minuscule bathroom, a few chairs, a roll top desk, and an old, ratty-looking rug which reminded me of a leprous distant cousin of the Shroud of Turin. The wallpaper was stained with giant red and purple blotches, as if the walls behind the paper were made up of rotten flesh ravaged by some Venusian venereal disease. Above the bed was a framed print depicting a Buddhist Bhavacakra, or Wheel of Becoming. The Bhavacakra was a symbolic representation of the concept of samsara, the endlessly repeating cycle of birth, life, death, and rebirth. The Bhavacakra itself was held by the jaws, hands and feet of a monstrous, black-skinned, three eyed demon, who was said to be either Yama, the God of Death, or Kala, the Lord of Time. I studied the print for a few moments, then rested my suitcase down on the bed, which creaked under the additional weight.

Once I had gotten myself settled, I left my room and headed down to the lobby, where I was able to get my hands on a map of Owlminster.

When viewed from above, I couldn't help but notice that the streets of Owlminster looked like whorls, as if the city were nothing more than the greasy fingerprint of some degenerate giant. Map in hand, I left the Inn, began heading in the direction of Arka Street, which was located in the exact center of the town. It only took me a few minutes to walk there. Once at Arka Street, I headed over to the spot where the church was said to be located, in the center of a small park named Wormblot Woods. I arrived at the park, headed towards the center, and saw: nothing more than an empty patch of land surrounded by a few dead trees.

I frowned and checked my notes. According to my research, I should have been staring at St. Dajjal's Cathedral. But there could be no doubt about it: the church was no longer there. Evidently it had been torn down some time ago.

To say that I was in a state of despair was putting it mildly. I had come all this way, only to find that the church no longer existed. I felt crushed by disappointment, and considered taking a train back to my town that very day. However, I had already paid for my hotel room, and I didn't want that money to go to waste. So I sighed and headed back in the direction of the Argos Inn, my shoulders slumped in defeat.

Back at the hotel, I walked across the musty lobby, the creepy clerk watching me pass by in a disinterested manner. A new song was playing on the jukebox now, another Current 93 tune, "The

Ballad of the Pale Christ." I took the elevator back to the fourth floor, returned to my room. I flopped down on my bed, unsure of how I should spend the rest of the day. Later on that evening, I would go try to find a restaurant, have a bit of dinner. Then I would probably return to my hotel room and spend the rest of the evening reading the books I had brought along with me to keep me occupied during the trip. Not how I intended to spend my time in Owlminster, but what could I do? St. Dajjal's Cathedral was apparently no more.

It was then that I noticed that the art hung on the wall above my bed had changed. No longer was it a framed print of the Buddhist wheel of existence. Now it was instead a framed print of Paul Delvaux's 1943 painting, *The Echo*. The painting in question depicted a nude woman wandering amongst Greek temples at midnight, and behind this woman were two other versions of herself, each one smaller as they receded further into the background of the painting. At first, I wondered why this painting, which I had never seen in my life, seemed so familiar to me. Then I recalled that J.G. Ballard had mentioned it in one of his short stories from the 1960's, "The Day of Forever," which I had read during my teenage years. I wondered who had changed the art... perhaps the maid, while I had been out strolling. More disconcerting, however, was the reason why the picture had even been changed in the first place. I couldn't even begin to guess why.

Around 6:00pm or so, I left the hotel and walked around the streets of Lamia Hill until I came across a Greek restaurant named "Garden of Thebes" that seemed clean enough to suit my tastes. I had a quick, inexpensive dinner, then left the restaurant. On my way back to the hotel, I asked every pedestrian I came across if they knew anything about a St. Dajjal's Cathedral. Naturally, like in a bad horror movie, no one had any idea of what I was talking about. It seemed the only thing that the inhabitants of the town wanted to discuss was a recent series of odd murders which had afflicted Owlminster that month. Frustrated, I returned to the Argos.

Back in my room at the hotel, I spent a few hours reading the books I had brought with me, even watched a bit of TV. Midnight rolled around, but I still wasn't all that tired. I looked out of my window, at the pointed rooftops of the town, roofs that were perched atop the houses like witch hats. It seemed like a tranquil place, the light of the full moon making it appear to be very peaceful. I decided to go for a small walk before bed, in an attempt to absorb the town's nocturnal aura. Making sure that I didn't forget to bring my hotel key, I shrugged on my jacket and exited my room. I took the elevator down to the lobby (which was deserted at this late hour: the clerk was nowhere to be seen), then left the hotel, stepping out into the brisk night air.

I began walking down the narrow, twisting streets of Lamia Hill, my hands in my coat pockets, my eyes taking in all of the sights. The streets were utterly barren of life: I didn't see a single soul during the first few minutes of my midnight stroll. I walked past more boarded-up apartment buildings, walls covered with old posters announcing winter carnivals dead and gone, a number of shops that had been closed for the evening: decaying bookstores, a clothing store whose front window displayed a number of skeletal, sinister-looking manikins draped in rags, toy stores whose display windows showcased children's toys that looked as if they had been imported straight out of some obscure German Expressionist film: dolls that appeared to be made of human bones, grotesque bird-headed jack in the boxes, toy trains whose passengers were dead spiders, doll houses whose interiors resembled that of crypts, and ghoulish marionettes who had the most lewd expressions carved onto their wooden faces. One shop I passed by seemed to sell nothing but spider webs.

As I walked on, I thought about a lot of things: St. Dajjal's Cathedral and its bizarre history, the mysterious girl with the discomposing eyes who I had tried to speak to at the train station platform, the deaths of both my parents and Fanny, and, most of all, the *Withering Echo* album, the object that had brought me to this town that I was now walking through on a cold October evening. None of it seemed to make a whole lot of sense to me:

everything seemed disjointed, and a curious sensation of melancholy coursed through my soul like a pitch-black river. Walking through the maze-like streets of Owlminster that evening, I felt so very alone.

I was so wrapped up in myself, I almost didn't even notice when the young girl I had met earlier in the day crossed my path like a black cat. I looked at her, saw that she was still dressed as she had been earlier in the afternoon: the same bulky winter coat, the mauve scarf wrapped around her nose and mouth, the red hat atop her head. Only now I could see a few strands of hair sticking out from under her cap, against the alabaster paleness of her forehead. Her hair was blond, golden curls. I stared into her widening eyes again, and in a moment of shock, I realized why her eyes had freaked me out earlier in the day: it was because they had reminded me of Fanny's eyes. And now that I could see a bit of her hair, the resemblance to Fanny was even more striking, though with the lower half of her face obscured, it was difficult to tell. But as I stood in the street that evening, staring into the frightened doe eyes of that little girl in the crepuscular light of the full moon, there was almost no doubt in my mind that I was reunited with my long-dead sister.

She backed away from me again, then took off running. I shouted out for her to wait, and when she didn't listen to me, began pursuing her down the curving, labyrinthine streets. As I chased her, I noticed two things: first of all, that the echoes created by our rapid footsteps seemed to linger in the air all around us in a manner reminiscent of the echo effect I had analyzed so often on the *Withering Echo* album, and secondly, that she was headed in the direction of Arka Street.

A few minutes later I noticed her running into the Wormblot Woods Park on Arka Street that I had visited earlier in the day, in my vain attempt to locate St. Dajjal's Cathedral. Perhaps her plan involved hiding from me by using the park's trees for cover. I ran into the park and stopped short. Rising up directly before me, on the spot which, that afternoon, had been nothing more than a blank patch of land, was St. Dajjal's Cathedral, looking exactly as it had in the drawings and photographs I had looked at in *Heretic Churches*. The Georgian English Baroque architectural style, the expertly carved gargoyles, the dramatic steeple rising high above the grand portico, which was itself adorned with massive Doric columns: the church I stood before was St. Dajjal's Cathedral, of that there could be no mistake. At first I thought the church was nothing more than an illusion, perhaps created by the light of the moon, but staring at the building, that seemed to be impossible; the edifice seemed as immobile as the Iron Mountains, something that would always be there, till the end of time itself.

And right now, the little girl who reminded me of Fanny was running up the front steps, to the main door of the cathedral, which she opened, then shut behind her. For a few seconds, I was too stunned to move. Then I raced after her.

I ran up the stairs under the grand portico, passed by the monolithic Doric columns. Horned gargoyles with cold and demonic eyes watched me gloomily as I made my ascent. The steeple, in the meanwhile, towered overhead, like a finger pointing accusingly at God in the heavens above. In seconds, I had reached the front door. Above this door, I noticed that a Latin phrase had been carved into the stone: Extra Ecclesiam nulla salus. "Outside the Church there is no salvation." I opened the door in a hesitant manner, then stepped into the great black space of the church, closing the door behind me as I did so.

I was now in the nave of the church, in the center aisle. On both sides of me were two holy water fountains, each of which was filled with honey, and trapped in this honey were halos of dead flies. At the end of the aisle, towards the back of the church, was the main altar. Behind the altar itself was a towering statue that had to be at least 50 feet tall. It depicted a triune figure: a three-headed monstrosity, a spawn of Hecate. The head on the left resembled that of a patriarchal-looking bearded old man, the head on the right was that of a green-skinned Egyptian pharaoh, while the head in the center was like that of a belligerent black goat, a Templar egregore. I realized with horror that the monstrous statue was meant to be a depiction of Jahbulon, the secret God of the Freemasons. At the base of this statue was a large wooden cross, and crucified to the cross was a large Noddy doll, a horrifed expression on its childlike face.

Standing on the raised platform before the altar, in the shadow cast by Jahbulon's statue and the crucified Noddy, was a small band of musicians, though in appearance they looked like one of Goya's series of "Black Paintings" come to life. The musicians resembled a motley assortment of withered old crones and wizened older men with blood-stained beards, the tails of serpents protruding from their drooling and feeble mouths. These disgusting human beings clutched in their wrinkled hands a variety of instruments: flutes, recorders, violins, percussive instruments, though some of the women held shriveled dead babies. The musicians were gathered around a giant male goat, who was himself perched before a microphone on a stand. The goat was easily as tall as a man and seated in an upright position, and his body was covered in black fur. Two giant curving devil horns grew forth from his head, and wrapped around these horns was a crown made out of poison ivy leaves. In some way, it looked very much like the He-Goat as captured in Goya's iconic 1798 "Witches Sabbath" painting.

I stared at this most curious band, and they stared back, almost as if they were expecting my arrival. Gradually, I became aware that the pews lining both sides of the cathedral's central aisle were occupied. I looked around me, saw that the congregation was made up of a crowd of skeletons, human skeletons that were seated in upright positions, dressed in musty yet elegant clothes, clothes that seemed like something right out of the 18th century. Mixed in with these skeletons were various birds and animals, all of whom were alive: I saw crows and owls perched atop the bony shoulders of the human skeletons, while wolves and foxes were seated calmly on the pews themselves. They were all staring intently towards the stage, towards the altar. They didn't even seem to be aware of my presence.

The interior of the church was quiet, save for the ghostly echoes of sound which seemed to swim in the air above my head like outlandish undersea monsters from prehistoric times. Echoes of music, haunting snatches of familiar music, and another sound: that of a little girl's frantic footsteps. The girl I had been chasing. I looked across the church at the goat. As if in response to my quizzical expression, he raised one of his front legs and pointed with his cloven hoof to the right. I turned and looked to see what he was pointing at. On the right of the nave I saw a door that opened onto a staircase, a staircase that descended downwards. Evidently, that was where the girl had run off to. I nodded, then strode down the central aisle, passing by row after row of finely-attired skeletons and pensive creatures of the night, a diabolic menagerie. At the foot of the stage, before the feral glares of the he-goat and his ancient musicians and the giant statue of Jahbulon, I took a right, to the staircase, noticing as I did so that a reel-to-reel tape recorder was located on the side of the stage, evidently recording the band's performance. I paused at the top of the stairs, then began heading downwards. When I was about halfway down the stairs, I heard the band above me begin to start playing their Walpurgisnacht folk rock, the eerie music accompanying my descent like a psychopomp guiding my soul to the realm of the dead.

By the time I had reached the bottom of the staircase, the band appeared to be wrapping up their final song. I found myself standing before a wooden door. Scrawled on the front in big letters of dried blood was the word RISE. Hesitantly, I opened the door and stepped into a small room: a room whose ceiling was made out of dirt, whose walls were of gray stone, a room lit only by candles. On one wall there was an alcove, and resting atop a pedestal in this alcove was a lonely human skull, a skull whose mouth was open in a silent scream. Crouched before this alcove was the little girl, huddled up in a ball, shivering. In the center of the room was a large black obelisk, and this obelisk was quivering like one of Harlow's mistreated monkeys, and from its base it was weeping a pool of blood. I walked across the room, past the quivering obelisk, its alien undulations mimicking that of the scared little girl. I stood over the girl, towering over her. She looked up, into my eyes, and once again I was confronted by eyes that reminded me of those of my dead sister. I knelt down so my face was closer to hers, and said, with a smile on my face, "Please don't be afraid. I don't want to hurt you."

Far above me, I could hear the he-goat speak into his microphone the following words: "Nothing ever dies: anything that ever happens leaves a fingerprint on time, a withering echo that reverberates for all eternity." He spoke in a male British accent. It was at that moment, as the band stopped playing, that the little girl removed her scarf, finally giving me an unobstructed view of the lower half of her face. I was presented with two shocks: first off, in the spot where her mouth should have been there was instead the head of a deranged-looking vampire bat, its open mouth resembling a wound on the body of Christ, and secondly, that it was, undoubtedly, the face of my dead Fanny. Only what horrible fate had befallen her to disfigure her in such a manner?

I tried to back away in horror, but I was too slow. Feelers shot out from her stigmata-mouth and latched onto my face, leech-like, their hook-teeth sinking into my skin. As they began to drain me of my blood, I screamed, but my scream was cut short by some more of her mouth-feelers slithering into my mouth, these feelers giving off a grotesque gurgling sound, and then:

The ringing of hundreds of bloody church bells, the peals of Stedman Caters/ The stained-glass rose window of a futuristic church spinning like a nauseating kaleidoscope before it shatters into nothing/ A lone spermatozoon swimming in Daddy's testicular palaces/ Daddy and his unicorn horn porn/ Mummy posing for Daddy in the art studio, one female breast exposed, 20th-century Whore of Babylon, mimicking Dali's 1944 portrait Galarina/ *Sweating out the fever of scorpions in a lonely cradle while Mummy sat nearby singing nursery rhymes: "Scorpio Rising on the horizon, black sun & bloody moon, here comes Dogether, here comes Dogether, La la la la, La la la la"/ Fanny and I lighting bonfires during the locust summers/ Fanny and I seated at the kitchen table while Daddy ate a robin and told us about the Circe Order of Dog Blood and the Gospel of Hooves/ Fanny floating face down in the red water of the marsh, a pre-adolescent Ophelia/ a train whistle going "Choo Choo"/ An empty coffin being lowered into the ground, earth covering earth, ashes to ashes, dust to dust/ Myself seated in the library at Uni, studying a book concerning blood-suckers/ Diana and I screwing on LSD in the center of Stonehenge that Halloween night/ Lucifer over London, a Delacroixian Mephistopheles over Paris/ The mast of a ship sinking into the Aegean sea/ The horrible visage of Hacamull, servitor of Beelzebub, perhaps Greek, or really Hebrew?/ Diana breaking up with me that November evening after we left the theaters: we had just seen* Don't Look Now/ *A box of records with my name on it/ A labyrinth in black and white/* California Dreamin' *playing on an infinite loop/ A voice chanting "Destruction" over and over again/ The girl on the train platform with the scarf hiding her face/ Yama chewing on the Bhavacakra/ Delvaux's* The Echo/ *The claustrophobic and twisting streets of Owlminster/ St. Dajjal's Cathedral in the pale October moonlight/ The He-Goat and his Satanic musicians playing for the congregation of the dead and damned/ A quivering obelisk drinking my blood, whispering sweet nothings.*

On my knees, my very life itself being sucked away by the mutant corpse of my undead sister, I received, in a moment of perfect lucidity, a final vision: I saw a cartoon version of myself, and this cartoon me was wearing a red long-sleeve shirt, a yellow tie with red polka dots, blue shorts, big red shoes with blue laces, and atop my head was a blue elf cap with a big jingling bell. In one hand I held a book about leeches, in the other a copy of *The Withering Echo* album. I was dancing around, doing a childish jig, a clueless expression on my cartoon face. And soon I was joined by a cartoon version of Fanny, then of my mother and father, then of my ex-girlfriend Diana, then of everyone I had ever known in my life, then of everyone on Earth. Billions of dancing puppets, jerking about in a sort of syphilitic playroom, a room with mauve-colored stage curtains, enormous children's building blocks decorated with extraterrestrial letters, our mass gyrations accompanied by a music box remix of *The Withering Echo's* sound. I then noticed how all of us had black strings attached to our arms and legs. With my eyes, I followed the path of all of these strings up, up, up, and I could then see, looming above the stage, a bloated giant manipulating all of us with billions upon billions of hands. In place of a head, there was instead a gigantic human ear, and the inside of this ear was lined with millions of mouths, mouths that were drooling and devouring serpents, mouths that were grinning in the most mindless, idiotic fashion. Perched atop the rim of the ear-head's auricula (which is known as the helix) was a set of Mickey Mouse ears, tipped at a jaunty angle.

Writhing behind the back of this Idiot God like mutated peacock feathers was a mandala of monsters: they had long, spiky bodies that were half-centipede, half-tentacle, while their heads resembled giant leaves, only leaves adorned with snake eyes and cavernous gaping mouths, like vertical vaginas lined with hundreds of pointy teeth. Behind these leaf-headed creatures was a backdrop of utter madness, the chaos that arises from the long-dead, half-forgotten nightmares of Lemuria: a seething flesh-sculpture of rapidly mutating and shape-shifting forms, screaming bird and lizard and fish faces melting together into each other like wax, a vortex of howling mouths and unblinking eyes. The Agony of Hyle, the Crucifixion of Matter, the Revolting Science of Abbalath.

I realized the sobering truth: there was no such thing as Free Will. We were nothing more than flimsy paper dolls, poorly constructed marionettes, all of our actions controlled by some blind, idiotic, ridiculous-looking God, a God who ruled over a schizophrenic Heaven. Reality as we knew it was nothing more than a galactic puppet show, a silly song put on by idiots for an audience of fools. None of it was fair, none of it made sense, none of it amounted to anything important.

The vision faded away. Back in reality, with nature once again veiled, I looked up into the eyes of Fanny, saw her pupils begin to dilate, then multiply like breeding rabbits as she sucked my body dry. Then I couldn't see anything anymore, just blackness. But I could still hear: all around me were the echoes. The echoes of the band's musical performance and the audience's skeletal applause of bone, fur and blood, the echoes of the lead singer's final world-weary lyrics, and finally, the echo of my scream and Fanny's ghoulish gurgling. I knew then that I would never die, that I had become immortal: forevermore I would be an echo of a scream, trapped like a bird in the echo of a church.

THE INMOST DARKNESS
Robert M. Price

"If the light within you is darkness, how deep is that darkness." (Matthew 6:23)

1.

Daniel was a first year student at the Miskatonic University Divinity School, a venerable if lately dubious institution for the study of theology. Venerable because of its many decades of service to the Congregational Church, dubious because of the declining rate of ministers produced over the last ten or twenty years. True, admission applications had fallen off a bit, concurrent with the shrinkage of the sponsoring denomination, along with all the formerly mainline Protestant bodies. But the dearth of graduating candidates for the parish ministry was inversely proportional to the number of students attracted to purely intellectual pursuits, which led them into the search for academic posts, even though these, too, were becoming rarer than hens' teeth. Why? It seems that Miskatonic Divinity possessed a rather unique collection of ancient Aramaic, Coptic, and Greek manuscripts, many of them unknown to conventional scholarship or else branded as spurious forgeries, albeit without much in the way of close examination. Many of these writings were the fruit of delvings by one Reverend Enoch

Bowen during a tour of Egyptian synagogue and mosque genizahs. Our Daniel was one of the many attracted to the prospect of new revelations in the crumbling pages (though now protected under glass) of these still-untranslated texts. He was at a distinct advantage, having devoted himself to Near Eastern linguistics while an undergraduate. Thus he found himself pretty much at home in what frustrated numerous others who sooner or later turned away in the hope that someone like Daniel should undertake a translation. The Miskatonic faculty had proven curiously reticent about taking on the job, perhaps because they already had some inkling of what the manuscripts contained. Indeed, Daniel had now received an unprecedented University scholarship, as well as a sabbatical from second-semester coursework, to begin the task. He approached the texts with a mix of thirsty eagerness and uneasy trepidation.

Learning of his mission, many of his erstwhile classmates and dormitory neighbors began to avoid his company, almost as if some threatening clouds were gathering about him. But Daniel, always a bookish and introspective fellow, hardly noticed. He was keeping company with spirits long dead, the authors of the old and quite heretical scriptures. As Daniel got an impression of the lay of the land, he began to surmise, perhaps to fear, that he had in hand the makings of a new and disorienting testament. There were several gospels of the Nag Hammadi type, though most were damnably clearer, not couched in the cryptic terminology, bordering on gibberish, of the published Gnostic treatises. There were a few revelation texts, too, though, in the style of Gnostic scripture, the gospel and apocalyptic genres largely overlapped. Granted, most of the conventionally religious would recoil from these texts as they had from the Gospel of Philip and the Apocryphon of John, discovered in 1945, provided they had even heard of them. But such intriguing documents often served as seed for the formation of new mystical sects like those who produced the books to begin with. Daniel idly wondered if such might be the effect of his own translation. It even crossed his mind whether he might want to join such a group. That was certainly premature, but the "new" texts were surely fascinating. There were *The Discourses of the Logos*, *Revelations of the Demiurge*, *The Gospel of Herod*, *The Acts of the Iscariot*, and more. He had decided to begin with *The Apocalypse of Darkness*. It sounded pretty interesting!

Before long, Daniel's progressing work was being whispered far and wide, if such a thing is appropriate to say about so small a fish bowl as the quiet seminary community. And this despite Daniel's hermit habits. Even those timid souls who disapproved of his delvings could hardly contain their curiosity, and soon Daniel was quite surprised to find a many-headed shadow looming over him from across the cafeteria table where he sat, as he always did, alone. He looked up and into the faces

211

of a handful of fellow students and was momentarily surprised to see polite interest, not superstitious fear and hostility, etched on their bright young faces.

"Dan, we've, ah, heard the rumors about your translations, and we were wondering if you'd be willing to meet with a group of us, maybe every week or so. We'd be very interested to hear what you're coming up with!" Another quipped, "Your own seminar! How about it, old man?"

He hadn't laughed in a long time, but now he did. A little popularity was good! Even though he knew it was the manuscripts that possessed the popularity, not him. But Daniel didn't mind taking what he could get. Besides, some of them might have some helpful suggestions. A couple of them, he knew, had a passing interest in Gnosticism and other heresies. He had seen them in certain classes the first semester. So he readily agreed. The others left him to his light lunchtime reading, a lexicon of ancient Coptic.

But the enterprising young scholar was called away from the turgid page again in less than a minute. Could he have become this much of a "Big Man on Campus" already? So he asked himself sardonically, as he raised his spectacled eyes to rest on the lined and reddened face of Professor Oldstone.

"Yes, sir? What can I do for you? Would you, uh, like to join me? Say, I really enjoyed your Philosophical Theology course last fall…"

The paunched and balding man had removed his wire rims and was rubbing the bridge of his nose between closed eyes. "Daniel, I don't make a habit of eavesdropping on my students. On anybody, for that matter. But I simply could not help overhearing just now."

"You mean," and here he glanced in the direction of his new friends, who were retreating from the dining hall, "the thing about the study group?"

"Study group. If you wish to call it that, yes. I know this is going to sound strange to you, but let me urge you to think twice about that. About the whole damn project."

Startled to hear such bluntness from the erudite old veteran, Daniel said all he could say: "But why?"

"My boy, haven't you ever wondered why those manuscripts are secured under lock and key? And haven't you asked yourself why no one has translated any of them before now?"

"Well, yes, Professor, I suppose I have. I guess I just assumed the faculty thought the books were heretical and worthless. And the school already has something of a controversial reputation... So I kind of figured..."

"To say the least, it does. But that's not why. In fact, it's not even true that certain of the faculty have not undertaken to translate the material before now."

"You mean they were shut down? Censored or something?"

With a weary chuckle, Professor Oldstone said, "No, my boy, nothing like that. *Self*-censorship of a sort, I suppose you could say. Better not to get into it. But this was some years ago. The matter was kept quiet, and that is why this new administration is willing, indeed eager, to have you work on the project. They have short memories. But I do not. There are some things one does not easily forget. And I do not want you to have to try to forget one day."

Daniel, now bemused and a bit worried, whispered, "Is that all you can tell me, Professor?"

"*This* ought to tell you enough. At any rate, it will have to do." Withal the old man unbuttoned his cuff and pulled back his left sleeve a few inches, revealing a white scar running up and down his wrist. With no further comment, he rebuttoned the cuff, arose, and left the dining hall.

Daniel was left nonplussed. But the Professor's words communicated one thing: pity. Fear that the old man was losing his mind. If there was any danger here, that was it. He liked the old scholar and resolved to tell no one what had passed between them.

2.

He decided, once two weeks had passed, that he had enough done to call a meeting to share his results. He left a message with Professor Oldstone's secretary, inviting him to join them, as a matter of courtesy, though he didn't much think he'd show up. They gathered at a cafeteria table long after dinner time, when no one was about, and Daniel laid out his notes before a surprisingly large group of twenty or so. He did sort of feel like a professor! He knew, though, that he mustn't let it go to his head. As soon as everyone was seated (including one or two staunch conservatives he would never have expected to see, as well as one of the newest faculty members) he started to read from his draft translation.

"This one is called *The Apocalypse of Darkness.* Somehow I felt drawn to do it first. Anyway, here goes. **One rested in silence before the beginning of all things. He should have known all things, only there was yet nothing to know. And he grew ill with boredom.** Or maybe that should be translated 'disinterest,' or 'apathy.' I haven't decided yet. **A darkness of nullity filled him. In the fullness of time, the One said to the One that he might lighten the burden of his sorrows if he imagined a thing as yet unknown, even a world. And it was so. And that One knew the world he had imagined. And for a time the terrible cloud of darkness within him lightened. But he again grew bored. And this time his voice said to him he might imagine living creatures, and generations of creatures. And these were soon found busy with all** manner of pass times, as men and women did love and kill and create and destroy and desire and discover and believe and deny and make wealth. And all this they did to distract themselves from the aching darkness of despair that lay within them, for their existence was no more than a pretense and a diversion. Nor was it even their own pretense, but another's diversion. That of the One who had created them that he might forget his own terrible black nullity."

Daniel stopped for a sip of water and glanced at the faces nearest him. All appeared rapt with interest, but no less downcast. He could not account for this. Wasn't the text he was reading basically one more exotic bit of ancient eccentricity? He recalled how one of the greatest Gnosticism scholars had frankly admitted that Gnosticism was but "a queer farrago of nonsense." Saul Lieberman had once caused an audience to gasp as he introduced Gershom Scholem, the world's authority on the Kabbalah, with the words, "Mysticism is nonsense." All breathed easy again when he continued, "But the history of nonsense is scholarship!" Daniel had expected all these listeners to share Lieberman's view, as he himself did. But it didn't look that way!

As he made his way out of the building and back toward the dorm, he thought he saw a figure looking at him from outside of the chapel building. Turning to get a better look at the watcher, he saw a man dashing as swiftly as he could around a concealing corner. But he could not move very fast. It was Professor Oldstone, who it seemed had taken up eavesdropping after all.

<h2 style="text-align:center">3.</h2>

Daniel sat down with his dictionaries, commentaries, notes, and of course the glass-sheeted text of *The Apocalypse of Darkness* arranged round the desktop in the Restricted Room of the Hoag Library as carefully as the Old Vedic priests used to lay out the ritual grass square as an altar to invoke Agni, High Priest of the Gods. He easily found the place he had stopped and made ready to take up where he had left off. He worked late into the night, glad they had given him his own key. His posterior ached frightfully, as did his poor bladder, once he pulled his head out of his books. He hit "save" on his laptop before pacing through the darkened hall to the Men's Room.

When he returned, considerably refreshed, he noticed at once various hints of disarray and interference. Nothing seemed to be missing, and his text was intact. He breathed a sigh of relief, as it would have been an easy matter for someone to destroy his labors, even if not necessarily beyond the reach of recovery specialists. But he didn't want to have to bother with that. What troubled him more was the implied snooping. That didn't add up to anything good. And he had a strong suspicion as to who it must have been. It had to be someone with his own keys to the building as well as the Restricted Room.

With a quick look around, Daniel scrolled back up the page a bit. He wanted to review his draft of the new translation before turning in for the now-shortened night.

And it came to pass that more and more of the creatures of the One succumbed to the darkness at their core, when they could no longer pretend and laugh and hope. And this was because the One, who lived in all their lives and sought by this means to distract himself from the paralyzing darkness within him, had grown listless and bored with his imaginings. As his darkness billowed and expanded to fill him once more, so did it commence to spread like a poison miasma among his imagined creatures. And the One knew not what he might do to contain and to stem the all-encroaching shadow of ennui. And his voice said to him that he might imagine a prophet to go among his figments to spread the lie of hope. And he did send the Prophet of False Hope once he had dreamed him. And for many ages false hope distracted his creatures from the knowledge of their nothingness. And as with renewed delusions of hope and promise they returned to their futile wind-chasing, the One shared their diversion.

Until the day came when one of the figments had suffered so terribly and had become smitten with the equal and greater suffering of others that he had a revelation, not from the One, but from the voice of his own nullity and darkness. He sat beneath the skeletal branches of a lightning-blasted tree and resolved to remain there until it should occur to him what to do next. And in a single hour the darkness fell. And he knew what steps to take. He would go forth into all the empty world and call all men to pretend no more, to embrace the gnawing darkness within and to seek the only salvation from their endless pain. For he knew that in the end, when all men accepted the black truth, the illusion with which the One had entertained itself should collapse forever. And the One itself should retract into sheer nullity, and there should be no more world, not even any more vacuum to contain a world. So he set out along the roads of the mist-world preaching the Nothing.

That night Daniel slept deeply and with no dreams, except that when he awoke, he felt strangely that the lack of a dream amounted to a dream of something that had no positive existence and so could not contain anything for him to recall. Thinking this gave him a sudden headache, though it passed soon enough when he tried his childhood technique of thinking hopeful thoughts. Once he felt a bit better, in the early afternoon, he decided to call up some of those who had attended his reading a couple of weeks before, to see if any of them were still interested. He rather suspected they had had enough of his depressing revelations, but he did not expect a couple of rude, even wordless, hang-ups. And no one else even answered. He didn't want to dig himself deeper by leaving some pathetic message. He sighed, resigned to being *persona non grata* once more.

Daniel was single-minded in his dedication to his task, and he had paid no attention to televised news or even campus scuttlebutt. That's why he never heard about the suicides.

4.

There wasn't much more of *The Apocalypse of Darkness* to translate. There was a good bit of space following the last few words, so it looked as if the document had reached an abrupt conclusion, but he could not be sure, since the bottom edge of the manuscript was jagged, leaving the leaf noticeably shorter than the previous manuscript pages. That was sure to occasion scholarly debate for years to come among the tiny circle of scholars who would be interested.

This thought sparked another: Daniel knew there was always a lot more popular interest among the self-educated, eccentric and lop-sided as their home-cooked erudition might be. Credentialed scholars publicly rued such interest and did not hesitate to express their contempt for such amateurs, regarding them as little more than cranks and nerds. But Daniel himself had begun as one such amateur, and it was his fascination with these esoteric matters, which one never heard discussed in church, that had led him precociously down the scholarly path to begin with. He knew that many more like him lurked out there, and it galled him that, even with the University's support, his efforts stood little chance of escaping, like Rapunzel, from the lonely ivory tower. Well, he'd think about those depressing matters another time. Might as well finish the translation. Tomorrow or the next day he would start, oh, maybe *The Gospel of Herod*, then return to this translation for a second look with a fresh eye later on.

And so the Prophet of False Hope, sent out to comfort men in their facile faiths, strove ever and again with the Revealer of Darkness as each sought to win the hearts of the men and women who were the stage props for the shadow play with which the One attempted to distract and to amuse himself. And the darkness waxed and waned as each for a time prevailed.

Daniel thought it sounded a bit like Zoroastrian dualism with a tinge of Ecclesiastes' pessimism thrown in. Pretty inconclusive ending, but then the author must have seen the struggle continuing in his own day with no end in sight. These were, Daniel reminded himself, ancient religious fanatics with few resources for spreading their respective messages very far. He had never heard of any sect with beliefs quite like this, which must mean they had long since died out from attrition, like the modern-day Shaker sect, or just never got off the ground. What was surprising was that anyone had preserved the manuscript at all. But that was not unheard of. Both the Qumran library of the Essenes and the Nag Hammadi collection guarded by the monks of St. Pachomius had apparently contained many works preserved for academic and antiquarian interest alone.

5.

He decided to take a couple of days to catch up on sleep, food, and some lighter reading. But after that he betook himself back to the Restricted Room. He decided he'd dive into what looked to be less foreboding territory. *The Gospel of Herod?* On second thought, maybe *The Discourses of the Logos.* This one looked like a resurrection dialogue, a group interview with the risen Jesus by the apostles, eager to get their last questions in before he returned to heaven. There were many known works of the same kind already familiar to scholars, such as *Pistis Sophia* and *The Dialogue of the Savior*.

Daniel had ventured a few lines, relieved to discover that he was right, and the text did not present nearly the challenge *The Apocalypse of Darkness* had, when a small noise told him he had a visitor in the otherwise deserted building. He was not surprised to hear Professor Oldstone's voice greeting him.

"I see you've finished *The Black Apocalypse*. At least that's the title I used when I did my translation many years ago. I see also that you remain unmoved by it. Your scholarly detachment is greater than mine was. Or perhaps there is another reason you remain so blithe."

Daniel's conviction that his professor's sanity had faded was now a certainty. The sense of dramatic urgency, even of subtle threat, convinced him of that.

"Uh, what do you mean, Professor Oldstone?"

"That ancient book is poison, and its potency has only increased over the centuries. It has done much damage in its quiet way in the ages in which it has been known and read, but then it was long lost until its rediscovery some decades ago. Since then, as you know, it has been kept under lock and key."

"But if it's so malignant, so dangerous, Professor, why didn't you destroy it?"

"That I could not bring myself to do. I suppose it was very foolish, but as a scholar I am sworn to protect knowledge and the sources of knowledge. Even dangerous knowledge is knowledge, and thus, in a way, sacred. I always thought it best simply to keep it under wraps. That is why what you are doing worries me so. I thought long and hard about how to reason with you, to help you see that you must not propagate the terrible knowledge of the darkness within every man and woman, within God, within the flimsy universe itself. I thought you might listen to me. That is, until the realization hit me just last night."

"What... what realization is *that*, sir?" Daniel did not like the way the Professor started to reach into his pocket.

"I always expected, once I translated the text years ago, that a new Apostle of Darkness would appear, but I assumed he would be some easily recognized villain or criminal. Probably a Jim Jones or Manson-type figure. But then that would be too obvious. People would see the danger he presented and stop him, even if they didn't suspect the nature of the threat he represented. But then it occurred to me that the best and most effective way of spreading the gospel of the Nihil would be for one insensitive to its danger to pass it on as an innocent curiosity. People would be curious to read it and, despite themselves, it would begin to ring true to them. And as soon as enough people fell under its sway, well, you know the rest. Indeed, it's already started."

Out came the pistol.

Daniel's eyes did not move from it as he asked, "You really think *I'm* this Apostle of... *any*thing? You're not serious, right?"

"Oh yes. Yes, I am. And I'm sure of something else. If you're the Dark Apostle, and I'm the only one who knows it, that makes me the Prophet of False Hope. I can't allow you to spread your poison. There's too much at stake. And I realize now how foolish I was not to destroy the manuscript. That's what I'll do once we're done here."

The gun went off. The old man's aim was surprisingly good. Daniel sank under the table. But, punctuating his words with spit blood, he was able to say one thing more.

"You're too late. I posted it on the Internet."

The campus police were underway as soon as they heard the first shot. They got to the door of the Restricted Room just after they heard the second. When they entered, there were two bodies on the carpeted floor, spilling their blood in widening circles. Soon there would be many more.

when the twilighttwilight of nihil.nihil chimes…

Joseph Pulver Sr.

for fair-hearted, David Tibet, our LIGHT, and often, our VOICE! !!

Mixed feelings in cahoots with some way, some *how*…

BLAT!

Slants coded when and did…

"ah… ah.ah.ah… ah.CAN'T.well sure.*ok*.maybe."

Landmine Saber-dance—a dollop in her eyes, FED UP in yours (even after the valiums), lousiness and caterwaulin'…

(fogged out of invention since widethroated.) Dragged and turned over, ex-vivants (channeling basement hours) bawl…

BLAT!

and television bacteria…

and the list beats on—

"piss off . . . *please*."

It's never easy in The Nation for a human. There were trials . . . Followed by failures, some stacked too high to climb over, had to walk the long way 'round the gravity-colored matineebreath of Cossacks and scarecrows. There were RUNAWAY exits; trojan egos negotiating riddles in vacant houses; the omissions, veils, and vigors, of countless Scheherazades (. . . the tall one in Manhattan, the lily-pale queen who held you in the wee small hours of indigo, Mary, Shirley, Suzanne—Sasha: tidal, seamless grey . . . *Je m'appelle Amour*: the pretty flower of ice you misunderstood . . .), and licks in D and F and G. There were. Some came with words, some with large specters that could (and most often did) breed like a thunderbolt of sudden birds from a Before wrapped in plain curiosities. Others were edgeless, rising dust piled up.

Tears or a smile, he tried. *Tried...* even when there was blood on it. Studied the malaise-stampede of every Ahab and Achilles and Aleister fastened to the thistled totems. Studied the betweens and ladders that were wide open on the kaleidoscope bookshelves. Ate scraps, many his own, with crows. Learned when and where and as soon as he could. Faced the commentaries poised in his mirror. Found. Funneled. FEARED. Stepped in and out of SUM and go-go, many times, and many times again—Even asking (multiplied by each new turn of self;or sun;or stars; or rain;or snow;or quoting April unearthed) how many is too damnmany to play-out this noose of sorcery? Naked as rock 'n' roll, under or over lesser crocodiles, his fabric OD'ed on bitter autumn AND/or cherrygrammarKISSes, "Sister Ray" fastened to his telescope or feathers swigging "Children of the Grave", he played on~ ~~

Tried to.

Some called it searching. Some a career.

It's never easy for a human in The Wasteland—the ghosts and the stars won't allow it.

~*~

The Poppyman was sleeping. Trying to… again. Trying to touch dreams. Dreams outside this urban mess.

Tonight was no different from the last. And the 10 before that.

A few drinks, or a pleasant cup of tea? Sitting quietly? Hope in his dark isolato. Hope tonight was the night it clicked. An hour ago he rose and walked softly across the dusk-colored fur of the bedroom carpet. Undressed and slipped under the comforter. Held and supported in soft he closed his eyes. Mentally grinned at the thought of wooly sheep. Did people really do that? 1-1000… 2-1000… 3… Did they hop over something? Each other… leaping light as feathers? Some fence?

Beyond the lavender-painted casement where no light came tapping, fence, barrier, wall that kept out light. All these streets were barriers. All his dramas, fear-fraught or laced sad, each large or not, a mess-quake that broke crosses and bonds, or an easy vote for *kind; with dove wings please*, seemed more immense as he struggled to find calm enough to sleep.

"Today is *done*."

No sheep replied.

But he heard the fox bark.

Looked at his window. "They all hear the fox bark." *Each of us… In our time.*

The breeze came through his upper room window and caressed the strings of an untuned acoustic guitar but no sound was made. Outside he heard the autumnal tones of an owl. *"Let your shoes follow the language of the hills. Follow the soft-souled butterfly to the Glade of Aeons. But beware the snicker-snack of the BAALstorm, Dear David. The fox and his slicked skulk are sly. He will take. He will take everything fair and dear."*

There's a flutter of departing wings and a soundless cathedral of soft black wanders in . . .

Finally a dent. And a long pair of yawns.

Sinking. The sequence of weathered waves blur… Mounting the sea of textured sleep…

After a hands/legs;tuck&fit of snarly tossing and the bleach of slow void, sleep found him and he traveled in deep soft BLACK until he came to the Doors of Perception where he was granted access to the ancient hall (built with bricks of WishShaped GRACE and wild, sunbelted-dreams) beyond. There, where all the days are bones divided by rows of dust and the choice-missed DIDN'T (still plump as undone chores) are weighed to measure direction, he sat on a trance-dune with the Lizard King and the ever-calm River Man. Mojo and magicks spun from solid air and autumnal-tongues (perfumed with winds that carried isolation from the hollow lands) brewed around him.

The Lizard King set the weight of the long neck bottle he was holding aside. "We have a task for you, David."

Setting aside a book of old apologies, the River Man made a sign with his long fingers. "A walk, if you will... Down a rather dark road."

"Long, and often narrow enough to strangle, is the way," Mr. Mojo Risin' added.

Nick winked. "Conviction you'll need. Necessary as air, but you'll need a few transformatives too."

"What would you have me do?"

"What *The Others* could not."

Mr. Mojo Risin' nods his cheerless concurrence.

The River Man reached in the soft closets of his coat pockets. "These will aid you."

David stared at what rested in the River Man's hands as he was given 10 blackmoth-wing rings.

Morrison muttered something about Ziggy failing and offered him a pipe. "You are to be our Johnny Appleseed. Each song you sing is a kernel. Each verse a leave that weaves its Sunday, giving dandelion and daughters the compass of balance... and hope.'

"They need you."

"Armed with impulse and desire we give you luck and the 10 rings of Will and Power. Use these gifts well. The flower-laughter of dawn needs the berries in your songs," the River Man said.

"But . . . I'm just a man. I have trouble tuning my hands and feet, and *my head is*—"

On their dune in the Great Hall David's teachers spoke of blasphemies and revelations. Of things that fell 8 miles and things that were made low, of aeons-old woes and evil things—demons, strange skulls with rattlesnake-eyes that touched the Earth and scorched it. Lemongrass and sandalwood and patchouli burned in the iron braziers and perfumed the air . . .

David listened, kept the brook on his lips and fingers quiet. His eyes held all his what and where and how.

Morrison's face grew dark, weighted by a slop of gloom his eyes tightened. "The core of unquiet is in Laufenburg. In the fog of Strangled Light where the sparrows have fallen, UN's seizure awaits.'

"The fountains are closed, Little Brother. S'all tyranny."

Nick Drake took a hit off the hookah and offered it to the Lizard King. He waved it off, saying. "Fear's grammar, the coils of rape and the murder's claws… No kindness. No giddy, just the scorpion clip-clops of Caesar's demons . . . The Children… stripped and silenced, their spirits are waiting for new voltage." Morrison handed him a small stone. "This is the Butterfly Stone. Plant it there."

Young David was about to rush into his sea of questions—

"Go, but remember the path is long *and skillfully ill.*" Nick Drake said.

231

Morrison smiled and passed his hand over a cold blue fire. "The river waits. Remember to stretch tall."

The River Man blew out the candle.

The Child of Wonder—suddenly grace-renewed, back to chipped and the splintered, blasting its apathetic and obscene loneliness. Returned to the world puzzle and the mob puffing and snapping with surprise at being punished... millions dwindling . . .

Whim.

Power.

Hand to hand. Hand to mouth. FranticTEETH and steel doors

~*~

SunsightREVOLUTION knows the flavors of his bed. Morning sounds. Sweating in his bed. Post-"Where?"-eyes not ready for seeking or gallop. Not yet. Lifts his hand. 10 rings. 10 blackmoth wings. One on each finger.

Huh?

Nick Drake?

Was... really—"Holyshit."—

The reality of his dream in the room. He's soaked in the shaman-Niagara that burned on the lips of Morrison and the River Man.

"Me?"

I did sit there... Did. In the epicenter hall with the commissars... As they "spoke of mancy and glinting poems returning to candleheart of humanity."

"Me?'

"Mere flesh and sin speeding into mistakes…
Every color hungry.'

"I was there as the lantern-loaves came from
their lunar-mouths. When they spoke of the
SnufflingDevil plying his Hellsewer rites of
torture… Was. Watching. Listening… On my
knees in the garden of dunes . . .'

"BAAL—*scum*. Ringmaster of the
DAMNATIONgame that rips heart-time with
black diamond flocks, and poisons bedsheets and
fountains with blood and grief and mud."

He rose and turned, checking the familiar of his
room. His bed. His mirror that does not hide the
small lies. His carpet was still on the floor. The
friendly eyes in a painting from his *Some Gnostic
Cartoons* series purred at him. His wardrobe, his
boots, the shelf of Glorious Names and his treks in
text… A small detail of his solitary… The white
paper beach of newborn lyrics, the top page bore
the stain of tears . . . Yesterday afternoon's *Billion
Dollar Babies* still on the turntable. No *Hail Atlantis*
he thought . . . A mirror with his proportions… A
handwritten sip of requests, more misdemeanors
than portly bothers, that should have had a 60's spy
movie soundtrack… His—

A guitar made of bones and ash stood in the
shaded corner. It had strings made of cobwebs.

"That isn't—"

Owl sat on his window sill. In the River Man's

voice Owl said, "She was made to silence a roar. To dispel fear and sin. Her name is, Bluebird."

"Exorcise broken from hearts? With these hands? I don't know how to play guitar."

Owl fluttered. "She does."

David folded his hands together, pulled them apart and flipped them over. Lifelines and flex. Opposable thumbs. Fingers made to use a butter knife and chalk. A man's fingers. Effort, traffic with parts, and press-until-it-hurts . . . and labyrinths.

The River Man said his right hand was a lamp, the left a staircase. How could that be? They looked so small to him. Too pale to hold fire, much less mold it.

"How do I begin? Where?"

A jubilee of sunlight strolls on the strings of Bluebird. They resonate. Solid as the skinless rivers of faith, the River Man's voice fills the air, "Cross the Muddy River. Follow your soul.'

"Flow where the currents of Owl flow until you find your feet there."

The muntin bars in his windowpane disappear and a street in a shabby foreign town appears.

"But how do I find it?"

"Go to Taxxol and follow Owl when he comes."

Walking to the guitar he said, "I will."

~*~

Imagining colors and plump carnival streets, flowers defying Death, and free horizons, and receptive stages, Tibet spent sunshine days and moon-claimed evening corridors holding Bluebird, not daring to touch her strings. But his eyes mapped them. The afternoon he touched her strings, chords as shores, chords as atlas—traffic with Amazement . . . She sang. And he joined in.

One hour.

4+.

Basked in her geography of milk and silvery affection. She was silk and magic and stars, all soaked in honey and almonds and cherries. Shimmery, David, inhaling *Possible* bubbles, began to climb the mountain of Belief.

In the NightDark garden where plans are dreamed, The River Man drew smoke from the *Shisha* and passed it to his friend's mojo hand. Exhaling he said, "He's learning."

Morrison smiled. "Yes, he is . . . Time for his boots to ink the miles."

~*~

Voyage: ship of fools. Cell compartments (two bunks and a single bare bulb) & below, Angry and End packed pretty tight. wOW & flutter; nihilist observation noise; bawlers pushing never will; LOWdown; lies; fish; cut to pieces . . . sadness assault . . .

WavEs, cold. Urgent rolling . . . Day after day,

WILD this side, sloshy leeward . . . No Aphrodite
to be gazed upon. Half empty bottles and cigarettes.
A few pistols tucked away for Judgment Day or
friends like these. Day after mariner-day, dice and
cards and AGES and depth and SALT . . . Night
after grey day, grey-bread freighter slopingSLOW
to Dracula's East~ ~~

~*~

Docks. A foreign town, dragged from warmth
and comfortably-worn, sick with strangeness,
masked. Today, tomorrow, believing, no visible
feast or festival. No safe in the nervous, bent
streets where the grip of neglect controls . . .

David frees his lungs of it quickly.

Days with no pansies, and guessing about the
enemy's growl . . .

The ox-drawn carriage left him at the gate to
Taxxol. A bombed-out city that had changed its
borders a dozen times in as many years and half as
many nameless military debates. Never really rebuilt,
it's poor elbowed by lack of crop or thread or the
bridge of a candle's warmlight; it was a cancer of
grey. Every street was a seething-cold feeble
trapped in some starless digestion. Everywhereing
men drank whatever grain-piss their hands could
clutch to quicken death. Women, 35-year-old crone
or underage girl thumped into signing-up or on for
slave-wages or mail order bridehood, offered pussy
or their mouths for a cigarette or pennies,

"Whatever you have."

He could fall down and cry. Blood and rain and pathological deep-by-deep-at-the-speed-of-wide trembling bought and sold. He heard Brando whisper over a tear that echoed his own, "The hor-ror. *The hor-ror.*" His grief had no desire to stand, but his boots had their task and moved . . .

Steered him to a street, a cruel drug. All it wanted was another she (with terrified eyes) or he (howling inside) to eat through... and another open door. Debris, gunfire and carrion—All that glistens is irretrievable (The bayonet in your gut does not lie.) . . . Tibet looked at a club called The Devil's Balls. No one out front giggling or sharing a smoke or just fuckinaround, no neon, just the cavern club on the corner throbbing with jackboot basslines and twin 6string napalmRAGE. He thought to enter the steel doors and sing, begin the greening. Owl perched on a horse-post. "This is not the station. The thing in the east waits." He took wing.

Guitar slung on his back, faint stars overhead, lantern with a rusted door in his hand, he walked . . . Passed through Drossk and Su-Yood, and when there were no more fingerposts pointing to dying villages and crater-heavy roads he took to the mummified fields and thicket-mazed valleys.

Owl flew overhead, said, follow me. Winged on. pictures.
no.promenade in tulip corridors or gallery.
an
exhibition.

a gnome (thinking of running—if the dead and dying would allow it) and a sage.both
bent.
hut.a quarrel.about
the gate and the
catacombs.
old.no castles.no troubadours singing.
curses.
no.promenade.
bent
crone.whispering (under her moving telescope) of demon vigors and baba yoga.
no children.no
nurses.
old.cart.(in the dust.low side of the road).no oxen.no crop in the field frosted to ZERO.
no.
promenade—
David, carrying travel's proof (each overlay.the lungs and notice of it's reflexes.), looks up—
follows wings that have not been eroded by the weirdings and crags of unwholesomeness . . .

On a hill with a little gate. A yard of thorned crosses and faint headstones, tall weeds and flowers shorn of sun-fueled changing. He strums Bluebird and flowers with yellow cargo bloom.

A day and a night he rests. Among new lush clover, reds and bunched pinks and blues-heavenward and oriental pastels laugh at the illness that surrounds them. When he departs, a sapling stands where he sat . . .

Boots back to their undertaking.

In the fields where the plague burns . . . Day after day: *grey*.

Armed with his poems he sets out again and again. Ill-lit objects he found in the square blocks of the decaying towns. Wind and rain and things with thunder...

Smoke chokes the roots of trees fed by the rivers of Hell...

Fog and salt in the barrens near the small eastern sea. Boat. No ferryman. He took it. He rowed . . . rowed . . .

The mysterious voices that roiled in the white-cap waves urged him to leave the icy-winds and settle below in the undergrowth. Come swim. Come sway. Come live with us and be careless. But he rowed on . . .

White whales (with sourCARTOONeyes and crosses for horns) eyed him and yawned as he rowed o'er their kingdom. No bye-bye, just split to DEEP where the roaming hooves of the stars can't step in . . .

Row (choo-choo) upon row (chooglin) of WARshadow-submarines slowed and turned their jaw-gun racks on his small boat. They sniff for range, then not measuring him a Jonah or Ahab, quickly recolored their punishments, changed their bar-soap tongues for bluer, and flew pass . . .

Little bird, unkilled & dreaming, ROW...

heart never ceasing it's prayer~~

    ROW~ ~~

    as an act of flesh,

              seize the wish of Will,

                      discard

minus

                      and fear,

          raise Maximus,

          cast aside Minimus

                      ~

~~ROW! Set your Spartacus teeth, loud as cantos
epic, to Odyssey –hero, when the enemy laughs…

    "There will be a grove in sun for the lost."

    Row~ ~~

Over the water~ ~~in his little stallion-boat,
gripping the Nightcrests~ ~~Drawn, staying,
though storm-swell hungry to claim him~ ~~

                      Above, a
grey-shaded moon noosed by a ghost~train of
blackBLOOD clouds—a CrowConstellation, beak-
eyes scrubbing his arc&pull, beats its wings and
laughSSSsssssS—"Children should be home." "In
bed." "Between the sheets." "Between the sheets."
"TIEDdown." "Gagged." "Not little rebels out on
REVOLUTIONS. Not full of UNmasked faces
headed for off with HIS head."

    ROWharder~ ~~

elbow and shoulder and all the passion of an
exorcist, wings shod with the hope of Clearlight.

    Row. Over every claw and blister of rain.

    Believe that in sorrow mighty can be found.

Believe that from death corn can rise again. Believe in jasmine and lilies and honeysuckle and sunflower and trees—benediction, blessings (created by the grace in the bower of singsong brothers and sisters) flowing as fire in eye and INMOST, and the signs in the stars—and BELIEVE this shining shining world is a rose.

Row~ ~~

like the painters who were not afraid of galaxies and rivers,

like the writers (with unmasked hands) who offered halos and revolutions,

like the other exorcists (locked in the towers of blackness or boiled in earthquakes) before

him~ ~~

Sing *and put his back into it.*

"Harbor.

By the sea—I look windward, whilst the moon is nailed behind clouds.

By the sea—I search the lee, with hope unfurled.

Venture forth, MandalaBeacon.

Shape an EYElight in this prison dark and dreary.

Reveal gates and WarmHearth;
return me to boulder
and branches and voices of forest-flame.
Shorelight unleashed,
come from your kingdom to my acts
o please. Please."

Just him and his little song burning in his lantern of courage . . .

Red coral sand raked by tidal foam. A stony beach. The great mouth of rambling net-waves funneled him onto the deadshore.

Solid under his heels. Uphill, that doesn't want the effort he carries, uphill—telescope far, before him—

Into wild hills . . . Walked the fossil tundra . . . Corridors of rubble and mud, told his boots about dryness...

Three days under the sorrow-haunted evening spires of the Pass of Soanthrakka until the exotic perfumes of the Vultloth opened the way to the Dark East.

Grey swells, darkens. A. M. (with its sick, weak luminosity) comes, TANKshadows invade. This bleached land holds no memories . . .

Walked, stoutly, deftly when the clay didn't argue with his soles. Rain and November. Holes in his shoes, a kingfisher's feather in his hatband. Saw hedgehogs and a minotaur that complained about what it saw in the cyclops-eye of Fate. Guitar in hand—waiting to laugh.

Gray city in sunlight. Honest broken. Everyone shaken . . . tear.tears.

Another corner. Some woman or thing that was struck until she looked like shit. no coat. her dress torn and missing 4 buttons and something dark like blood was dripping down her leg. bottle of dirty hands. mind on knife or a gun...

Another hill…

Another field: Divine—NO! Comedy—NO!
Indigo phantasmagoria of dead cats… Black
Halloween's massacre is spread before his open
wounds, opening his tongue with unfathomable
with despair… Eyes crippled by split, behold open
puppy skulls… Giddy pazuzuRATS and craving-
bugs take red and the empire that was flesh and
experience, leave no face, no springing muscle, no
BRIGHT happyeyes to gladness-texture your
heart… And above, fully unfolded and drenching
the sky, cautionless heathen vultures—meteor-swift,
are a whirlwind trotting down from the clouded
ashland for the swallowing…

And tangled in the bloodlet he cries. And
remembers. *There were lotuses in the River Man eyes.*
"We write in you. Give you reborn, as Appleseed, as Aleph,
the beginning—man as SpiritSun hopeful and shining,
carrying the songs of Paradise.'

"Arise unveiled, David. Wear Heaven's smile. The
shadows will be long and you will be rubbed by ashes, every
act of Death's knifemouth will be a mountain you must
overcome. Don't not fear the walls, or shackled to deep
burdens and weariness, fall to the flavors of hate. His black
ships fear ChristLight. Write new books for the Children of
the Sun . . . Be Dawn's star. Shine."

David walked faster. He had to get there. He
had to stop the crying. He had to.

(another) City decked in another NIGHT—all
the lights (and—barbwire—hearts, controls set for
the OVERdose-core) and the tattoos of GUNS

and BLOOD must be TRUE! No one wants to remember prior. Not with all this sweetcreamFAKE frosting Mind-Body trajectories (with no aversion to pacts with the DARKside or just plain STUPID) . . .

over daubs and

misshapen hill.
through abandonment, extracted,

and dale muddied by
terminal wind.

Town. without. seeing awe. without discover. to another

Soup and a roll. Lot of dead leaves under his boots.

Village. after. sunset. waiting. alone. in. silence. forgetting green . . .

Voices. looking out at What's OVER. Cigarettes. All looking for games and faces, or maybe something that didn't lose what happed an hour go.

David's eyes wander. "I don't know why." And no one answers . . .

David is dozing. Wants to reach up beyond reflex and faith to that ancient country and ask the River Man if they're sure he's the right man for this. But he's covered, cheeks and hands and every damn inch, in the thick filth of his travels and the doors won't open for him . . .

Owl's urging awakens him. His wings are fire, creating deeds to do in David's heels.

"I'm coming. I'm coming."

Runs—tires to keep the wings close and the spiked blurs of doubt out of focus . . .

But pain leaks in.

Dues you can't push away and Sahara's weathered by endless loops and resets of RE; and vice versa gates that don't change the bad in done; and Zarathustra; cults of MoonCrazed jesters raking dead SunFlowers with hands that can't find a big-red-X or Galilee; dulsatory; and the True Believer philippics stamped in the 2nd and 5th ("color-corrected") printings of the Down-to-Earth only found on handbills for Over-the-Rainbow; 8 days a week; and they, Mutha (that never heard poem) and Father (tactics springing from NO) and (boiler room) CHURCH and OVERLORD-STATE, shoveled an undertow of "It's FUCKED" and "Nevermind" in your jungle until you were stoned-until-DEAD, no resurrection allowed by law.

over and
under and
THROUGH (broken ideas and silted-full-of-lies, and reeling Sunday morning bums—devouring eyes frantic as spinning pigeons—wielded to bottom), or
around if need offered it from burning lips . . . FATBLACKnight (croaking and scraping and sticking to everything) and day with little light to snow . . . Sisyphean rolling, groaning . . .

40 weary days. 40 grim-as-the-bottom-of-the-

world nights. Led.driven.to.barren. Haul foot another step . . . episode . . . of unholy BLACKNESS. the outside that gets in. and no medicine or lobotomy or breathe or thrashing will turn its wicked . . .

Under a dome of (struggling-to-be-seen and losing the game) rose-rich stars and galaxies sown by the skills of celestial spiders whose garden is a treasure chest of FURTHER David sleeps in a vast field of DEADpoppies. And cries.

"All this is too grave for a head to hold.'

Looks at the conquered moon with clouds in its eyes. "When?"

Owl alights on the 12o'clock of a headless scarecrow. Holds up FARTHER.

Tibet nods his yes, yes. "Learning to live on faith alone ain't easy." Marches on . . .

Soup and a roll, and a dream of warm. Lot of dark dirt under his boots.

Arrives: once a golden-shouldered canvas of shelter, Laufenburg (every invalidated clause and cranny and silent berth without a transcendental tomorrow) is a ghost town after the Apoppylypse of BAAL's ironfist-Nihil.

Broke and broken, mind, frame and glance of seer. Every pliant-Yesterday possession sunken— extinct . . . dropped—or in shadow's scimitar hands . . .

Up 1,000 sorrowstairs to the court of Broken Birds. To the court where the stars are Not Balanced.

"Take the narrow way down, Starchild," directs Owl.

"Is this the place?"

"Soon. Soon."

A twist in the street. Corner, weeds, a 9mm fuck Bukowski's steel wouldn't give you directions to—they don't take references here. Street that never felt the sun between its legs . . . Crippled dreams hissing... and no revolution . . . One last block, teeth-marks on every window. An intersection of muck-smeared anti-Rothko. In a cramped alley of formless garbage, a scruff pantry of broken languages and puked-up sewage. A backalley dead-end, sign say Famine Street. No door was left calm by bad temper, no pasture of softYes left to hum in irises. There is a lot, a crowbar-bruised amphitheatre of shattered bricks and glass, splinters of wood that may have been casements or formed stairs . . . Did this devastate ever hold fine? Development? Hope? The answer that grips him is unbearable. Above the small wasteland, the bombed out ruins of an old castle— an ugly lair, where philosophies failed to see eye to eye.

A slab of industrial grey (part of a wall?piece of a floor?) where moments, expelled from the sky where you get a voice, their shoulders in the dust, huddled . A steel stake. What was a tenderhearted young girl bound to the staff of BAAL's pleasure. Pocks of emptiness fester on her skin. Poison imprisons the life in her bloodstream.

And **BAAL** (larger than what was in David's mind), WHITEHOT, ready to burst into dance. "As you see, I'm a painter too, boy."

One tear was David's reply.

Behind BAAL, a fire of shadows and his reavers. MAL (on percussive thunder—lunge of pissMEAN with rough to trade) and nihil (spiderfingers keyed to his STORMcasket of minor-toned sadnessETUDES—hot ANVIL smile, one corner leering, one an exhibit of FUCKem) and BLACKNESS (grips 4strings of bansheeDENY—fulla AllyGRIME and SCREAM).

"Took your time, boy."

"There were many of your rivers to cross, Murderer."

BAAL's furnace-eyes gleam. "So you enjoyed my gifts."

"If you were watching, you know what was in my heart."

The tip of BAAL's tongue is split into three red serpents. Fatter than the right or left, the middle opens its mouth and hisses, "So the tiny boychild seeks to become a man." Then it laughs. Longest of the trio, the left, joins in, "Brings his bluebird to change reality." It too, laughs. The right, most often a shriek that just spits FUCK or KILL-IT, adds, "Do you carry some sweet dazzlement of love?"

"Heaven," says the middle.

"Heaven," injects the right.

"Heaven. Heaven. Heaven," three sizzling as

one, "is **FUCKED**."

"I carry love and hope."

BAAL's laugh licks his fangs. "Your poppies fell down the sickstairs and are corpses. The hourglass is broken."

Dancing, shedding their skins as they rub BAA's lips, the trio chimes in, "Null." "Null." "Null." "Poor boy. Poor boy, no lambs to light."

"You are The Tumbler. *Mur-der-er* . . . And Orphan Maker, the anvil sprang from the sewers."

A great laugh painted the unfurled feathers on the great devilface. "I am the Devourer, the wolfserpent of the Charnel House. You stand there with your open red shirt and arteries and think to create JOYcontinents in *My Wood*."

"Drake and his fool-friend have smoked the dream-pipe too long. Did they smile and promise you Eternal reward, rest in azure peace? You think they'll pin nice white wings on you?"

Over a thunderclap rimshot, MAL flaps his great black wings and laughs.

"Their aspirations can't sustain the note. You think the hoodoo trinkets they gave you are armor.'

"You're peasants. They send *Little David* with his song to stand in for them in on the Last Day and you, full of Goliath ways, think you can win the day . . . I'll wager your soul for hers you cannot.'

"Sing softly and bravely, boy, and this Desolation Row and all around it will flower with safely and warm. You are mad to think to stand in

My Empire and circle my claws with your threadbare poppyskins. Your watery brew of wings and dreamy psalms *cannot*." BAAL walks to the pale grey girl and marks her chest with a foul stain. "Sanctity and beauty to transform." He spits at David's feet. "Lyricism over howl, and timid souls can rest? *Fool.* If you can outplay me, I'll give you her soul. And if your song cannot best mine, you join the skeletal family in the emptiness of **BLACKtime**. Do you dare?"

David does not step back.

"Tibet climbing. Are you some tiger carrying water to crush my fire? You believe love is a part of you, breathing within. David the dreamer, David looking for the Palace of Love . . . Another damnfool, merely some puny song-tailor who believes Glory is possible. You are a mere beast, a starburst poet, like the others before you . . . Did your new masters not tell you each failed. They too stood there like St. George. I laughed. And they cried. In a few moments you, little lark, will cry as they did.'

"How will you replace Absolute, boy? Even now your pawn-mouth fails you."

And the serpent chorus rang. Left: "Little shit-boy." Right: "nihil boy." Middle: "Hopeless little horsey." As one, with venom for all: "KILLKILLKILL—the fool"

BAAL adjusts his guitar strap. "Are you better than the River Man? He could not walk among the Harms Tremendous I made solid in this air. And I broke the Lizard King's mojo; he did not last as long as a Shakespearian play in my rollicking darkness. I am terror and violence, the starving black fleece of hate. Ziggy knew this. You think to cast my void aside with your song? I will have *all your children* and you will have **My Sword**."

BAAL steps upon the slab stage.

"Age before beauty, boy." And the Devourer, BAALstorm, set a claw upon a string. "This is Murderer. Forged in the sewerCUNT of Hell. Sit, boy. Listen to RED-DEATH utter flame."

No -4 -3 -2 . . . No "Hit me, band." With DEATHFIRE fingers BAAL stuck his first blow. Up jumps THUNDER's BLACKonslaught-vultures out of the box, Nihil's penetralia in D minor flares from his axe. Constellations waver. The gale of deconstruction, thick and foaming with FOUL & BANErape & NULLuntoyou came upon David, cut flesh and blackened INMOST. BAALstorm's eyes laugh.

His escalating hands a slowvoltage-frost of HEX and flutter, **MALEDICTION** swings low... Each UNCLEAN line (stapled to the wounded.and dying) and UNCLEAN phrase (stapled to the wounded.and dying) and UNCLEAN acid-barked clutter of tones (stapled to the wounded.and dying) rang with Nothing. Ups the wattage to rank and churn—the FuryFist, impure, blood—GORE—souls. Shred-grammar: ornaments of precious and foolish mouths, and feathers that drew juices from sun-essence, withered. Demons were in milk.

Barbers clutched their heart when mirrors handcuffed them to ugly.

One—no time to scream.by.one. corridors of harmony-strung stars—attacked, bleached, are squeezed...

Birds tumble from the sky and smolder.

PanzerBAALchord, sucking up souls. METHdiveBAALchord, sucking up souls. Eyes (after all the books that spoke of rivers of blood and years of darkness and true were reddened by arson's hoes and all the pictures that flowed from the land were erased by sand) ate the unfurled venom and were muzzled by out of tick-tock tears.

"**Disaster** and burgeoning rust—*squalor* . . . and nothing more." BAAL screams unholy pronouncements. His flint-sharp, black-corby knifefangs bite into the world's meat with bitter music.

A man of StarryTruth, a man that will not take ash and End into his mouth, stands and waits his turn.

BAAL's RapeSermonTHUNDER batters David.

"Fleshworms
SIXSIXSIXsicksicksick.
Fleshworms
choking on **SHITSHITSHIT.**
GloryGloryGlory *dismembered.*
Christ's little children are falling.
FallingFallingFalling."

Hate-fueled, the Last Ceasar's WARmachine

rages… Christgau called sonic incinerate *skronk*, Lester Bangs , something plainer, like NOISE— Lester would have added FUCKING noise—the bad, useless kind, but... Had either been frontrow ready to spit a review, might have been along the lines of *This Slice 'N' Dice Horseshit Ain't Rock 'N' Roll And I Sure As Hell Don't Like Having it In My Earhole*. **E -**

No stars loud with eyes. No eyes loud with olive tree home. No kittens or blossoms brimming with the shapes of summer. Collapsed hedges, collapsed names, collapsed anointed, self tricked out of heart—snuffed in the bump and thighs of WAR, crushed pink faces of peace covered in horned masks, burdened by what the teeth of BAALflame has cursed.

BAAL's rapeWiRES buzz and shut, scrape and soil all the ascendant Us that was marvelous, each soul that was trying to download lambmilk-song from the Rosy Palace of GloryLight.

BAAL shits on human.

BAAL shits on OM

and LightMagic

and the embrace of kitten-soft

sunset.

BAAL shits on Christ

and the dream of a

GoodUniverse.

Above the great sucking sounds of the Black Cosmic Sewer sucking up rag-field flesh and bone and cindered souls, BAAL laughs (one last crushing

253

chord) at God, as Murderer's grunt/bullet-assault/chainsaw strides . OUT-FUCK-THAT-fangs welded on 11. Last slashed INTO THE BLACK-skronk slams to cessation. "Now, boy, bark your useless bark."

David takes off his boots. Barefoot, to FEEL the Earth. Sets the Butterfly Stone between them. Tells himself he has but one chance.

He draws a breath, seeking INMOST. Feel its warmth.

"This is for all the children who shake off littleness and accept the OM of Evergreen."

Bluebird quivers in David's hands as he kisses each moth-ring. Hope empowered, one by one they float above Bluebird's strings. Yes occurs as each moth, summerhouse-measured, settles on a string and the cobweb transforms into strings of stars, the chords of life revealed. David's drying tears do not dilute the flowering wheel of velocity angels in his heart. He strikes sinless notes formed in Ankaa, Tarazed, and Terebellum, each expands and rings strong and soft as the velvet of a rose. And as his gentle fingers conduct the moths' galaxy-song he begins to sing.

"I, poet of Apollo and RA,
I, Blake-child and HEART-voyager,
who will not play with the dicecast of flies
Mount Diablo spits,
believe LOVE can . . .
and will.
Its wings and banners gleam.

The bells grow, as I, initiating *OPEN*,
unseal my pact with *HOLY LIGHT*."
Above one bird does not fall. Owl soars in
circles.

From the rubble at his feet hyacinths,
remembering the science of God and the sun,
bloom. Generous comes into the map of the world
again.

Wearing love woven of song, David, eager,
skilled in the starhum of up with no downs, plays.
"I am. We, of can and will, the pure, are." At the
speed of We Can tonebeams perfume the eggs of
Enlightenment. Lavender dances. The ashclouds
above turn their faces. Dead birds are reanimated,
and ruby-throated, lark into the mosaic-sky of
molten novature.

With no soft goodbye for BAAL's TEETH,
Bluebird's unsullied rush unbuttons iron.
BAALstorm is chained to Tibet's stake of songly.
Notes of Glory bind him. Chords of feathered love
married to prettyFLOWERING and rooted in
serene, tie him. And with pure GODlight *gleaming;
PleasantSweetness*, BAAL, anguishDEEP in UN,
begins his slow pilgrimage to cremation.

David's song of RA and the perfection of
SUNglitterSpringfoam-and-GREENfield-flaming is
a molten glow of LovelyLovelyLovely.

Pushing Heaven's sake, carnivals of splendor-
hued orchids stretch tall. Woodland glad, blessed in
dawn apples, bearded by stars and seedsof
BLESSED and silk, a new aroma flavors the breeze

as it paints rainbows dispelling the grim greys and beast-roared null.

Hips and smile and hands in it, I LOVE is David's SWEET heartsong, a song that will not dent under BLACKfire, a song high, high as rocky mountainsHIGH or silver clouds that see far.

BORN, opening a sky without hungry or wrong, is born.

BAAL, inverted, wavering, stapled to what vertigo's breath enacts, cringes.

Bluebird's incredible HAPPINESSstrings decry blacken with luminous ringing tones. David, Believer—Midas Man reversed, WHITEknight souljer, SINGS.

"Lovely GRACE.
GODlight,
more solutions,
more horizons,
filled by HIGH fresh skies."

Clamped to less, forced into undo, BAAL's time dissolves. Swell leaves his chest. His horns chip and fall away. The FATBLACK of his pot, no longer roilingHOT with the constrictions of seizure's eels, shrinks.

Larking stars, enlarged by angels, dance.

Bluebird laughs. In her magnet MAL's percussive thunder runs, Nihil's spiderfingers break, and BLACKNESS is denied everything but it's final SCREAM.

"Balance.

Balance. *Yes and believe*. High and here, it's

JOYwind.

Balance—LovelyLovelyLovely LOVE.
OverPlanetEasy."

David, faith's child, Earth's cup of nature
FULL, sang.

BAAL's grimIRON fingers lose history in
David's waves of LOVE. He—now less and on the
way to over, quaking, failing, is an ocean of blind.

"Balance.

Fields with no down narrowed by BAD, no
hung.

Fields living—
understanding.

The light of BALANCE,
molded in RA~lifted meditations,
in JOY's RosyCHRIST."

Flowering tide a-flowing, Bluebird's Eden
anthem offers BAAL no fare thee well . . .

The girl's underworld-black bonds fall away. An
aphrodisia of velvet color and softness paints her
skin.

"BALANCE REX, sweet king,
STARHOPE-free, moon-clad anatomy of
ANGELbells, wise,
wise and FINE and filling gaze.
Balance outhere and INMOST, shore to shore.
Balance for every human grain of sand.
Balance.
Believe in SAVE. Believe in
Balance . . . BALANCE, sweet heavenly song."

David (SOUL with no doubt) shining, spa-spa-

sparkling. LARKsoaring, all his brooches, sweet cream smooth, and fruit HELLO-bright, ripe.

BAAL, no longer mighty, no longer swelled with many bought and sold, falls.

David wears love's mountains. Sweet the full heart who rises to wear balance and break bread with Paradise. LOVE ripples.

David wins. "You are nothing. You hold nothing. Your eyes touch nothing. You do not even possess a name now . . . I breathe mighty waters and release angels ticking with fullness."

The long shadows of nihil recede.

Crushed by LOVE, mal is a pool of nothing sucked up by the sewer. Crushed by LOVE nihil is a pool of nothing sucked up by the sewer. Crushed by LOVE blackness is a pool of nothing sucked up by the sewer.

CRUSHED by the pungent glow of fragrant marigolds and morning glories and sweet smelling roses and butterflies, baal is a pool of nothing sucked up by the sewer.

David Appleseed has freed one soul; she stands with clear eyes, the first young branch in his garden.

"I am, Anastasia, again." Extending the wands of her fingers, she says, "Eastersong cleansed my veins, heart, and eyes. I see love's golden sea. I am no longer a thing of The Plague."

Shining with Rosy-ripe, David takes her hand and kisses it gently.

On their soft round dune in the Star Chamber

of the Great Hall the River Man sees the chrysanthemum-sun color a bee's race to aromatic and the Lizard King speaks, "From one spark comes The Cascade. Passion for the Shining Light on the shore of peace is a fire once again burning in the heart of humankind . . . People will be fair again."

The River Man flashed a MileWideSmile. There were stars in his hair.

David looks up at the stout breast of Owl. "Where are we bound next, Brother?"

On the woody branch now ripe with healthy green leaves, Owl says, "For you, after toast and tea and a few winks, *Glory*."

~*~

Coda:

Calm Sunday, spring- flavored, spring-scented. Dark, but not stormy night. Not far from the simple village green, and the steeple of hope, and the nightingale verbs of the fable (laced with a pint of bitters) in The Frolicking Horsey, and Desmond and Martha having strawberry jam and a cuppa tea with their picture book memories, sits the Swanson's bungalow house on a wooded lane of broadleaf green.

tick.tock.tick.tock. almost 8 o'clock . . .

The dial set.

Kiddies and kittens. Elbows and swaying tails on the magic carpet floor, leaning at the great

rosewood cabinet. Mum & Dad ready for the
Poppyman's aural rainbows to repaint their blues
with cheer. All eyes huddled for the days of yore—

tick.tock.tick.tock. The tubes inside the '39
RCA A33 Globe Trotter console radio glow, the
15-inch speaker is eager for the supple textures
nature, each giant step of good, flowing.

8soft *chimes*.

David's LovelyLovelyLovely welcome. "Good
evening, my dear friends. I am delighted and
honored to sing for you tonight." The Poppyman's
Appleseed-alchemic song comes down from the
mountain . . .

Kiddies (in their softly pj's) and SoftlyWarm-
kittens loved in Mum & Dad's eyes. Smiles—quiet
joy.

Everywhere: the velvet of poppies

*{various selections from 35 Current 93 recordings [1986-
2011], the Doors "The End" and "THE WASP (Texas
Radio And The Big Beat), Fairport Convention "Matty
Grooves", David Bowie "Ziggy Stardust" and "Future
Legend", ELP Pictures At An Exhibition, Nurse With
Wound "Black Is The Color Of My True Love's Hair",
Donovan "Wear Your Love Like Heaven", Strawberry
Alarm Clock "Sit With the Guru", various Nick Drake
songs, and the Charlie Daniels Band "The Devil Went
Down To Georgia"}*

CHRIST BEGAT THE PERVERSIONS

Dustin Reade

In the beginning was the word. That word was passed down through the generations and perverted by tongues. John the Baptist had it right. His biggest misfortune, however, was having no one better than Christ to relay his message to. Christ begat the perversions.

After he was beheaded, Christ kept a locket full of John the Baptist's hair around his neck. The locket begat the miracles.

We see all religions at their uppermost point end in mysticism and mysteries: in darkness and oblique obscurity.

Upon how many donkeys did Christ ride into Jerusalem? Answer: one.

Christ fell from the ass and buried his hands in the mud. From this mud was born countless demons. They bubbled and boiled from the sludge and repeated his tainted dogma like trained puppets.

Before his career as the Messiah, Christ apprenticed as a carpenter. Upon cutting his palm open on a splinter, he discovered he bled not blood, but a green compound which was highly acidic. The blood he gathered up into a locket which he carried with him until falling from the ass on Palm Sunday.

In the blood: a splinter of wood.

John the Baptist allowed his hair to be carried by the faux Messiah into Jerusalem on the back of an ass.

The mud demons carried the locket of blood and wood with them to the four corners of the earth, believing it to be a holy relic.

Christ could heal the sick with his hands and raise the dead with his words. His blood could do both. It could also eat through anything, corrosive as it was.

Think of the nails melting in his palms.

Think of the sting as it hit his eyes.

The mud demons spent decades searching for the original cross. They scavenged wood piles in backyards and railway stations in search of the stake.

Jesus was whipped before the crucifixion. Think of his blood melting stones.

On his sweet sixteen, Christ was given a large slab of black wood. He carved the wood into a ship and watched as it flew away, inking a black line across the sky.

It was not his last words he spoke on the cross, but those of John the Baptist.

"Forgive them, for they know not what they do." **Luke 24-34.**

This has been taken to be Jesus' final plea to his "Father" to show mercy on those who put him to death. Others believe it to be a plea for all of humanity. John the Baptist, however, was speaking of those who were born of the mud.

The mud people discovered the original cross—old, rugged—in a cemetery in Bethlehem. Nails melted into the shape of hands, complete with fingerprints jutted from the sides. Immediately, the mud people poured the acid-blood from the locket over its surface. The blood ate a face into the wood. The tiny eyes opened, and a boy was made.

Christ died on the cross and was wrapped in a shroud. His blood burned cigarette circles into the fabric and left a stain of his body on its surface.

After the face was burned into the wood, the mouth began to speak. The message was pure, free of perversion, undiluted truth from the puppet of Christ.

In the beginning was the word, and the word was warped and distorted. John the Baptist held his head in his hands and waited.

The mud people fashioned arms and legs from the wood of the cross and affixed them to the wooden boy. In three days' time, he was walking, plodding over the earth with tiny wooden feet.

When Christ awoke in the darkness, he heard a tapping at the vault door. Thinking he was dreaming, he moved the rock aside. There, floating before him was the black ship he had whittled on his sweet sixteen.

"We shall call him Noddy," said the mud people. Their voices crackled like television static. The puppet nodded his head and said, "Noddy."

Christ rode the black ship through the early morning sky. It sailed over the landscape. Christ leaned over the side and defecated. Where his shit fell, millions became sick. Fences folded over with the weight, and trees surrounded the ship as it fell to heaven.

Heaven is mud. Heaven is within us all.

Noddy stormed through the world like the apocalypse. He plugged into the television and preached electric nonsense to the people.

John the Baptist took the locket from Christ's neck and proceeded to use the strands of hair to sew his head back to his neck. Once finished, he whispered in a husky voice, "There, I have been completed." He then leapt on the black ship and ascended back to the earth, bubbling forth from the muddy pits.

In the beginning was the word, and the word remained and distorted. Christ died on the cross. The greatest tragedy on that day was that the word did not die with him. Imagine millions of tongues drying out in the sun. Shriveled, and without words, thirsty for moans and pleas.

Satan stretched his wings and watched as Noddy imitated Christ on the cross, inspiring others to do the same. Countless corpses nailed to telephone poles as far as the eye can see. The new American landscape.

John the Baptist clambered from the ship and sank to his knees in the mud. The moon dissolved.

The sky was red. Kissing the rudder, he sent the ship away.

Christ watched the world from heaven. He raised his robes and defecated over the side. The shit came down in clumps. Mud puddles where it landed birthing still more believers. With mouths wide open, they screamed: "we will swallow anything!"

The word.

The world was ending in slow burps. Horses gathered at the edges of cliffs.

The word.

Forgive them, for they know not what they do.

The word.

The horses raced over the edge, landing in a heaping puddle of Christ shit.

"This is the last day," Noddy said, climbing aboard the black ship and flying quietly away.

The sky was red the day Christ was crucified.

We sat and drank cherry cola and watched the end of the world.

SHADOWS AND ABYSS
Michael Göttert

The sky was wan and pale and everything was dreariness: The horizon seemed to flee and beyond the horizon he could only see another beyond, ungraspable, yet strangely alluring in its desire to show him the infinity of his journey. His way was paved with stones that were the colour of blood – not quite dry but not fresh either. For others the sun shone like a beacon whereas for him it was a hidden, but still blinding and piercing eye that watched his every move. He felt naked and was looking for another robe to clothe him; what he found in the vast space of a restless mind was neither a robe of water nor a robe of air but a robe woven from the promises of a girl named Mary Joyce - or was it Martha? This robe promised redemption and salvation. Of that he was sure.

He thought it would be best to follow the river. Because what else could there be but life, purpose, direction, and some kind of end - even if the end was the sea in its greyish infinity. He was wondering why no birds were singing. It was not a violent winter that may have prevented them from singing their praises and no carrion crows were in sight to scare them like rocking horses that rock on their own accord scare children. But the silence was deafening and his head was too clear and the thoughts too numerous to let him come to rest. He remembered something from a distant past: A low beach, a low ceiling that was terror, the fear of terror and terror itself, doors and walls the colour of spit and spite and the howling of those damaged and destroyed – but he had survived. He had followed the rules and pretended to be awake the way required and he had written endlessly: The darkening days had been filled with the singing of sparrows, blackcaps, thrushes and others too precious to be tainted by a name that imprisoned them the same way as he had been locked up. The people had been nice but what did they know about the seasons? The perfect moment of a snowflake melting on one's tongue and renewing one's spirits? For them a cat was a domestic convenience and not one of God's wonders speaking in tongues both ancient and pure. They were mind people. There was no room in their bloated heads for the cry of the seagull or the blinding vision of truth. One of the mind people had laughed when he had mentioned the shadows; for him a shadow was just an area of darkness and not a pale second self. They didn't see the trees they passed and had long forgotten that the sky could be a shelter as well as an oracle that spoke of stars and moons and the infinity of words and worlds and whirlpools of stars marching sadly and rejoicing in their endless parade of proud perfection.

After a while somebody emerged from the landscape that despite its green trees and woods beyond the world was fear and desire. It was a hooded man, tall but strangely crooked. "Who is it that breaks the peace of a hapless man?", were the words uttered from a mouth that was all teeth. He wanted to answer that he had no intention to break the peace because peace was what he sought, desired and needed. But the mouth did not seem to wait for an answer, so quick was the reply. "You don't have to answer. I must apologize. Too late did I see that you are a fellow traveler. A master of the void, voiceless and yet all voice. Years ago I would not have made this mistake, but my journey has already taken me to all four corners of the world and back again and my perception is wearing thin."

"If you've been to all of these places, then you can tell me where I must go."

The teeth chattered and uttered: "I've been nearly everywhere and still I am a seeker, my desire to find is a burden that keeps dragging me down. I can't help you because my way is not yours and yours is that of two men. Just keep in mind that your dream is just a shadow of another shadow and this shadow may have long since lost its way. But beyond that shadow that you can sometimes glimpse in moments of great clarity - even though others my chide you for that and may want to send you straight down the road to Bedlam - lies something that may be real. The Ambul, a creature of great wisdom you may have never heard of before, once told me that you just have to go back far enough and every dream can be real." With that he left and left him wondering how much of this had been real. But it didn't really matter as the man was gone and he was alone again. And what else could and should he do but walk on, in his head the faiths and faces that had already turned into fragments of rags and fragrances.

It grew darker and for one moment he thought he had seen something in the distance, some kind of creature, but it was just a dead fox, lying near the way in a posture that reminded him of a picture he had once dreamt. It had been a spring day and he had just returned from a visit to his father. On his way home he had suddenly seen a girl dressed in white sowing the seeds of life and welcoming the birds of passage. From her hands the seeds had fallen like honey and it had been impeccable. Here on the road the paws of the fox were raised as if the animal wanted to welcome him. That clearly was a sign that his journey was not in vain. Even though he had not eaten or drunk anything for the last hours, he felt renewed and rejoiced in what had been shown to him.

After a while he saw the river crossing his way and he did not know what to do. But then he noticed a figure that was present and absent, it seemed to bleed into the meadows and the branches of the river. But he was not afraid because he knew that now was the time to finally ask the question that had troubled him for such a long time: "Am I?" The creature, whose name might have been spoken of in forgotten lore and scriptures in cuneiform, spoke, but the voice was not that of thunder, not that of fire, but a voice of all the sounds of all the worlds combined, neither silence nor sound: "I am the abyss and I am light" were his words and then the figure retched and seemed to melt and freeze at the same time and it was everything and not nothing and he had to kneel down before him; and all the nothings of the past - the twitching mouths and broken limbs, the drowned and drowning hopes, the laughing faces in the city that had mocked him and his words and the tongues that had laughed behind his back, calling him names and spreading pity, disdain's younger brother - no longer mattered. He was there now and there was no scorn or noise, sound or fury, he no longer felt a shipwreck, but he was the whole that had been there when he had first looked into the mirror and had realized that it was him reflected in the glass. The River Tweed was like a snake acknowledging his presence now, at the same time giving light and life. What else was there to do now but to embrace it and feel its warmth? All the words he had written and spoken and all the paintings that had left the retina of his eyes were there. And they all were one and once. And then there was a candle burning bright and the voice that was there and everywhere told him about saints and sinners and the first word and the last breath.

THE INVOCATION OF NODDY
Dinah Prim

The Hill of Crucifixion in the Town is a big one, and it is full of people.

Well, not *people* exactly. They are toys. Giant toys suffering on the wooden emblems embossed in blood. They are bathed in taboric light, satisfied in their bliss, in their eternal supplication. They make no moves for resurrection. There is no need to try so hard to become *real*.

Buses drive down the road on the bottom of the hill. The occupants take pictures and wave their souvenirs (cheaply-made puppets and water pistols in the shape of mummified messiah figures).

After visiting the hill, the buses will drive to the sea. They will watch the fog move over the water and the occupants will throw their souvenirs into the greenish blue abyss.

The residents of the Town watch.

A boy exits the bus. He looks out at the ocean and then back at the hill. He spies on cross in particular, a cross on which hangs a skinny little thing.

The boy puts his hands to his mouth and shouts. 'Do look out, Noddy!'

There is no answer from the cross. Just a shimmer of light.

The boy shouts again. 'Cheer up, little Noddy!'

Again, no response but a slight shimmer.

The boy tries one more time. 'You funny little Noddy!'

The boy walks back onto the bus and sits down next to his sister who is fiddling with the ribbons in her hair.

She says, 'Did you see them?'

'See what?'

'The black ships.'

'The black ships?'

'Yes, the black ships that will eat the hill.'

The boy scoffs. 'Nothing can eat that hill. That hill is gigantic. That hill is the biggest hill in the Town. It is the biggest in the *world*.'

'Oh, but the ships...they are the biggest *ships* in the world.'

The boy dismisses his sister with a gesture of his hand. He has no time for foolish superstition. He looks out the window back at the hill and watches as the skinny little thing on the cross pulls itself off the wood and falls clumsily to the earth.

The boy sticks his head out the window and shouts.

'Be brave, little Noddy! Be brave...'

NIGHTMARE FOR THE IRON YOUTH

Chris Kelso

The witching hour.

A peel of thunder rattles over the valley. You can hear the awful growl of slumbering trolls in caves. Alluvium trails all lead to the heel of Achilles...

It is nigh.

A boy wandering through the haze of trees looks up at the Demiurge's moon as it forms a perfect, horned crescent. The forest has lured and consumed so many of the town's children beneath its penumbra - this one should've known better than to stray from the beaten path.

- I never saw the dead man, I never saw the dead man – repeats the boy through fits and shakes.

Clouds streaked purple become thin as vapour and an all-seeing eye blinks open, peering through, unto the valley. Cloying copper spice of blood hangs thickly in the air.

There is nothing inspirational about the boy – nothing beyond his presence here in the darkest, most dangerous of woodland jungles. The forest is burdened by evil ether. Naked trees haemorrhage from the thorax under scabs of bark and bone.

The boy, once blonde and lit by innocence, now bedimmed by shadow, has heard all about the demons that lurk in the forest at night tide. Sweat sleeks his palms and forehead, twigs crack under invisible feet and a million sets of yellow eyes watch from the rotten palace apertures mortared in swathes their own feculence.

He forges westward, gripped in fear.

- *I never saw the dead man, I never saw the dead man...*

He too knows *it* is nigh.

Time passes quickly. The boy can see the vague contours of a cottage roofed in shingles and timber purlins. Giddy with excitement he clambers towards it. When the boy reaches the maple door, he composes himself and knocks politely to the tune of pop-goes-the-weasel. It creaks open. In his terrified haste, the blonde child pushes the door inward and enters the cottage.

Inside there is a hall with archways leading into each of the separate rooms, bisected by a large staircase. He is percolated by the warmth. The boy turns left through the first archway and sees a man sitting at a desk. He is a young man with hair pulled back into a ponytail and a linen shirt stained red beneath an open doublet – he is excruciatingly skinny, bones poke out from the face in jagged scaffolding.

- I'm sorry sir... - the boy apologizes, fearful that the well-dressed man will strike him for trespassing.

To the boy's relief the man's face softens into a smile.

- Come in my boy, out of the cold with you!

Relieved to have escaped the vigil of night tide, the boy sits in the opposite chair and shakes off his coat.

- Thank you.

- You shouldn't be out in the forest by yourself.

- I know sir.

- There are things in this valley that pray upon vulnerable spirits like you, things your small, innocent mind cannot fathom. Still, you display courage. This might make a man of you yet.

The man materializes a large blister steel cutting knife and hacks off a slice of bread for the wayward boy. He forwards it and the child gratefully stuffs the entire rectangle of bread into his mouth with reckless abandon.

- What's your name?

The boy tries to swallow the bread quickly to answer but chokes on the crust.

- Take your time, boy.

He clears his throat and reveals his name – I am Cleve.

- Ah, Cleve, what an unusual name.

- What is your name, sir, if you don't mind my asking?

- Not at all. I'm Rafael. I'm a painter.

The boy cannot contain his glee, for he is an avid admirer of his nation's art.

- May I see your work?

- I'm not sure.

- Why not?

- Well, I only show it to certain people and…we just met, you and I.

- Please sir!

- Well…if your heart and soul desires it…very well.

Rafael leads the boy up the wooden staircase, warning him to mind his head on the exposed beams.

- I am more than an artist, young Cleve, I'm also a prophet.

- A prophet, really?

- Really. The Gods speak to me. I have seen how this all ends.

- How *what* all ends sir?

Rafael gives a theatrical sigh of righteous indignation.

- This! *Everything!*

At the apex of the stairwell, Rafael turns to the boy, kneels down and looks him in the eye.

- You are a guest here in my home. I have sheltered you, protected you, even fed you, so I ask you to please reserve your criticism of my work.

- Sir, I'm sure they will be masterful.

The painter smiles and tousles Cleve's hair.

- Come, follow me.

Cleve is taken to a loft space full of canvas panels, paint brushes and barrels of gesso. There must be over a hundred paintings.

- They're quite beautiful sir.

- Ah now, let me explain each piece. They were communicated to me by a divine force. I feel it only right to explain the history of each canvas.

- That's not necessary. I enjoy just looking.

- This, St Sebastian. This is St George and the Dragon...oh and then there's this. You might be interested in this, young Cleve.

Rafael goes over to a canvas covered by a white tarp. He grabs the sheet at the bottom and unveils the painting beneath.

- I call it "Nightmare for the Iron Youth." *It* is nigh.

Cleve is frozen. He stares at the picture disbelievingly. How can this be? Rafael has drawn a picture of a boy bearing an uncanny resemblance to him – a boy with scraped and bloody knees being chased through the woods by a creature.

- How...?

- I told you, I am a conduit...

Cleve sees a framed contract hanging on the wall, binding and signed by Mephistopheles himself. His instincts tell him to get out of the cottage. He turns away, scarpering down the staircase, two steps at a time, minding his head on the exposed beams. He powers through the hallway. Through each archway he sees a different image of horror - a crucified boy, a weeping girl, all manner of monstrous abominations waiting in the dimmet. Cleve throws the front door open and runs back into the forest. He can hear Rafael laughing maniacally.

The slumbering troll opens its eyes. Eventide will never come again.

It is nigh.

IN A FOREIGN TOWN, IN A FOREIGN LAND

Thomas Ligotti

HIS SHADOW SHALL RISE TO A HIGHER HOUSE

In the middle of the night I lay wide awake in bed, listening to the dull black drone of the wind outside my window and the sound of bare branches scraping against the shingles of the roof just above me. Soon my thoughts became fixed upon a town, picturing its various angles and aspects, a remote town near the northern border. Then I remembered that there was a hilltop graveyard that hovered not far beyond the edge of town. I have never told a soul about this graveyard, which for a time was a source of great anguish for those who had retreated to the barren landscape of the northern border.

It was within the hilltop graveyard, a place that was far more populated than the town over which it hovered, that the body of Ascrobius had been buried. Known throughout the town as a recluse who possessed an intensely contemplative nature, Ascrobius had suffered from a disease that left much of his body in a grossly deformed condition. Nevertheless, despite the distinguishing qualities of his severe deformity and his intensely contemplative nature, the death of Ascrobius was an event that passed almost entirely unnoticed. All of the notoriety gained by the recluse, all of the comment I attached to his name, occurred sometime after his disease-mangled body had been housed among the others in the hilltop graveyard.

At first there was no specific mention of Ascrobius, but only a kind of twilight talk – dim and pervasive murmurs that persistently revolved around the graveyard outside of town, often touching upon more general topics of a morbid character, including some abstract discourse, as I interpreted it, on the phenomenon of the grave. More and more, whether one moved about the town or remained in some secluded quarter of it, this twilight talk became familiar and even invasive. It emerged from shadowed doorways along narrow streets, from half-opened windows of the highest rooms of the town's old houses, and from the distant corners of labyrinthine and resonant hallways. Everywhere, it seemed, there were voices that had become obsessed to the point of hysteria with a single subject: the 'missing grave.' No one mistook these words to mean a grave that somehow had been violated, its ground dug up and its contents removed, or even a grave whose headstone had absconded, leaving the resident of some particular plot in a state of anonymity. Even I, who was less intimate than many others with the peculiar nuances of the northern border town, understood what was meant by the words 'a missing grave' or 'an absent grave.' The hilltop graveyard was so dense with headstones and its ground so riddled with interments that such a thing would be astonishingly apparent: where there once had been a grave like any other, there was now, in the same precious space, only a patch of virgin earth.

For a certain period of time, speculation arose concerning the identity of the occupant of the missing grave. Because there existed no systematic record-keeping for any particular instance of burial in the hilltop graveyard – when or where or for whom an interment took place – the discussions over the occupant of the missing grave, or the *former* occupant, always degenerated into outbursts of the wildest nonsense of simply faded into a vaporous and sullen confusion. Such a scene was running its course in the cellar of an abandoned building where several of us had gathered one evening. It was on this occasion that a gentleman calling himself Dr Klatt first suggested 'Ascrobius' as the name upon the headstone of the missing grave. He was almost offensively positive in this assertion, as if there were not an abundance of headstones on the hilltop graveyard with erroneous or unreadable names, or none at all.

For some time Klatt had been ˉadvertising himself around town as an individual who possessed a distinguished background in some discipline of a vaguely scientific nature. This persona or imposture, if it was one, would not have been unique in the history of the northern border town. However, when Klatt began to speak of the recent anomaly not as a *missing* grave, even an absent grave, but as an *uncreated* grave, the others began to listen. Soon enough it was the name of Ascrobius that was mentioned most frequently as the occupant of the missing – now *uncreated* – grave. At the same time the reputation of Dr Klatt became closely linked to that of the deceased individual who was well known for both his grossly deformed body and his intensely contemplative nature.

During this period it seemed that anywhere in town one happened to find oneself, Klatt was there holding forth on the subject of his relationship to Ascrobius, whom he now called his 'patient.' In the cramped back rooms of shops long gone out of business or some other similarly out-of-the-way locale – a remote street corner, for instance – Klatt spoke of the visits he had made to the high backstreet house of Ascrobius and of the attempts he had made to treat the disease from which the recluse had long suffered. In addition, Klatt boasted of insights he had gained into the deeply contemplative personality whom most of us had never met, let along conversed with at any great length. While Klatt appeared to enjoy the attention he received from those who had previously dismissed him as just another imposter in the northern border town, and perhaps still considered him as such, I believe he was unaware of the profound suspicion, and even dread, that he inspired due to what certain persons called his 'meddling' in the affairs of Ascrobius. 'Thou shalt not meddle' was an unspoken, though seldom observed, commandment of the town, or so it seemed to me. And Klatt's exposure of the formerly obscure existence of Ascrobius, even if the doctor's anecdotes were misleading or totally fabricated, would be regarded as a highly perilous form of meddling by many longtime residents of the town.

Nonetheless, nobody turned away whenever Klatt began talking about the diseased, contemplative recluse: nobody tried to silence or even question whatever claims he made concerning Ascrobius. 'He was a monster,' said the doctor to some of us who were gathered one night in a ruined factory on the outskirts of the town. Klatt frequently stigmatized Ascrobius as either a 'monster' or a 'freak,' though these epithets were not intended simply as a reaction to the grotesque physical appearance of the notorious recluse. It was in a strictly metaphysical sense, according to Klatt, that Ascrobius should be viewed as most monstrous and freakish, qualities that emerged as a consequence of his intensely contemplative nature. 'He had incredible powers available to him,' said the doctor. 'He might even have cured himself of his diseased physical condition; who can say? But all of his powers of contemplation, all of those incessant *meditations* that took place in his high backstreet house, were directed toward another purpose altogether.'

Saying this much, Dr Klatt fell silent in the flickering, makeshift illumination of the ruined factory. It was almost as if he were waiting for one of us to prompt his next words, so that we might serve as accomplices in this extraordinary gossip over his deceased patient, Ascrobius.

Eventually someone did inquire about the contemplative powers and meditations of the recluse, and toward what end they might have been directed. 'What Ascrobius sought,' the doctor explained, 'was not a remedy for his physical disease, not a cure in any usual sense of the word. What he sought was an absolute *annulment*, not only of his disease but of his entire existence. On rare occasions he even spoke to me,' the doctor said, 'about the *uncreation* of his whole life.' After Dr Klatt had spoken these words there seemed to occur a moment of the most profound stillness in the ruined factory where we were gathered. No doubt everyone had suddenly become possessed, as was I, by a single object of contemplation – the absent grave, which Dr Klatt described as an uncreated grave, within the hilltop graveyard outside of town. 'You see what has happened,' Dr Klatt said to us. 'He has annulled his diseased and nightmarish existence, leaving us with an uncreated grave on our hands.' Nobody who was at the ruined factory that night, nor anyone else in the northern border town, believed there would not be a price to pay for what had been revealed to us by Dr Klatt. Now all of us had become meddling accomplices in those events which came to be euphemistically described as the 'Ascrobius escapade.'

Admittedly the town had always been populated by hysterics of one sort or another. Following the Ascrobius escapade, however, there was a remarkable plague of twilight talk about 'unnatural repercussions' that were either in the making or were already taking place throughout the town. *Someone would have to atone for that uncreated existence*, or such was the general feeling as it was expressed in various obscure settings and situations. In the dead of night one could hear the most reverberant screams arising at frequent intervals from every section of town, particularly the backstreet areas, far more than the usual nocturnal outbursts. And upon subsequent overcast days the streets were all but deserted. Any talk confronting the specifics of the town's night terrors was either precious or entirely absent: perhaps, I might even say, it was as uncreated as Ascrobius himself, at least for a time.

It was inevitably the figure of Dr Klatt who, late one afternoon, stepped forward from the shadows of an old warehouse to address a small group of persons assembled there. His shape barely visible in the gauzy light that pushed its way through dusty windowpanes, Klatt announced that he might possess the formula for solving the new-found troubles of the northern border town. While the warehouse gathering was as wary as the rest of us of any further meddling in the matt of Ascrobius, they gave Klatt a hearing in spite of their reservations. Included among this group was a woman known as Mrs Glimm, who operated a lodging house – actually a kind of brothel – that was patronized for the most part by out-of-towners, especially business travelers stopping on their way to some destination across the border. Even though Klatt did not directly address Mrs Glimm, he made it quite clear that he would require an assistant of a very particular type in order to carry out the measures he had in mind for delivering us all from those intangible traumas that had lately afflicted everyone in some manner. 'Such an assistant,' the doctor emphasized, 'should not be anyone who is exceptionally sensitive or intelligent.

'At the same time,' he continued, 'this person must have a definite handsomeness of appearance, even a fragile beauty.' Further instructions from Dr Klatt indicated that the requisite assistant should be sent up to the hilltop graveyard that same night, for the doctor fully expected that the clouds which had choked the sky throughout the day would linger long into the evening, thus cutting off the moonlight that often shone so harshly on the closely huddled graves. This desire for optimum darkness seemed to be a conspicuous giveaway on the doctor's part. Everyone present at the old warehouse was of course aware that such 'measures' as Klatt proposed were only another instance of meddling by someone who was almost certainly an imposter of the worst sort. But we were already so deeply implicated in the Ascrobius escapade, and so lacking in any solutions of our own, that no one attempted to discourage Mrs Glimm from doing what she could to assist the doctor with his proposed scheme.

So the moonless night came and went, and the assistant sent by Mrs Glimm never returned from the hilltop graveyard. Yet nothing in the northern border town seemed to have changed. The chorus of midnight outcries continued and the twilight talk now began to focus on both the 'terrors of Ascrobius' and the 'charlatan Dr Klatt,' who was nowhere to be found when a search was conducted throughout every street and structure of the town, excepting of course the high backstreet house of the dreadful recluse. Finally a small party of the town's least hysterical persons made its way up the hill which led to the graveyard. When they approached the area of the absent grave, it was immediately apparent what 'measures' Klatt had employed and the fashion in which the assistant sent by Mrs Glimm had been used in order to bring an end to the Ascrobius escapade.

The message which those who had gone up to the graveyard carried back to town was that Klatt was nothing but a common butcher. 'Well, perhaps not a *common* butcher,' said Mrs Glimm, who was among the small graveyard party. Then she explained in detail how the body of the doctor's assistant, its skin finely shredded by countless incisions and its parts numerously dismembered, had been arranged with some calculation on the spot of the absent grave: the raw head and torso were propped up in the ground as if to serve as the headstone for a grave, while the arms and legs were disposed in a way that might be seen to demarcate the rectangular space of a graveyard plot. Someone suggested giving the violated body a proper burial in its own gravesite, but Mrs Glimm, for some reason unknown even to herself, or so she said, persuaded the others that things should be left as they were. And perhaps her intuition in this matter was felicitous, for not many days later there was a complete cessation of all terrors associated with the Ascrobius escapade, however indefinite or possibly nonexistent such occurrences might have been from the start. Only later, by means of the endless murmurs of twilight talk, did it become apparent why Dr Klatt might have abandoned the town, even though his severe measures seemed to have worked the exact cure which he had promised.

Although I cannot say that I witnessed anything myself, others reported signs of a 'new occupation,' not at the site of the grave of Ascrobius, but at the high backstreet house where the recluse once spent his intensely contemplative days and nights. There were sometimes lights behind the curtained windows, these observers said, and the passing figure outlined upon those curtains was more outlandishly grotesque than anything they had ever

288

seen while the resident of that house had lived. But no one ever approached the house. Afterward all speculation about what had come to be known as the 'resurrection of the uncreated' remained in the realm of twilight talk. Yet as I now lie in my bed, listening to the wind and the scraping of bare branches on the roof just above me, I cannot help remaining wide awake with visions of that deformed specter of Ascrobius and pondering upon what unimaginable planes of contemplation it dreams of another act of uncreation, a new and far-reaching effort of great power and more certain permanence. Nor do I welcome the thought that one day someone may notice that a particular house appears to be missing, or absent, from the place it once occupied along the backstreet of a town near the northern border.

THE BELLS WILL SOUND FOREVER

I was sitting in a small park on a drab morning in early spring when a gentleman who looked as if he should be in a hospital sat down on the bench beside me. For a time we both silently stared out at the colorless and soggy grounds of the park, where things were still thawing out and signs of a revived natural life remained only tentative, the bare branches of trees finely outlined against a gray sky. I had seen the other man on previous visits to the park and, when he introduced himself to me by name, I seemed to remember him as a businessman of some sort. The words 'commercial agent' came to my mind as I sat gazing up at the thing dark branches and, beyond them, the gray sky. Somehow our quiet and somewhat halting conversation touched upon the subject of a particular town near the northern border, a place where I once lived. 'It's been many years,' the other man said, 'since I was last in that town.' Then he proceeded to tell me about an experience he had had there in the days when he often traveled to remote locales for the business firm he represented and which, until that time, he had served as a longterm and highly dedicated employee.

It was late at night, he told me, and he needed a place to stay before moving on to his ultimate destination across the northern border. I knew, as a one-time resident of the town, that there were two principal venues where he might have spent the night. One of them was a lodging house on the west side of town that, in actuality, functioned primarily as a brothel patronized by traveling commercial agents. The other was located somewhere on the east side of town in a district of once-opulent, but now for the most part unoccupied houses, one of which, according to rumor, had been converted into a hostel of some kind by an old woman named Mrs Pyk, who was reputed to have worked in various carnival sideshows – first as an exotic dancer, and then later as a fortune-teller – before settling in the northern border town. The commercial agent told me that he could not be sure if it was misdirection or deliberate mischief that sent him to the east side of town, where there were only a few lighted windows here and there. Thus he easily spotted the VACANCY sign that stood beside the steps leading up to an enormous house which had a number of small turrets that seemed to sprout like so many warts across its façade and even emerged from the high peaked roof that crowned the structure. Despite the grim appearance of the house (a 'miniature ruined castle,' as my companion in the park expressed it), not to mention the generally desolate character of the surrounding neighborhood, the commercial agent said that he was not for a moment deterred from ascending the porch steps. He pressed the doorbell, which he said was a 'buzzer-type bell,' as opposed to the type that chimed or tolled its signal. However, in addition to the buzzing noise that was made when he pressed the button for the doorbell, he claimed that there was also a 'jingle-jangle sound' similar to that of sleigh bells. When the door finally opened, and the commercial agent confronted the heavily made-up face of Mrs Pyk, he simply asked, "Do you have a room?'

Upon entering the vestibule to the house, he was made to pause by Mrs Pyk, who gestured with a thin and palsied hand toward a registration ledger which was spread open on a lectern in the corner. There were no other visitors listed on the pages before him, yet the commercial agent unhesitatingly picked up the fountain pen that lay in the crux of the ledger book and signed his name: Q.H. Crumm. Having done this, he turned his back toward Mrs Pyk and stooped down to retrieve the small suitcase he had brought in with him. At that moment he first saw Mrs Pyk's left hand, the non-palsied hand, which was just as thing as the other but which appeared to be a prosthetic device resembling the pale hand of an old manikin, its enameled epidermis having flaked away in several places. It was then that Mr Crumm fully realized, in his own words, the 'deliriously preposterous' position in which he had placed himself. Yet he said that he also felt a great sense of excitation relating to things which he could not precisely name, things which he had never imagined before and which it seemed were not even possible for him to imagine with any clarity at the time.

The old woman was aware that Crumm had taken note of her artificial hand. 'As you can see,' she said in a slow and raspy voice, 'I'm perfectly capable of taking care of myself, no matter what some fool tries to pull on me. But I don't receive as many gentleman travelers as I once did. I'm sure I wouldn't have any at all, if it were up to certain people,' she finished. *Deliriously preposterous*, Mr Crumm thought to himself. Nevertheless, he followed Mrs Pyk like a little dog when she guided him into her house, which was so poorly lighted that one was at a loss to distinguish any features of the décor, leaving Crum with the heady sensation

292

of being enveloped by the most sumptuous surroundings of shadows. This feeling was only intensified when the old woman reached out for a small lamp that was barely glowing in the darkness and, with a finger of her real hand, turned up its wick, the light pushing back some of the shadows while grotesquely enlarging many others. She then began escorting Crumm up the stairs to his room, holding the lamp in her real hand while simply allowing her artificial hand to hang at her side. And with each step that Mrs Pyk ascended, the commercial agent seemed to detect the same jingle-jangle of bells that he had first heard when he was standing outside the house, waiting for someone to answer his ring. But the sound was so faint, as if heavily muffled, that Mr Crumm willingly believed it to be only the echo of a memory or his wandering imagination.

The room in which Mrs Pyk finally deposited her guest was on the highest floor of the house, just down a short, narrow hallways from the floor leading to the attic. 'By that time there seemed nothing at all preposterous in this arrangement,' Mr Crumm told me as we sat together on the park bench looking out at that drab morning in early spring. I replied that such lapses in judgment were no uncommon where Mrs Pyk's lodging house was concerned; at least such were the rumors I had heard during the period when I was living in the town near the northern border.

When they had reached the hallway of the highest floor of the house, Crumm informed me, Mrs Pyk set aside the lamp she was carrying on a table positioned near the top of the last flight of stairs. She then extended her hand and pushed a small button that protruded from one of the walls, thereby activating some lighting fixtures along either wall. The illumination remained dismal – actively dismal, as Crumm described it – but served to reveal the densely patterned wallpaper and the even more densely patterned carpeting of the hallway which led, in one direction, to the opening onto the attic and, in the other direction, to the room in which the commercial agent was supposed to sleep that night. After Mrs Pyk unlocked the door to this room and pushed another small button upon the wall inside, Crumm observed how cramped and austere was the chamber in which he was being placed, unnecessarily so, he thought, considering the apparent spaciousness, or 'dark sumptuousness,' as he called it, of the rest of the house Yet Crumm made no objection (nor felt any, he insisted), and with mute obedience set down his suitcase beside a tiny bed which was not even equipped with a headboard. 'There's a bathroom just a little way down the hall,' Mrs Pyk said before she left the room, closing the door behind her. And in the silence of that little room, Crumm thought that once again he could hear the jingle-jangle sound of bells fading into the distance and the darkness of that great house.

Although he had put in quite a long day, the commercial agent did not feel in the least bit tired, or possibly he had entered into a mental state beyond the boundaries of absolute fatigue, as he himself speculated when we were sitting on that bench in the park. For some time he lay on the undersized bed, still fully clothed, and stared at a ceiling that had several large stains spread across it. After all, he thought, he had been placed in a room that was directly below the roof of the house, and apparently this roof was damaged in some way which allowed the rain to enter freely through the attic on stormy days and nights. Suddenly his mind became fixed in the strangest way upon the attic, the door to which was just down the hall from his own room. *The mystery of an old attic*, Crumm whispered to himself as he lay on that miniature bed in a room at the top of an enormous house of enveloping shadows. Feelings and impulses that he had never experienced before arose in him as he became more and more excited about the attic and its mysteries. He was a traveling commercial agent who needed his rest to prepare himself for the next day, and yet all he could think about was getting up from his bed and walking down the dimly lighted hallway toward the door leading to the attic of Mrs Pyk's shadowy house. He could tell anyone who cared to know that he was only going down the hall to use the bathroom, he told himself. But Crumm proceeded past the door to the bathroom and soon found himself helplessly creeping into the attic, the door to which had been left unlocked.

The air inside smelled sweet and stale. Moonlight entered by way of a small octagonal window and guided the commercial agent among the black clutter toward a lightbulb that hung down from a thick black cord. He reached up and turned a little dial that protruded from the side of the lightbulb fixture. Now he could see the treasures surrounding him, and he was shaking with the excitation of his discovery. Crumm told me that Mrs Pyk's old attic was like a costume shop or the dressing room of a theater. All around him was a world of strange outfits spilling forth from the depths of large open trunks or dangling in the shadows of tall open wardrobes. Later he became aware that these curious clothes were, for the most part, remnants from Mrs Pyk's days as an exotic dancer, and subsequently a fortune-teller, for various carnival sideshows. Crumm himself remembered observing that mounted along the walls of the attic were several faded posters advertising the two distinct phases of the old woman's former life. One of these posters portrayed a dancing girl posed in mid-turn amidst a whirl of silks, her face averted from the silhouetted heads representing the audience at the bottom of the picture, a mob of bald pates and bowler hats huddled together. Another poster displayed a pair of dark staring eyes with long spidery lashes. Above the eyes, printed in a serpentine style of lettering, were the words: Mistress of Fortune. Below the eyes, spelled in the same type of letters, was a simple question: WHAT IS YOUR WILL?

Aside from the leftover garments of an exotic dancer or a mysterious fortune teller, there were also other clothes, other costumes. They were scattered all over the attic – that 'paradise of the past,' as Crumm began to refer to it. His hands trembled as he found all sorts of odd disguises lying about the floor or draped across a wardrobe mirror, elaborate and clownish outfits in rich velvets and shiny, colorful satins. Rummaging among this delirious attic-world, Crumm finally found what he barely knew he was seeking. There it was, buried at the bottom of one of the largest trunks – a fool's motley complete with soft slippers turned up at the toes and a two-pronged cap that jangled its bells as he pulled it over his head. The entire suit was a mad patchwork of colored fabrics and fitted him perfectly, once he had removed all of the clothing he wore as a commercial agent. The double peaks of the fool's cap resembled the twin horns of a snail, Crumm noticed when he looked at his image in the mirror, except that they drooped this way and that whenever he shook his head to make the bells jangle. There were also bells sewn into the turned-up tips of the slippers and hanging here and there upon the body of the jester's suit. Crumm made them all go jingle-jangle, he explained to me, as he pranced before the wardrobe mirror gazing upon the figure that he could not recognize as himself, so lost was he in a world of feelings and impulses he had never before imagined. He no longer retained the slightest sense, he said, of his existence as a traveling commercial agent. For him, there was no only the jester's suit hugging his body, the jingle-jangle of the bells, and the slack face of a fool in the mirror.

After a time he sank face-down upon the cold wooden floor of the attic, Crumm informed me, and lay absolutely still, exhausted by the contentment he had found in that musty paradise. Then the sound of the bells started up again, although Crumm could not tell from where it was coming. His body remained unmoving upon the floor in a state of sleepy paralysis, and yet he heard the sound of the jangling bells. Crumm thought that if he could just open his eyes and roll over on the floor he could see what was making the sound of the bells. But soon he lost all confidence in this plan of action, because he could no longer feel his own body. The sound of the bells became even louder, jangling about his ears, even though he was incapable of making his head move in any way and thus shaking the bells on his two-pronged fool's cap. Then he heard a voice say to him, 'Open your eyes ... and see your surprise.' And when he opened his eyes he finally saw his face in the wardrobe mirror: it was a tiny face on a tiny fool's head ... and the head was at the end of a stick, a kind of baton with stripes on it like a candy cane, held in the wooden hand of Mrs Pyk. She was shaking the striped stick like a baby's rattle, making the bells on Crumm's tiny head go jingle-jangle so wildy. There in the mirror he could also see his body still lying helpless and immobile upon the attic floor. And in his mind was a single consuming thought: *to be a head on a stick held in the wooden hand of Mrs Pyk. Forever ...forever.*

When Crumm awoke the next morning, he heard the sound of raindrops on the roof just above the room in which he lay full clothed on the bed. Mrs Pyk was shaking him gently with her real hand, saying, 'Wake up, Mr Crumm. It's late and you have to be on your way. You have business across the border.' Crumm wanted to say something to the old woman then and there, confront her with what he described to me as his 'adventure in the attic.' But Mrs Pyk's brusque, businesslike manner and her entirely ordinary tone of voice told him that any inquiries would be useless. In any case, he was afraid that openly bringing up this peculiar matter with Mrs Pyk was not something he should do if he wished to remain on good terms with her. Soon thereafter he was standing with his suitcase in his hand at the door of the enormous house, lingering for a moment to gaze upon the heavily made-up face of Mrs Pyk and secure another glimpse of the artificial hand which hung down at her side.

'May I come to stay again?' Crumm asked.

'If you wish,' answered Mrs Pyk, as she held open the door for her departing guest.

Once he was outside on the porch Crumm quickly turned about-face and called out, 'May I have the same room?'

But Mrs Pyk had already closed the door behind him, and her answer to his question, if it actually was one, was a faint jingle-jangle sound of tiny bells.

After consummating his commercial dealings on the other side of the northern border, Mr Crumm returned to the location of Mrs Pyk's house, only to find that the place had burned to the ground during the brief interval he had been away. I told him, as we sat on that park bench looking out upon a drab morning in early spring, that there had always been rumors, a sort of irresponsible twilight talk, about Mrs Pyk and her old house. Some persons, hysterics of one sort or another, suggested that Mrs Glimm, who operated the lodging house on the west side of town, was the one behind the fire which brought to an end Mrs Pyk's business activities on the east side. The two of them had apparently been associates at one time, in a sense partners, whose respective houses on the west and east sides of the northern border town were operated for the mutual benefit of both women. But a rift of some kind appeared to turn them into bitter enemies. Mrs Glimm, who was sometimes characterized as a 'person of uncanny greed,' became intolerant of the competition posed by her former ally in business. It came to be understood throughout the town near the northern border that Mrs Glimm had arranged for someone to assault Mrs Pyk in her own house, an attack which culminated in the severing of Mrs Pyk's left hand. However, Mrs Glimm's plan to discourage the ambitions of her competitor ultimately backfired, it seemed, for after this attack on her person Mrs Pyk appeared to undergo a dramatic change, as did her method of running things at her east side house. She had always been known as a woman of exceptional will and extraordinary gifts, this one-time exotic dancer and later Mistress of Fortune, but following the dismemberment of her left hand, and its replacement by an artificial wooden hand, she seemed to have attained unheard-of powers, all of which she directed toward one aim – that of putting her ex-partner, Mrs Glimm, out of business. It was then that she began to operate her lodging house in an entirely new manner and in accordance with unique methods, so that whenever traveling commercial agents who patronized Mrs Glimm's west side lodging house came to stay at Mrs Pyk's, they always returned to Mrs Pyk's house on the east side and never again to Mrs Glimm's west-side place.

I mentioned to Mr Crumm that I had lived in that northern border town long enough to have been told on various occasions that a guest could visit Mrs Pyk just so many times before he discovered one day that he could never leave her again. Such talk, I continued, was to some extent substantiated by what was found in the ruins of

Mrs Pyk's house after the fire. It seemed there were rooms all over the house, and even in the farthest corners of its vast cellar regions, where the charred remains of human bodies were found. To all appearances, given the intensely destructive nature of that conflagration, each of the incinerated corpses was dressed in some outlandish clothing, as if the whole structure of the house were inhabited by a nest of masqueraders. In light of all the stories we had heard in the town, no one bothered to remark on how unlikely it was, how preposterous even, that none of the lodgers at Mrs Pyk's house had managed to escape. Nevertheless, as I disclosed to Crumm, the body of Mrs Pyk herself was never found, despite a most diligent search that was conducted by Mrs Glimm.

Yet even as I brought all of these facts to his attention as we sat on that park bench, Crum's mind seemed to have drifted off to other realms and more than ever he looked as if he belonged in a hospital. Finally he spoke, asking me to confirm what I had said about the absence of Mrs Pyk's body among those found in the ashes left by the fire. I confirmed the statement I had made, begging him to consider the place and the circumstances which were the source of this and all my other remarks, as well as his own, that were made that morning in early spring. 'Remember your own words,' I said to Crumm.

'Which words were those?' he asked.

'Deliriously preposterous,' I replied, trying to draw out the sound of each syllable, as if to imbue them with some actual sense or at least a dramatic force of some kind. 'You were only a pawn,' I said. 'You and all those others were nothing but pawns in a struggle between forces you could not conceive. Your impulses were not your own. They were as artificial as Mrs Pyk's wooden hand.'

For a moment Crumm seemed to become roused to his senses. Then he said, as if to himself, 'They never found her body.'

'No, they did not,' I answered.

'Not even her hand,' he said in a strictly rhetorical tone of voice. Again I affirmed his statement.

Crumm fell silent after that juncture in our conversation and when I left him that morning he was staring out at the drab and soggy grounds of that park with the look of someone in a hysterical trance, remaining quietly attentive for some sound or sign to reach his awareness. That was the last time I saw him.

Occasionally, on nights when I find it difficult to sleep, I think about Mr Crumm the commercial agent and the conversation we had that day in the park. I also think about Mrs Pyk and her house on the east side of a northern border town where I once lived. In these moments it is almost as if I myself can hear the faint jingle-jangle of bells in the blackness, and my mind begins to wander in pursuit of a desperate dream that is not my own.

Perhaps this dream ultimately belongs to no one, however many persons, including commercial agents, may have belonged to it.

A SOFT VOICE WHISPERS NOTHING

Long before I suspected the existence of the town near the northern border, I believe that I was in some way already an inhabitant of that remote and desolate place. Any number of signs might be offered to support this claim, although some of them may seem somewhat removed from the issue. Not the least of them appeared during my childhood, those soft gray years when I was stricken with one sort or another of life-draining infirmity. It was at this early stage of development that I sealed my deep affinity with the winter season in all its phases and manifestations. Nothing seemed more natural to me than my impulse to follow the path of the snow-topped roof and the ice-crowned fence-post, considering that I, too, in my illness, exhibited the marks of an essentially hibernal state of being. Under the plump blankets of my bed I lay freezing and pale, my temples sweating with shiny sickles of fever. Through the frosted panes of my bedroom window I watched in awful devotion as dull winter days were succeeded by blinding winter nights. I remained ever awake to the possibility, as my young mind conceived it, of an 'icy transcendence.' I was therefore cautious, even in my frequent states of delirium, never to

304

indulge in a vulgar sleep, except perhaps to dream my way deeper into that landscape where vanishing winds snatched me up into the void of an ultimate hibernation.

No one expected I would live very long, not even my attending physician, Dr Zirk. A widower far along into middle age, the doctor seemed intensely dedicated to the well-being of the living anatomies under his care. Yet from my earliest acquaintance with him I sensed that he too had a secret affinity with the most remote and desolate locus of the winter spirit, and therefore was also allied with the town near the northern border. Every time he examined me at my bedside he betrayed himself as a fellow fanatic of a disconsolate creed, embodying so many of its stigmata and gestures. His wiry, white-streaked hair and beard were thinning, patchy remnants of a former luxuriance, much like the bare, frost-covered branches of the trees outside my window. His face was of a coarse complexion, rugged as frozen earth, while his eyes were overcast with the cloudy ether of a December afternoon. And his fingers felt so frigid as they palpated my neck or gently pulled at the underlids of my eyes.

One day, when I believe that he thought I was asleep, Dr Zirk revealed the extent of his initiation into the barren mysteries of the winter world, even if he spoke only in the cryptic fragments of an overworked soul in extremis. In a voice as pure and cold as an arctic wind the doctor made reference to 'undergoing certain ordeals,' as well as speaking of what he called 'grotesque discontinuities in the order of things.' His trembling words also invoked an epistemology of 'hoe and horror,' of exposing once and for all the true nature of this 'great gray ritual of existence' and plunging headlong into an 'enlightenment of inanity.' It seemed that he was addressing me directly when in a soft gasp of desperation he said, 'To make an end of it, little puppet, in your own way. To close the door in one swift motion and not by slow, fretful degrees. If only this doctor could show you the way of such cold deliverance.' I felt my eyelashes flutter at the tone and import of these words, and Dr Zirk immediately became silent. Just then my mother entered the room, allowing me a pretext to display an aroused consciousness. But I never betrayed the confidence or indiscretion the doctor had entrusted to me that day.

In any case, it was many years later that I first discovered the town near the northern border, and there I came to understand the source and significance of Dr Zirk's mumblings on that nearly silent winter day. I noticed, as I arrived in the town, how close a resemblance it bore to the winterland of my childhood, even if the precise time of year was still slightly out of season. On that day, everything – the streets of the town and the few people traveling upon them, the store windows and the meager merchandise they displayed, the weightless pieces of debris barely animated by a half-dead wind – everything looked as if it had been drained entirely of all color, as if an enormous photographic flash had just gone off in the startled face of the town. And somehow beneath the pallid façade I intuited what I described to myself as the 'all-pervasive aura of a lace that has offered itself as a haven for an interminable series of delirious events.'

It was definitely a mood of delirium that appeared to rule the scene, causing all that I saw to shimmer vaguely in my sight, as if viewed through the gauzy glow of a sickroom: a haziness that had no precise substance, distorting without in any way obscuring the objects behind or within it. There was an atmosphere of disorder and commotion that I sensed in the streets of the town, as if its delirious mood were only a soft prelude to great pandemonium. I heard the sound of something that I could not identify, an approaching racket that caused me to take refuge in a narrow passageway between a pair of high buildings. Nestled in this dark hiding place I watched the street and listened as that nameless clattering grew louder. It was a medley of clanging and creaking, of groaning and croaking, a dull jangle of something unknown as it groped its way through the town, a chaotic parade in honor of some special occasion of delirium.

The street that I saw beyond the narrow opening between the two buildings was now entirely empty. The only thing I could glimpse was a blur of high and low structures which appeared to quiver slightly as the noise became louder and louder, the parade closing in, though from which direction I did not know. The formless clamor seemed to envelop everything around me, and then suddenly I could see a passing figure in the street. Dressed in loose white garments, it had an egg-shaped head that was completely hairless and as white as paste, a clown of some kind who moved in a way that was both casual and laborious, as if it were strolling underwater or against a strong wind, tracing strange patterns in the air with billowed arms and pale hands. It seemed to take forever for this apparition to pass from view, but just before doing so it turned to peer into the narrow passage where I had secreted myself, and its greasy white face was wearing an expression of bland malevolence.

Others followed the lead figure, including a team of ragged men who were harnessed like beasts and pulled long bristling ropes. They also moved out of sight, leaving the ropes to waver slackly behind them. The vehicle to which these ropes were attached – by means of enormous hooks – rolled into the scene, its green wooden wheels audibly grinding the pavement of the street beneath them. It was a sort of platform with huge wooden stakes rising from its perimeter to form the bars of a cage. There was nothing to secure the wooden bars at the top, and so they wobbled with the movement of the parade.

Hanging from the bars, and rattling against them, was an array of objects haphazardly tethered by cords and wires and straps of various kinds. I saw masks and shoes, household utensils and naked dolls, large bleached bones and the skeletons of small animals, bottles of colored glass, the head of a dog with a rusty chain wrapped several times around its neck, and sundry scraps of debris and other things I could not name, all knocking together in a wild percussion. I watched and listened as that ludicrous vehicle passed by in the street. Nothing else followed it, and the enigmatic parade seemed to be at an end, now only a delirious noise fading into the distance. Then a voice called out behind me.

'What are you doing back here?'

I turned around and saw a fat old woman moving toward me from the shadows of that narrow passageway between the two high buildings. She was wearing a highly decorated hat that was almost as wide as she was, and her already ample form was augmented by numerous layers of colorful scarves and shawls. Her body was further weighted down by several necklaces which hung like a noose around her neck and many bracelets about both of her chubby wrists. On the thick fingers of either hand were a variety of large gaudy rings.

'I was watching the parade,' I said to her. 'But I couldn't see what was inside the case, or whatever it was. It seemed to be empty.'

The woman simply stared at me for some time, as if contemplating my face and perhaps surmising that I had only recently arrived in the northern border town. Then she introduced herself as Mrs Glimm and said that she ran a lodging house. 'Do you have a place to stay?' she asked in an aggressively demanding tone. 'It should be dark soon,' she said, glancing slightly upward. 'The days are getting shorter and shorter.'

I agreed to follow her back to the lodging house. On the way I asked her about the parade. 'It's all just some nonsense,' she said as we walked through the darkening streets of the town. 'Have you seen one of these?' she asked, handing me a crumpled piece of paper that she had stuffed among her scarves and shawls.

Smoothing out the page Mrs Glimm had placed in my hands, I tried to read in the dimming twilight what was printed upon it.

At the top of the page, in capital letters, was a title: METAPHYSICAL LECTURE I. Below these words was a brief text which I read to myself as I walked with Mrs Glimm. 'It has been said,' the text began, 'that after undergoing certain ordeals – whether ecstatic or abysmal – we should be obliged to change our names, as we are no longer who we once were. Instead the opposite rule is applied: our names linger long after anything resembling what we were, or thought we were, has disappeared entirely. Not that there was ever much to begin with – only a few questionable memories and impulses drifting about like snowflakes in a gray and endless winter. But each soon floats down and settles into a cold and nameless void.'

After reading this brief 'metaphysical lecture,' I asked Mrs Glimm where it came from. 'They were all over town,' she replied. 'Just some nonsense, like the rest of it. Personally I think this sort of thing is bad for business. Why should I have to go around picking up customers on the street? But as long as someone's paying my price I will accommodate them in whatever style they wish. In addition to operating a lodging house or two, I am also licensed to act as an undertaker's assistant and a cabaret stage manager. Well, here we are. You can go inside – someone will be there to take care of you. At the moment I have an appointment elsewhere.' With these concluding words, Mrs Glimm walked off, her jewelry rattling with every step she took.

Mrs Glimm's lodging house was one of several great structures along the street, each of them sharing similar features and all of them, I later discovered, in some way under the proprietorship or authority of the same person – that is, Mrs Glimm. Nearly flush with the street stood a series of high and almost styleless houses with institutional façades of pale gray mortar and enormous dark roofs. Although the street was rather wide, the sidewalks in front of the houses were so narrow that the roofs of these edifices slightly overhung the pavement below, creating a sense of tunnel-like enclosure. All of the houses might have been siblings of my childhood residence, which I once heard someone describe as an 'architectural moan.' I thought of this phrase as I went through the process of renting a room in Mrs Glimm's lodging house, insisting that I be placed in one that faced the street. Once I was settled into my apartment, which was actually a single, quite expansive bedroom, I stood at the window and gazed up and down the street of gray houses, which together seemed to form a procession of some kind, a frozen funeral parade. I repeated the words 'architectural moan' over and over to myself until exhaustion forced me away from the window and under the musty blankets of the bed. Before I feel asleep I remembered that it was Dr Zirk who had used this phrase to describe my childhood home, a place that he had visited so often.

So it was of Dr Zirk that I was thinking as I fell asleep in that expansive bedroom in Mrs Glimm's lodging house. And I was thinking of him not only because he had used the phrase 'architectural moan' to describe the appearance of my childhood home, which so closely resembled those high-roofed structures along that street of gray houses in the northern border town, but also, and even primarily, because the words of the brief metaphysical lecture I had read some hours earlier reminded me so much of the words, those fragments and mutterings, that the doctor had spoken as he sat

312

upon my bed and attended to the life-draining infirmities from which everyone expected I would die at a very young age. Lying under the musty blankets of my bed in that strange lodging house, with a little moonlight shining through the window to illuminate the dreamlike vastness of the room around me, I once again felt the weight of someone sitting upon my bed and bending over my apparently sleeping body, ministering to it with unseen gestures and a soft voice. It was then, while pretending to be asleep as I used to do in my childhood, that I heard the words of a second 'metaphysical lecture.' They were whispered in a slow and resonant monotone.

'We should give thanks,' the voice said to me, 'that a poverty of knowledge has so narrowed our vision of things as to allow the possibility of feeling something about them. How could we find a pretext to react to anything if we understood … everything? None but an absent mind was ever victimized by the adventure of intense emotional feeling. And without the suspense that is generated by our benighted state – our status as beings possessed by our own bodies and the madness that goes along with them – who could take enough interested in the universal spectacle to bring forth even the feeblest yawn, let along exhibit the more dramatic manifestations which lend to unwonted color to a world that is essentially composed of shades of gray upon a background of blackness? Hope and horror, to repeat merely two of the innumerable conditions dependent on a faulty insight, would be much the worse for an ultimate revelation that would expose their lack of necessity. At the other extreme, both our most dire and most exalted emotions are well served every time we take some ray of knowledge, isolate it from the spectrum of illumination, and then forget about it completely. All our ecstasies, whether sacred or from the slime, depend on our refusal to be schooled in even the most superficial truths and our maddening will to follow the path of forgetfulness. Amnesia may well be the highest sacrament in the great gray ritual of existence. To know, to understand in the fullest sense, is to plunge into an enlightenment of inanity, a wintry landscape of memory whose substance is all shadows and a profound awareness of the infinite spaces surrounding us on all sides. Within this space we remain suspended only with the aid of strings that quiver with our hopes and our horrors, and which keep us dangling over the gray void. How is it that we can defend such puppetry, condemning any efforts to strip us of these strings? The reason one must suppose, is that nothing is more enticing, nothing more vitally idiotic, than our desire to have a name – even if it is the name of a stupid little puppet – and to hold on to this name throughout the long ordeal of our lives as if we could hold on to it forever. If only we could keep those precious strings from growing frayed and tangled, if only we could keep from falling into an empty sky, we might continue to pass ourselves off under our assumed names and perpetuate our puppet's dance throughout all eternity ...'

The voice whispered more words than this, more than I can recall, as if it would deliver its lecture without end. But at some point I drifted off to sleep as I had never slept before, calm and gray and dreamless.

The next morning I was awakened by some noise down in the street outside my window. It was the same delirious cacophony I had heard the day before when I first arrived in the northern border town and witnessed the passing of that unique parade. But when I got up from my bed and went to the window, I saw no sign of the uproarious procession. Then I noticed the house directly opposite the one in which I had spent the night. One of the highest windows of that house across the street was fully open, and slightly below the ledge of the window, lying against the gray façade of the house, was the body of a man hanging by his neck from a thick white rope. The cord was stretched taut and led back through the window and into the house. For some reason this sight did not seem in any way unexpected or out of place, even as the noisy thrumming of the unseen parade grew increasingly loud and even when I recognized the figure of the hanged man, who was extremely slight of build, almost like a child in physical stature. Although many years older than when I had last seen him, his hair and beard now radiantly white, clearly the body was that of my old physician, Dr Zirk.

Now I could see the parade approaching. From the far end of the gray, tunnel-like street, the clown creature strolled in its loose white garments, his egg-shaped head scanning the high houses on either side. As the creature passed beneath my window it looked up at me for a moment with that same expression of bland malevolence, and then passed on. Following this figure was the formation of ragged men harnessed by ropes to a cage-like vehicle that rolled along on wooden wheels. Countless objects, many more than I saw the previous day, clattered against the bars of the cage. The grotesque inventory now included bottles of pills that rattled with the contents inside them, shining scalpels and instruments for cutting through bones, needles and syringes strung together and hung like ornaments on a Christmas tree, and a stethoscope that had been looped about the decapitated dog's head. The wooden stakes of the caged platform wobbled to the point of breaking with the additional weight of this cast-off clutter. Because there was no roof covering this cage, I could see down into it from my window. But there was nothing inside, at least for the moment. As the vehicle passed directly below, I looked across the street at the hanged man and the thick rope from which he dangled like a puppet. From the shadows inside the open window of the house, a hand appeared that was holding a polished steel straight razor. The fingers of that hand were thick and wore many gaudy rings. After the razor had worked at the cord for a few moments, the body of Dr Zirk fell from the heights of the gray house and landed in the open vehicle just as it passed by. The procession which was so lethargic in its every aspect now seemed to disappear quickly from view, its muffled riot of sounds fading into the distance.

To make an end of it, I thought to myself – *to make an end of it in whatever style you wish.*

I looked at the house across the street. The window that was once open was now closed, and the curtains behind it were drawn. The tunnel-like street of gray houses was absolutely still. Then, as if in answer to my own deepest wish, a sparse showering of snowflakes began to descend from the gray morning sky, each one of them a soft whispering voice. For the longest time I continued to stare out from my window, gazing upon the street and the town that I knew was my home.

WHEN YOU HEAR THE SINGING, YOU WILL KNOW IT IS TIME

I had lived in the town near the northern border long enough so that, with the occult passing of time, I had begun to assume that I would never leave there, at least not while I was alive.

I would die by my own hand, I might have believed, or possibly by the more usual means of some violent misadventure or some wasting disease. But certainly I had begun to assume that my life's end, as if by right, would take place either within the town itself or in close proximity to its outskirts, where the dense streets and structures of the town started to thin out and eventually dissolved into a desolate and seemingly endless countryside. Following my death, I thought, or had begun unwittingly to assume, I would be buried in the hilltop graveyard outside the town. I had no idea that there were others who might have told me that it was just as likely I would not die in the town and therefore would not be buried, or interred in any way whatsoever, within the hilltop graveyard. Such persons might have been regarded as hysterics of some kind, or possibly some type of impostor, since everyone who was a permanent resident of the northern border town seemed to be either one or the other and often both of them at once. These individuals might have suggested to me that it was also entirely possible neither to die in the town nor ever to leave it. I began to learn how such a thing might happen during the time I was living in a small backstairs apartment on the ground floor of a large rooming house located in one of the oldest parts of the town.

It was the middle of the night, and I had just awakened in my bed. More precisely, I had *started into wakefulness*, much as I had done throughout my life. This habit of starting into wakefulness in the middle of the night enabled me to become aware, on that particular night, of a soft droning sound which filled my small, one-room apartment and which I might not have heard had I been the sort of person who remains asleep all night long. The sound was emanating from under the floorboards and rose up to reverberate in the moonlight darkness of the entire room. After a few moments sitting up in my bed, and then getting out of bed to step quietly around my small apartment, it seemed to me that the soft droning sound I heard was made by a voice, a very deep voice, which spoke as if it were delivering a lecture of some kind or addressing an audience with the self-assured inflections of authority. Yet I could not discern a single word of what the voice was saying, only its droning intonations and its deeply reverberant quality as it rose up from beneath the floorboards of my small backstairs apartment.

Until that night I had not suspected that there was a cellar below the rooming house where I lived on the ground floor. I was even less prepared to discover, as I eventually did, that hidden under a small, worn-down carpet, which was the only floor covering in my room, was a trap door – an access, it seemed, to whatever basement or cellar might have existed (beyond all my suspicions) below the large rooming house. But there was something else unusual about this trap door, aside from its very presence in my small apartment room and the fact that it implied the existence of some type of rooming-house cellar. Although the trap door was somehow set into the floorboards of my room, it did not in any way appear to be *of a piece* with them. The trap door, as I thought of it, did not at all seem to be constructed of wood but of something that was more of a leathery consistency, all withered and warped and cracked in places as though it did not fit in with the roughly parallel lines of the floorboards in my room but clearly opposed them both in its shape and its angles, which were highly irregular by any standards that might conceivably apply to a rooming-house trap door. I could not even say if this leathery trap door had four sides to it or possible five ides or more, so elusive and misshapen was its crude and shriveled construction, at least as I saw it in the moonlight after starting into wakefulness in my small backstairs apartment. Yet I was absolutely certain that the deeply reverberant voice which continued to drone on and on as I inspected the trap door was in fact emanating from a place, a cellar or basement of some kind, directly below my room. I knew this to be true because I placed my hand, very briefly, on the trap door's leathery and irregular surface, and in that moment I could feel that it was *pulsing* in a way that corresponded to the force and rhythms of the voice which echoed its indecipherable words throughout the rest of that night, fading only moments before daylight.

Having remained awake for most of the night, I left my backstairs apartment and began to wander the streets of the northern border town on a cold and overcast morning in late autumn. Throughout the whole of that day I saw the town, where I had already lived for some time, under an aspect I had not known before.

I have stated that this town near the northern border was a place where I had assumed I would one day die, and I may even say it was a place where I actually desired to make an end of it, or such was the intention or wish that I *entertained* at certain times and in certain places, including my residence in one of the oldest sections of the town. But as I wandered the streets on that overcast morning in late autumn, and throughout the day, my entire sense of my surroundings, as well as my intuition that my existence would be terminated within those surroundings, had become altered in a completely unexpected manner. The town had, of course, always displayed certain peculiar and often profoundly surprising qualities and features. Sooner or later everyone who was a permanent resident there was confronted with something of a nearly insupportable oddity or corruption.

As I wandered along one byway or another throughout that morning and into late afternoon, I recalled a specific street near the edge of town, a dead-end street where all the houses and other buildings seemed to have grown into one another, melding their diverse materials into a bizarre and jagged conglomerate of massive architectural proportions, with peaked roofs and soaring chimneys or towers visibly swaying and audibly moaning even in the calm of an early summer twilight. I had thought that this was the absolute limit, only to find out at exactly the moment of having this thought that there was something further involved with this street, something that caused persons living in the area to repeat a special slogan or incantation to whomever would listen. *When you hear the singing,* they said, *you will know it is time.* These words were spoken, and I heard them myself, as if the persons uttering them were attempting to absolve or protect themselves in some way that was beyond any further explication. And whether or not one heard the singing or had ever heard what was called the singing, and whether or not that obscure and unspeakable *time* ever came, or would ever come to those who arrived in that street with its houses and other buildings all mingled together and tumbling into the sky, there nevertheless remained within you the feeling that this was still the place – the town near the northern border – where you came to live and where you might believe you would be a permanent resident until either you chose to leave it or until you died, possibly by violent misadventure or some wasting disease, if not by your own hand. Yet on that overcast morning in late autumn I could no longer maintain this feeling, not after having started into wakefulness the night before, not after having heard that droning voice which delivered some incomprehensible sermon for hours on end, and not after having seen that leathery trap door which

I placed my hand upon for only a brief moment and thereafter retreated to the furthest corner of my small apartment until daylight.

And I was not the only one to notice a change within the town, as I discovered when twilight drew on and more of us began to collect on street corners or in back alleys, as well as in abandoned storefront rooms or old office buildings where most of the furniture was badly broken and out-of-date calendars hung crooked on the walls. It was difficult for some persons to refrain from observing that there seemed to be fewer of us as the shadows of twilight gathered that day. Even Mrs Glimm, whose lodging house-plus-brothel was as populous as ever with its out-of-town clientele, said that among the permanent residents of the northern border town there was a 'noticeably diminished' number of persons.

A man named Mr Pell (sometimes *Doctor* Pell) was to my knowledge the first to use the word 'disappearances' in order to illuminate, during the course of one of our twilight gatherings, the cause of the town's slightly reduced population. He was sitting in the shadows on the other side of an overturned desk or bookcase, so his words were not entirely audible as he whispered them in the direction of a darkened doorway, perhaps speaking to someone who was standing, or possibly lying down, in the darkness beyond the aperture. But once this concept – of 'disappearances,' that is – had been introduced, it seemed that quite a few persons had something to say on the subject, especially those who had lived in the town longer than most of us or who had lived in the oldest parts of the town for more years than I had. It was from one of the latter, a veteran of all kinds of hysteria, that I learned about the demonic preacher Reverend Cork, whose sermonizing I had apparently heard during the previous night as it reverberated through the leathery trap door in my apartment room. 'You didn't happen to open that trap door, did you?' the old hysteric asked in a somewhat coy tone of voice. We were sitting, just the two of us, on some wooden crates we had found in the opening to a narrow alley. 'Tell me,' he urged as the light from a streetlamp shone upon his thin face in the darkening twilight. 'Tell me that you didn't just take a little peek inside that trap door.' I then told him I had done nothing of the sort. Suddenly he began to laugh hysterically in a voice that was both high-pitched and extremely coarse. 'Of course you didn't take a little peek inside the trap door,' he said when he finally settled down. 'If you had, then you wouldn't be *here* with *me*, you would be *there* with *him*.'

The antics and coy tone of the old hysteric notwithstanding, there was a meaning in his words that resonated with my experience in my apartment room and also with my perception that day of a profound change in the town near the northern border. At first I tended to conceive of the figure of Reverend Cork as a spirit of the dead, someone who had 'disappeared' by wholly natural means. In these terms I was able to think of myself as having been the victim of a haunting at the large rooming house where, no doubt, many persons had ended their lives in one way or another. This metaphysical framework seemed to apply nicely to my recent experiences and did not conflict with what I had been told in that narrow alley as twilight turned into evening. I was indeed *here*, in the northern border town with the old hysteric, and not *there*, in the land of the dead with Reverend Cork the demonic preacher.

But as the night wore on, and I moved among other residents of the town who had lived there far longer than I, it became evident that Reverend Cork, whose voice I had heard 'preaching' the night before, was neither dead, in the usual sense of the word, nor among those who had only recently 'disappeared,' many of whom, I learned, had not disappeared in any mysterious way at all but had simply abandoned the northern border town without notifying anyone. They had made this hasty exodus, according to several hysterics or impostors I spoke with that night, because they had 'seen the signs,' even as I had seen that leathery trap door whose existence in my apartment room was previously and entirely unsuspected.

Although I had not recognized it as such, this trap door, which appeared to lead to a cellar beneath the rooming house where I lived, was among the most typical of the so-called 'signs.' All of them, as numerous persons hysterically avowed, were indications of some type of *threshold* – doorways or passages that one should be cautious not to enter, or even to approach. Most of these signs, in fact, took the form of doors of various types, particularly those which might be found in odd, out-of-the-way places, such as a miniature door at the back of a broom closet or a door appearing on the inner wall of a fireplace, and even doors that might not seem to lead to any sensible space, as would be the case with a trap door in an apartment on the ground floor of a rooming house that did not have a cellar, nor had ever had one that could be accessed in such a way. I did hear about other such 'threshold-signs,' including window frames in the most queer locations, stairways that spiraled downward into depths beneath a common basement or led below ground level along lonely sidewalks, and even entrances to streets that were not formerly known to exist, with perhaps a narrow gate swinging open in temptation.

Yet all of these signs or thresholds gave themselves away by their distinctive appearance, which, according to many of those knowledgeable of such things, was very much like that withered and leathery appearance of the trap door in my apartment room, not to mention displaying the same kind of shapes and angles that were strikingly at odds with their surroundings.

Nevertheless, there were still those who, for one reason or another, chose to ignore the signs or were unable to resist the enticements of thresholds that simply cropped up overnight in the most unforeseen places around the northern border town. To all appearances, at that point, the demonic preacher Reverend Cork had been one of the persons who had 'disappeared' in this way. I now became aware, as the evening progressed into a brilliantly star-filled night, that I had not been the victim of a *haunting*, as I had earlier supposed, but had actually witnessed a phenomenon of quite a different sort.

'The reverend has been gone since the last disappearances,' said an old woman whose face I could barely see in the candlelight that illuminated the enormous, echoing lobby of a defunct hotel where some of us had gathered after midnight. But someone took issue with the old woman, or 'idiot-hag,' as this person called her. The preacher, this other person contended in exactly the following words, was *old town*. This was my first exposure to the phrase 'old town,' but before I could take in its full meaning or implications it began to undergo a metamorphosis among those gathered after midnight in the lobby of that defunct hotel. While the person who called the old woman an idiot-hag continued to speak of the 'old town,' where he said Reverend Cork resided or was originally *from*, the old woman and a few of those who sided with her spoke only about the *other* town. 'No one is *from* the other town,' the woman said to the person who was calling her an idiot-hag. 'There are only those who disappear *into* the other town, among them the demonic preacher Reverend Cork, who may have been a ludicrous impostor but was never what anyone would call *demonic* until he disappeared into that trap door in the room where this gentleman,' she said, referring to me, 'heard him preaching only last night.'

'You idiot-hag,' said the other person, 'the old town existed on the very spot where this northern border town now exists . . . until the day when it disappeared, along with everyone who lived in it, including the demonic preacher Reverend Cork.'

Then someone else, who was lying deep in the cushions of an old divan in the lobby, added the following words: 'It was a demon town and was inhabited by demonic entities of all sorts who made the whole thing invisible. Now they throw out these *thresholds* as a way to lure another group of us who only want to live in this town near the northern border and not in some intolerable demon town.'

Nonetheless, the old woman and the few others who sided with her persisted in speaking not about an *old town* or an invisible *demon town*, but about the *other* town, which, they all agreed, never had any concrete existence to speak of, but was simply a metaphysical backdrop to the northern border town that we all knew and that was a place where many of us fervently desired to make an end of our lives. Whatever the facts in this matter, one point was hammered into my brain over and over again:

there was simply no peace to be had no matter where you hid yourself away. Even in a northern border town of such intensely chaotic oddity and corruption there was still some greater chaos, some deeper insanity, than one had counted on, or could ever be taken into account – wherever there was anything, there would be chaos and insanity to such a degree that one could never come to terms with it, and it was only a matter of time before your world, whatever you thought it to be, was undermined, if not completely overrun, by another world.

Throughout the late hours of that night the debates and theories and fine qualifications continued regarding the spectral towns and the tangible thresholds that served to reduce the number of permanent residents of the northern border town, either by causing them to disappear through some out-of-the -way door or window or down a spiraling stairway or phantom street, or by forcing them to abandon the town because, for whatever reason, it had become, or seemed to become, something quite different from the place they had known it to be, or believed it to be, for so long. Whether or not they arrived at a resolution of their conflicting views I will never know, since I left the defunct hotel while the discussion was still going strong. But I did not go back to my small apartment in one of the oldest parts of town. Instead I wandered out to the hilltop graveyard outside of town and stood among the graves until the following morning, which was as cold and overcast as the one before it. I knew then that I would not die in the northern border town, either by means of a violent misadventure or a wasting disease, or even by my own hand, and therefore I would not be buried in the hilltop graveyard where I stood that morning looking down on the place where I had lived for so long. I had already wandered the streets of the northern border town for the last time and found, for whatever reason, that they had become something different from what they had been, or had once seemed to be. This was the only thing that was now certain in my mind. For a moment I considered returning to the town and seeking out one of the newly appeared thresholds in order to enter it before all of them mysteriously disappeared again, so that I might disappear along with them into the other town, or the old town, where perhaps I might find once more what I seemed to have lost in the northern border town. Possibly there might have been something there – on the other side of the town – that was like the dead-end street where, it was said, 'When you hear the singing, you will know it is time.' And while I might never be able to die in the town near the northern border, neither would I ever have to leave it. To have such thoughts was, of course, only more chaos and insanity. But I had not slept for two nights. I was tired and felt the ache of every broken dream I had ever carried within me. Perhaps I would one day seek out another town in another land where I could make an end of it, or at least where I could wait in a fatalistic delirium for the end to come. Now it was time to just walk away in silence.

Years later I learned there was a movement to 'clean up' the northern border town of what was elsewhere perceived to be its 'contaminated' elements. On arriving in the town, however, the investigators assigned to this task discovered a place that was all but deserted, the only remaining residents being a few hysterics or impostors who muttered endlessly about 'other towns' or 'demon towns,' and even of an 'old town.' Among these individuals was a large and gaudily attired old woman who styled herself as the owner of a lodging house and several other properties. These venues, she said, along with many others throughout the town, had been rendered uninhabitable and useless for any practical purpose. This statement seemed to capsulize the findings of the investigators , who ultimately composed a report that was dismissive of any threat that might be posed by the town near the northern border, which, whatever else it may have been, or seemed to be, was always a genius of the most insidious illusions.

OR ALONE
Hyacinthe L. Raven

When you wake,
you will find me—

Lying at your feet as
if I could root myself
up through your limbs, to
hold you there until the
snows freeze you still:
glass-shard sharpened and bare.

Or perhaps, if I am brave, a
chandelier in the half-light,
twisted of too-rosy pink
flesh, lips tenderly parted, as
though I were saying:
if only, if only, if only...

Will you know that I called
for you in my last pin-pricked
moments? That I saw your
face, so clearly unbroken while
the ice veins held me back,
tried to make me forget that
you had hung here once, a
pale offering too new to be
understood? You, who are my
father, my brother, my husband:
Oh Christ, Oh Christ, O Christus...

When you wake,
you will find me—

A silent sacrifice to your
porcelain heart, the three
stones upon your grave.

ABOUT THE CONTRIBUTORS

Andrew Liles

Andrew Liles is a prolific solo artist, producer, remixer and sometime member of Nurse With Wound and Current 93. He has been recording since the mid 80s and has appeared on well over 150 releases. He has worked with David Tibet live and in the studio as a member of Current 93 for past 7 years. You can visit him at www.andrewliles.com

Nikki Guerlain

Nikki Guerlain lives in Portland, Oregon. Her writing can be found online and in print. Her debut novel *Machine Gun Vacation* will be released by Thunderdome Press in 2014.

Michael Griffin

Michael Griffin's short fiction has appeared in the Thomas Ligotti tribute anthology *The Grimscribe's Puppets*, and such periodicals as Apex Magazine, Black Static, Lovecraft eZine and Phantasmagorium. His work is forthcoming in the King in Yellow special issue of Lovecraft eZine. He's also an electronic ambient musician and founder of Hypnos Recordings, an ambient music record label he operates with his wife in Portland, Oregon. Michael blogs about books and writing at griffinwords.com, and his Twitter feed is @griffinwords.

Ross E. Lockhart

Ross E. Lockhart is an author, anthologist, editor, and publisher. A lifelong fan of supernatural, fantastic, speculative, and weird fiction, Lockhart is a veteran of small-press publishing, having edited scores of well-regarded novels of horror, fantasy, and science fiction. Lockhart edited the anthologies *The Book of Cthulhu I and II*, *Tales of Jack the Ripper*, and *The Children of Old Leech* (with Justin Steele). He is the author of *Chick Bassist*. Lockhart lives in an old church in Petaluma, California, with his wife Jennifer, hundreds of books, and Elinor Phantom, a Shih Tzu moonlighting as his editorial assistant.

Daniel Mills

Daniel Mills is the author of *Revenants: A Dream of New England* (Chomu Press, 2011) and *The Lord Came at Twilight* (Dark Renaissance Books, 2014). His short fiction has appeared in various magazines and anthologies including Black Static, Shadows & Tall Trees, and The Mammoth Book of Best New Horror 23. His novella *Children of Light* is also available from Dunhams Manor Press. Visit him online at http://www.daniel-mills.net.

Nicole Cushing

Nicole Cushing's fiction has been praised by Thomas Ligotti, Jack Ketchum, Famous Monsters of Filmland and Ain't It Cool News. Her most recent work is the novella *I Am the New God* (DarkFuse, 2014). A Maryland native, she now lives with her husband in Indiana. Keep up with her online at nicolecushing.com.

Josh Myers

Josh Myers is the author of *Feast of Oblivion* and *Guns*. He lives in Lambertville, NJ.

Edward Morris

Edward Morris is a 2011 nominee for the Pushcart Prize in Literature, also nominated for the 2009 Rhysling Award. His second collection of published short stories (*Beyond the Western Sky*, Borgo Press) brings his total to over a hundred and twenty published short stories worldwide, most recently in THE MAGAZINE OF BIZARRO FICTION, Robert M. Price's *The Mountains of Madness*, and Glynn Barass'/Brian M. Sammons' forthcoming *World War Cthulhu*. He has been a Current 93 fan for one quarter of a century.

Ian Delacroix

Ian Delacroix is an Italian editor and professional writer. He writes horror, weird and grotesque fiction, he published his own very first anthology *Abattoir* in 2007. He translated Michael Laimo's short story "In The eyes of the Victim" in Italian for the anthology *Carnevale* (Edizioni XII, 2010). In 2011 he published the horror novel *Il Grande Notturno* (The Big Nocturne) with Edizioni XII.

Jon R. Meyers

Jon R. Meyers is the author of *The Dream Ward* (Dynatox Ministries) and a number of other various publications within the realms of Cult, Horror, and Weird Fiction. He is currently residing in the murky depths of Northwest Indiana.

Kent Gowran

Kent Gowran lives and works in Chicago. His stories have appeared in NEEDLE: A Magazine of Noir, Plots With Guns, Beat To A Pulp, and other wild venues. In

2011 he founded and edited the flash fiction site Shotgun Honey.

Michael Allen Rose

Michael Allen Rose is a Chicago based writer, musician and performer. He's been published in a variety of strange places including The Surreal Grotesque, the Bizarro Bizarro anthology and *Fifty Secret Tales of the Whispering Gash* as well as having books published by Eraserhead Press and Dynatox Ministries. Flood Damage is the name of his industrial music project. He likes to set things on fire and put on puppet shows when he does readings. He is currently dating a unicorn. He believes that the real conspiracy is born of those who say there is a conspiracy. He likes cats. He likes Indian food. He likes a lot of things, actually. He might even like you. Really. No, not like that. Okay, yeah, like that. Find him at www.michaelallenrose.com and send him presents.

Neal Alan Spurlock

Neal Alan Spurlock is an author, musician, and filmmaker devoted to creating the darkly beautiful. Also published as Neal Jansons.

D.P. Watt

D.P. Watt is a writer living in the bowels of England. He balances his time between lecturing in drama and devising new 'creative recipes', 'illegal' and 'heretical' methods to resurrect a world of awful literary wonder. His collection of short stories *An Emporium of Automata* was reprinted by Eibonvale Press in early 2013, a recent novella *Memorabilia* was published in *The Transfiguration*

of Mr Punch, and his latest collection, The
Phantasmagorical Imperative and Other Fabrications,
was published in February 2014 with Egaeus Press. You
can find him at The Interlude House:
www.theinterludehouse.webs.com

Bob Freeman

Bob Freeman doesn't just write and draw occult
detectives, he's also a card carrying paranormal
adventurer who founded Nightstalkers of Indiana in
1983. Bob's studies have focused on mythology,
witchcraft, magic, and religion and these interests are
reflected in his art, both as an author and illustrator.
Bob lives in rural Indiana with his wife Kim and son
Connor. He can be found online at occultdetective.com

Andrew Wayne Adams

Andrew Wayne Adams is the author of a novella (a
metaphysical comedy-romance-adventure called *Janitor
of Planet Anilingus*), as well as some short stories that
have appeared sporadically over the past decade. Born
in rural America, he is becoming Canadian.

Jayaprakash Satyamurthy

Jayaprakash Satyamurthy lives in Bangalore, India. He is
a musician and a writer and also the indentured slave of
a vast feline horde. Someday he will write a history of
modern India entitled 'Swastikas for Modi'.

James Champagne

James Champagne is the author of the short story
collection *Grimoire: A Compendium of Neo-Goth Narratives*
(Rebel Satori Press, 2012) and *Autopsy of an Eldritch City:*

Ten Tales of Strange & Unproductive Thinking
(forthcoming). His work has also appeared in *Userlands:*
New Fiction Writers From The Blogging Underground
(Akashic Books, 2007, edited by Dennis Cooper). A
native of Woonsocket, Rhode Island, his website is
http://onyxglossary.blogspot.com/.

Robert M. Price

Robert M. Price was the editor of *Crypt of Cthulhu* for
two decades, then began editing Lovecraftian fiction
anthologies for Fedogan & Bremer, Chaosium, Inc.,
Arkham House and others. His articles have appeared
in *Lovecraft Studies*, *Nyctalops*, and others. His Mythos
fiction is collected in *Blasphemies and Revelations*. Price
has been presiding at Cthulhu Prayer Breakfasts for
twenty years at NecronomiCon, Mythos Con, and the
H.P. Lovecraft Film Festival. And he is the host of *The*
Lovecraft Geek podcast. What a fanatic!

Joseph Pulver Sr.

Joseph S. Pulver, Sr., is the author of the novels *The*
Orphan Palace and *Nightmare's Disciple*, and he has written
many short stories that have appeared in magazines and
anthologies, including "Weird Fiction Review",
"Lovecraft eZine", Ellen Datlow's *Best Horror of the*
Year, S. T. Joshi's *Black Wings (I and III)*, *Book of Cthulhu*,
and many anthologies edited by Robert M. Price. His
highly–acclaimed short story collections, *Blood Will Have*
Its Season, *SIN & ashes*, and *Portraits of Ruin*, were
published by Hippocampus Press. He edited *A Season in*
Carcosa and *The Grimscribe's Puppets*. He is at work on
two new collections of weird fiction, *Stained Translations*

and *The Protocols of Ugliness*, both edited by Jeffrey Thomas.

Dustin Reade

Dustin Reade is the author of the immortal classic *Grambo*. He practices voodoo and street magic near upper-left-hand corner of the Pacific Northwest.

Michael Göttert

Michael Göttert has been writing about music (and occasionally literature) for the past seventeen years. His texts have appeared in Equinoxe Magazin, Taucher, Black and Auf Abwegen. He is currently one of two administrators of the website African Paper (africanpaper.com), a cultural magazine. Ever since he first listened to Current 93 almost 25 years ago, he has been fascinated by the work(s) and vision(s) of David Tibet and those around him.

Dinah Prim

Dinah Prim is a physical therapist and author. She lives in California. She is the author of *The Baffling Resurrection of Toyland*.

Chris Kelso

Chris Kelso is a writer, illustrator, editor and journalist. He has also been printed frequently in literary and university publications across the UK, US and Canada. His publications include *Schadenfreude* (Dog Horn Publishing), *Last Exit to Interzone* (Black Dharma Press), *A Message from the Slave State* (Western Legends Books), *Moosejaw Frontier* (Bizarro Pulp Press), *Transmatic* (MorbidbookS), *The Black Dog Eats the City* (Omnium

Gatherum), *Caledonia Dreamin' - Strange Fiction of Scottish Descent"* (ed.with Hal Duncan).

Thomas Ligotti

Thomas Ligotti is one of the foremost contemporary authors of supernatural horror literature. For his writings in the horror genre, he has been honored with several awards. These include the Horror Writers Association's Bram Stoker award for his collection *The Nightmare Factory* (1996) and short novel *My Work Is Not Yet Done* (2002).

Hyacinthe L. Raven

Hyacinthe L. Raven is known within the small press for her poetry, which has appeared in numerous publications such as *Not Dead But Dreaming*, *Thistle*, and *Blackbird*. She has been the editor of Via Dolorosa Press since 1994.

dynatoxministries.com

Printed in Great Britain
by Amazon.co.uk, Ltd.,
Marston Gate.